PRAISE FOR SARAH SULTOON

'A powerhouse writer' Jo Spain

'Gripping, intriguing, action-packed and powerful, I raced through this hard-hitting thriller in just two days!' Philippa East

'A bitingly sharp, pacy thriller. Devilishly good. I inhaled it' Freya Berry

'A brave and thought-provoking debut novel' Adam Hamdy

'Brilliant and gripping' S. J. Watson

'Full of danger and pulsating characters' Louise Swanson

'A taut and thought-provoking book that's all the more unnerving for how much it echoes the headlines in real life' *CultureFly*

'A tense thriller, a remarkable debut, heartbreaking, but ultimately this is a story of resilience and survival' *NB Magazine*

'A master of creating atmosphere and a sense of place in her writing' Hooked from Page One

'Once again, Sarah Sultoon pulls it out of the bag' Books 'n' Banter

'Highly entertaining fiction' From Belgium with Book Love

'Sarah Sultoon's writing is as sharp as ever as this taut, chilling political thriller is brought vividly to life' Cal Turner Reviews

'A compulsively immersive, enlightening political thriller; breathtakingly exciting yet frequently deeply poignant' Hair Past a Freckle

ABOUT THE AUTHOR

Sarah Sultoon is an award-winning journalist and writer, whose work as an international news executive with CNN and for Channel 4 News has taken her all over the world, from the seats of power in both Westminster and Washington to the frontlines of Iraq and Afghanistan. Her debut thriller, *The Source*, was a Capital Crime Book Club pick, won the Crime Fiction Lover Best Debut Award, was nominated for the CWA's New Blood Dagger, was a number one bestseller on Kindle and is currently in production with Lime Pictures. It was followed by the critically acclaimed *The Shot, Dirt* and *Death Flight*. Follow Sarah on X @SultoonSarah and Instagram @sarahsultoon.

Also by Sarah Sultoon and available from Orenda Books

The Source
The Shot
Dirt
Death Flight

Blackwater

Sarah Sultoon

Are they still lying to us?

Sarah
xx

**ORENDA
BOOKS**

Orenda Books
16 Carson Road
West Dulwich
London SE21 8HU
www.orendabooks.co.uk

First published in the United Kingdom by Orenda Books, 2025
Copyright © Sarah Sultoon, 2025

A catalogue record for this book is available from the British Library.

ISBN 978-1-916788-98-5
eISBN 978-1-916788-99-2

Typeset in Garamond by typesetter.org.uk
Printed and bound by Clays Ltd, Elcograf S.p.A

MIX
Paper | Supporting
responsible forestry
FSC® C018072

For sales and distribution, please contact info@orendabooks.co.uk

For Gill and Pete – even better friends than neighbours.

Prologue
Christmas Day, 1999

The child looked like a porcelain doll. Dark eyelashes resting on pale cheeks, softly pouting lips, sandy hair swept neatly under a flat brown cap. Delicate hands folded across a miniature cotton shirt and waistcoat. A figure of peace, placed in repose on the bracken as if simply lying down to rest next to a pyramid of rocks. Even the bluish tinge to the skin could have been explained away by the moonlight.

Except this was Blackwater Island. An uninhabited tidal landmass in the middle of Essex's Blackwater river. An ecosystem so rare and fragile that it was designated an official wildlife sanctuary and closed to visitors many years earlier. Until an anonymous call before dawn on Christmas Day, Essex police had only ever seen it from a distance, shrouded in the near-constant haze hanging low over the estuary. They weren't just wary of its protected status as a nature reserve. Blackwater was once a Viking stronghold. The myths and legends surrounding its fall to the Saxons dated back to the Dark Ages.

The caller had left a message on the automated answering service at the small police station in the nearby mainland town of Maldon. All Detective Inspector Gillian Peters overheard before the caller hung up was that an innocent child had died in Blackwater's wilderness. The only police officer permanently based in an area long overlooked in favour of London, she was used to feeling isolated and edgy. But she wasn't prepared to deal with the body of a child alone. There was just one person she could call who she knew would help her without question. The local pathologist. More used to dealing with dead bodies than she'd ever be.

By the time the two of them reached the copse at the centre of Blackwater's wilderness, the vegetation was almost over their heads. The all-pervasive estuary mist had turned to rain and the wind tearing through their sodden clothes felt like a lash. But they were coming up against far worse than the elements. For all Blackwater's mythical folklore, there was no escaping the reality of the scene before them.

A child was dead. Bearing no obvious signs of cause or recent injury. Laid next to a makeshift shrine, on an island long presumed to be largely untouched by human hands.

The two women paused, eyeing the child's chest, damp and still as a painting. Peters blamed the rain for the single tear escaping down her cheek. Turning, they did their best not to contaminate the scene and went to call for reinforcements. The only wet footprints left in the bracken were theirs.

Chapter One
Herefordshire, two days earlier

Sudden darkness. Total disorientation. Rising panic. Jonny Murphy is thrown the instant the hood is plunged over his head. He saw it coming – the edge of a black pillowcase was hanging out of one of his assailants' pockets. Why else would the man be carrying it? They're outside, on a farm in the middle of the English countryside. But that split second of anticipation has done nothing for Jonny's ability to fight back. He's suddenly moving like a rag doll, wrongfooted by more than just the dark. He's had a hood thrown over his head on the job before and was lucky to escape with his life that time.

His two assailants manhandle him at speed down the lane at the edge of the giant yellow field. Jonny knows where he's being taken – he saw that a split second earlier, too: an old shed by the boundary corner, rusty door already hanging open. Chosen exactly for this purpose, he realises with a sour rush of adrenaline, recalling the men's unsolicited offer of a ride out into the fields to help investigate reports of suspicious behaviour. Jonny is the journalist in this equation. He's operating alone in a tricky location that he knows is hiding something big. He shouldn't be taking offers of anything at face value. Stumbling, he lands hard on his knees in the undergrowth.

'Careful,' a voice warns, yanking his arms over his head so he can be hauled along the ground. 'We don't want to bruise the product.'

Product? Some of Jonny's spirit returns at that. He may have made mistakes. But he isn't a product of anyone or anything. Objective thought and independent action are at his fucking core. Digging his heels into the dirt, he pulls back with his arms as his assailants try to drag him forward.

'Oooh, got some fight in you after all.'

More jibes and taunts, but they are glancing off Jonny now. He works for a major international newspaper. He's driven to find out the truth at any cost. And the instructions clanging around in his mind are those he's successfully followed before. Leave footprints. Leave evidence. Fight for your life. He goes limp, dragging his feet until a pair of hands grabs at his ankles. Then he kicks out with as much strength as he can muster, heel connecting with something unmistakably solid.

'You jumped-up little shit,' a voice spits thickly. Jonny pictures blood collecting in the man's mouth, and he kicks out again with a wet thump. The scuffle escalates. There's a whole lot more swearing. An alarm sounds somewhere deep in Jonny's mind, but he refuses to acknowledge it. Not yet. Not until he's got the job done.

But then his leg is caught and immobilised. The cotton pillowcase is pulled tight across his face. And now he's off the ground, spreadeagled in the air, facing downward. He feels his notebook fall from his pocket, heart sinking with it. Proof of his entire investigation just disappeared on the wind.

Leave evidence, he reminds himself, even though he knows his notebook is the one thing that these men will spot and pocket immediately. They're after information. They want to know exactly what Jonny knows. And Jonny has most of it written down.

Grunting, the men carry him along until a scrape, creak and distinct change in the atmosphere confirms they're out of the open air. They must be inside the shed.

Jonny is bent into a chair, his hands quickly yanked behind his back and tied together. The stench of fertiliser assails him with such sudden intensity it threatens to make him gag inside the hood. His mind races. They're on a farm. Fertiliser's not unusual or especially dangerous – unless it is mixed with a combustible material. Then it becomes one of the two main ingredients needed to produce a homemade bomb. He starts sniffing wildly despite the stench, suddenly desperate to detect a whiff of diesel too. If he's right, then he's in the bomb's kill zone. And he'll have confirmed this farm's secret. He tunes out the alarm sounding deep in his mind again. He's still not ready to listen to its warning.

Then the pillowcase is yanked off his head as suddenly as it was plunged on. A row of giant fertiliser drums are all that he registers before two different assailants step heavily in front of him, unrecognisable in black gloves and balaclavas.

Jonny scrutinises each man, remembering to drop his head deferentially a split second too late. Don't make eye contact. Minimise aggression. Play for time. Instructions clatter around in his mind until a voice heavy with arrogance and entitlement rings around the shed.

'Start talking.'

Jonny flinches, keeping his gaze low. Keep calm. Concentrate on practical details. This man is trying to rattle him. He can't let himself rise to it. Twisting his hands behind his back to test the tension of their bindings, he is encouraged to find his chair demonstrably unstable, wobbling with his every movement.

'About ... about what?' he asks.

Now a second voice, reedy and sinister, redolent of intelligence – the brains of the operation. Not the brawn. 'You know exactly what.'

Jonny plays dumb. He's so close to finding out the truth about this farm he can literally smell it. But it's worth nothing if he spills his guts now or can't get out of this fucking shed. A gloved hand reaches out to chuck him under the chin before running a menacing finger down his chest.

'Don't make me wait, Jonny. We've got plenty of ways to loosen your tongue. And the longer I have to stand here staring at you, the more I like the idea of using some of them.'

The brawn lifts his shirt to show off the conspicuous lack of manual safety on the handgun tucked into his waistband. But it's the sight beyond him that makes Jonny catch his breath. A large, red, plastic fuel tank positioned directly in front of a giant fertiliser drum. Unmistakable evidence of a makeshift bomb factory. One instruction instantly supersedes the others clanging around in his head: play for time.

'You've already got my notebook,' he begins, rocking in mock panic on the increasingly feeble chair. 'Everything I know is written down in there.'

The finger jabs hard into Jonny's gut. 'Wrong answer. But since I believe in delayed gratification, I'll let you have another go.'

He rocks harder. 'I don't … I don't know what you mean.'

Breath, rancid and hot, is suddenly puffing directly into Jonny's face. 'You're sniffing around this farm for a reason. We want to know exactly what it is.'

But he doesn't have to reply. One last determined rock and the chair finally gives way. Jonny shoots both forward and down, angling his body so he thunders into his assailant like a rocket. The man groans as he sprawls in a winded heap.

Scrambling to his feet, Jonny bolts for the open shed door. Dives into the yellow meadows. Blunders on through a shower of pollen. *Leave footprints. Leave evidence. Fight for your life.* Then the thunder of heavy boots catches up with him. Rough hands grab at the arms still tied behind his back. Jonny falls to his knees as soon as he recognises the two men who drove him into the fields at the start. His assailants from inside the shed reach them seconds later.

Gazing up from his clump of felled yellow wheatgrass, Jonny can't disguise the desperation in his voice. He looks wildly between the four men, by now all arrayed brick-set in front of him, bright pollen dust splayed beneath their feet.

'Did I make it? Did I pass?'

'Sorry, son.' A balaclava comes off to reveal a face and a wry smile that Jonny recognises from a seminar on weapons held at the farm earlier in the week. 'You failed the minute you got on to the tractor alone with these two jokers.' The balaclava waves at the two men to his right. 'It couldn't have been more obvious they were leading you into a trap.'

All the fight is draining out of Jonny in disappointment. Suddenly that stupid alarm in his mind is ringing so loud it is deafening. Surely he isn't going to fail? He can never fail, no matter what it costs him.

'But I got the story. Isn't the whole point of this exercise to test whether I can get the story and get out safely? It was literally the first thing you said when I got here – that the aim of this course is to teach journalists how to do our jobs as safely as possible. That I had to find out what the farm was hiding but be prepared to fight my way out to report it. And it's a bomb factory – right? The empty tank of diesel that I couldn't miss right in front of the fertiliser drums? You even used a bright-red one. Nice touch, by the way—'

'No.' The man cuts him off with an expression caught somewhere between irritation and pity. Jonny feels marginally better as he registers the cut swelling on the man's bottom lip. 'You've completely missed the point of this exercise. We're all former special-forces soldiers. We don't care about the story. We just care about teaching you lot how to stay alive long enough to get it. That's what we're practising here. And you were toast the minute you agreed to get on that tractor without backup.'

He pauses to spit blood into the dirt before continuing.

'Better luck next time, eh? Look on the bright side. At least you're not dead. Or took a boot to the face. You wouldn't have had a hope in real life.'

Chapter Two
London, 30th December 1999

Jonny ferrets around for tea bags in the grimy cupboard above the coffee machine. The newsroom's windowless kitchen is still choked with the detritus of a Christmas spent in the office. Dirty dishes are piled high in the sink. There's a faintly rotten note in the air. A black bin bag is leaking empty microwave meal cartons directly on to the floor – along with the frayed edge of a red felt Santa hat.

Beside him, Paloma reaches for the glass jug on the machine's hotplate. She eyes its thick and murky contents. 'Think this is drinkable?'

Jonny sighs, taking down two mugs instead of the box of Tetley's he was hoping for. 'It'll have to be. We're out of tea bags.'

Paloma replaces the jug in mock horror, her American accent coming out with an exaggerated twang. 'Hold the front page. An English newsroom is out of tea bags?'

Jonny gazes at the empty workstations beyond the squalid kitchen, still strung with tired loops of tinsel. 'Listen, tea is no laughing matter around here. No one can get any work done without it. And anyway, not even breaking news stands a chance of making it into the paper at the moment – unless it's about the new millennium.'

Paloma pours herself some coffee. 'Still sore, I see.'

'About spending Christmas sitting around in here?'

She raises an eyebrow over the lip of her mug. 'No.'

Jonny broods on his failed training course. Proving he knows how to operate safely in warzones should have been easy for someone like him. He's a frontline news reporter. The *International Tribune* covers stories from all over the world. He's already had a lot more experience of warzones than most people ever have.

'I am still a bit pissed off about that course,' he admits. 'I just don't particularly want to talk about it any more, is all.'

'Even if it's just to remind you of how many sticky situations you've already extracted yourself from – successfully and without the help of former special forces?'

His mood lifts a notch or two. 'Well, since you put it like that.'

'There you go. And it's true. I was there for some of them too, remember?'

Jonny recalls the moment they first met. A violent street riot, a febrile South American city. Paloma had arrived from the US to try and find freelance work as a photographer while he had been attempting to make a name for himself covering Argentina's financial crisis.

'How could I forget,' he adds wryly. 'I suppose it just still winds me up that after repeatedly proving I can do the actual job I suddenly need to pass a test to keep doing it. And it's not even for anything related to journalism. It's just to tick a new box on the company's insurance policy.'

'It wouldn't be much of a training course if you didn't need to pass a test at the end.'

Jonny slops some more coffee into his mug. 'It didn't feel like much of a training course to start with. The whole thing was more of an advert for the army than anything else. We spent ages playing with guns and bullets. Did you know that special-forces soldiers don't carry pistols with manual safety catches these days?'

Paloma looks interested. 'Really? Since when?'

Jonny instantly regrets getting drawn back into discussing the bloody course again. The truth is he was so busy spinning out over the uncertain status of their relationship while he was doing it that he could hardly concentrate, let alone remember anything. Telling her how he really feels about her the night before it started was by far the most unnerving thing he's ever done. And for what? He still isn't sure how she really feels about him.

He tries to move on. 'I'm not sure. Something to do with the Cold War. That's when we got on to chemical weapons. Then it was every different kind of military operation in the book. Talking me through the logistics of attack helicopters, tanks, boats, even submarines. Marvelling at glossy photos of hardware.'

'I see what you mean about an advert for the army.'

'Right.' Jonny slurps his coffee, grimacing. 'Man alive, this stuff is disgusting.'

'Drink it fast,' Paloma says. 'You don't taste it that way.'

'If you say so,' he replies, gulping down the rest. 'Nope. Still absolutely rancid.'

She puts down her mug with a grin. 'So the whole thing was just military PR?'

'Basically. And we only got to the practical stuff right at the end. Which was mainly just a list of instructions about what to do in the event of an ambush or hostage situation. Leave evidence. Play for time. Fight for your life. The usual.'

'But I thought you said the ambush they staged was actually pretty realistic?'

'It was. They knocked me off my feet, put a hood over my head. Tied me up and tried to force me to spill my guts about a story they'd planted.'

Paloma frowns. 'Sounds a bit heavy.'

'Not really. I mean, we know it happens.'

Her face darkens. Jonny immediately feels guilty.

'I managed to kick one of them in the face though,' he adds.

'I bet that made you feel better,' she remarks.

'Only for about ten seconds. The truth is if I'd kicked anyone in the face the last time someone shoved a hood over my head we definitely wouldn't be here now.'

She rinses her mug in the sink. 'Then maybe it's a good thing that you failed.'

Jonny is silenced for a moment. Their reporting on Argentina's financial crisis had led to a far darker investigation, which seriously threatened both of their lives. Starting again in London hasn't been easy for either of them. He may have been raised in the UK but his upbringing wasn't exactly straightforward. And Paloma's story is almost worse than his. For at least the thousandth time he wonders whether the one person on earth he feels like he can actually relate to will ever feel the same about him.

'Maybe so,' he finally says. 'But now I'm stuck with reporting on the bloody new millennium every day that I don't have this damn certificate.'

Paloma clangs her mug on to the draining rack. 'Well at least you've only got two days of it left.'

'I suppose that's one advantage of covering a countdown,' he mumbles, still preoccupied, running an unconscious hand down the buttons of his shirt where days earlier he'd been repeatedly jabbed in the stomach. 'I know exactly when it is going to end.'

'But not *how* it is going to end, huh?'

He looks up to find her smirking. 'Don't you start. If I have to interview one more person about the risk of total digital meltdown at the stroke of midnight I will melt down the fucking computers myself.'

'Can you explain it to me? I still don't totally understand how they think it will work.'

'The millennium bug, you mean?'

'Yes. I know it's a computer virus but don't get how it could torpedo everything.'

'Experts are warning of a potential glitch in numerical recognition software that could see chaos take hold in the new year,' Jonny recites, as if by rote. 'A computer's ability to differentiate between—'

'In English, please. Preferably the American kind.'

'Look, I don't have any tea.' Jonny gestures at the coffee grounds in his own mug. 'So that's the best you're going to get right now.'

'Well no one is going to let you write about anything else if you can't even explain it to me.'

'OK, OK. It's simple, really. It's just about how computer programs interpret dates. For example, when's my birthday?'

Paloma's eyes narrow. 'Is this a test?'

'No,' he replies decidedly, even though it kind of is a test – just of nothing whatsoever to do with computers. 'It's an example. Just tell me when my birthday is.'

'July fifteen? And you're already a year older than me, so 1975.'

He tries and fails to stop himself beaming. So she knows when his birthday is. That doesn't mean she also knows and loves the recesses of his pathetic soul.

'Correct. July the fifteenth, 1975. Now picture the universal way we enter dates into computer systems. The two digits we use to represent the day, the month and the year. Can you see how straightforward it is for a computer program to interpret the difference between my birthday and your birthday on that basis?'

'And when's my birthday?'

He answers a little too quickly. 'January the twenty-fourth, 1977.'

'Very good,' she replies, raising an eyebrow. 'OK, I see what you mean. The numbers seventy-five and seventy-seven make it clear which date comes first. Right?'

'Exactly. The concern now is that when the year updates from 1999 to 2000 the computer might roll backward in time rather than forward because it's never had to deal with a year ending in two zeros before.'

Paloma's eyes widen with recognition. 'So loads of automated systems might collapse as a result?'

'Bingo. Software engineers have been speculating about it for years. The first sign things might go wrong was when an American woman born in 1888 got an automatic invite to join her local nursery when she was one hundred and four. A computer program in some tiny town in Minnesota interpreted the last two digits of her year of birth as 1988 and therefore thought she was four years old.'

'But surely advanced computer systems can cope with a simple variation in numbers.'

'That's why it's called a bug. Experts can't definitively predict how all the software is going to behave. Think of it like a variation in the virus that causes flu. Immune responses will differ and some patients will really suffer. But imagine if computers flying a packed passenger plane suddenly malfunction. Or billions of dollars are wiped off financial markets. All information held online is also potentially vulnerable – bank details, medical records, state secrets, the whole salad. Everyone thought what happened in Minnesota was funny until an industry magazine published an article called "The Doomsday Bug". Now total costs of counter measures are estimated at between three and five hundred billion. International action is being co-ordinated by the fucking United Nations.' He knows he suddenly sounds irritated, but he can't help it. He's been writing different versions of the same story for months.

'But most of these computer systems are still operated by actual people,' Paloma persists.

'That's part of the problem. Even just one person worrying about it is enough for millions to start panicking. The prospect of unpredictable systems failure is terrifying. What if nuclear weapons are accidentally discharged? Or planes start falling out of the sky?'

'And there we have the story to end the century,' Paloma finishes archly. 'I get it now. Even though it still sounds a little ridiculous.'

Jonny reaches into the sink to rinse out his mug. 'Right. Readers love a good conspiracy. And all this coverage just feels like we're giving them one because they want one, not because we know one actually exists. At least it'll be over soon, one way or the other. And you get to take beauty shots of fireworks and drunk people dancing all night.'

'I like how you think you're the one with the most boring assignment.'

'Well, you are going to be at one hell of a party.' He pauses. Then tries to ask his next question as if he doesn't care what the answer is. 'Do you know exactly where they're sending you yet?'

'Tower Bridge. They're trying to get me a second security pass so I can get closer to Westminster, but it's not looking good. I'm just happy I don't have to do any of the accreditation paperwork myself. The background checks are crazy. There are different identity badges for each press pen along the river bank. Arrangements for the pleasure boats on the Thames with the best view of the fireworks were finalised weeks ago. They're even calling the display the "River of Fire".'

'Right.' Jonny tries not to sound disappointed. 'I'm down at Westminster.'

'As you should be.' Paloma avoids his gaze. 'Hey, if senior reporters aren't right at the heart of things then...' She trails off into a shrug.

Jonny replies with a forced laugh.

'Come on.' She eyes the rest of the dirty crockery in the sink with distaste. 'It's time.'

Chapter Three

The London bureau chief – Lukas – frowns as Paloma and Jonny join the daily morning huddle at the newsdesk a few seconds late.

'As I was saying.' Lukas taps the edge of the desk with the rolled-up magazine in his hand, running the other through his shock of strawberry-blonde hair. 'There are some great angles on the millennium bug to pick up and run with today. The planning department has been working overtime. We've got an exclusive interview with the two pyrotechnicians in charge of the firework display by the Thames. The whole event is computerised and could, therefore, potentially fail—'

'The fireworks are computerised?' Jonny interrupts before he can catch himself. 'How is that even possible? Isn't this just about lighting a load of fuses?'

Lukas's eyes narrow behind the thick black frames of his glasses. 'That's why it's a doubly good get. They're having to set the rockets off from barges on the water because they're expecting a million people to gather and watch from the river banks. So a computer program is going to send radio cues to the technicians on each barge from an operations room at Tilbury Docks.'

'Which I suppose is why they're calling the display the "River of Fire".'

'Right. The route starts at Tower Bridge and ends in Vauxhall. Four miles of major London landmarks. It's all about maximising the beauty and impact of the spectacle. Gotta compete with all the displays due around the rest of the world. A snapper somewhere is going to win best picture and these guys are dead set on it coming from London.'

'I'll give it my best shot,' Paloma pipes up beside Jonny. He smarts as Lukas smiles at her. A murmur of encouragement ripples around the group.

'We've also got an interview lined up with a family of four who will be airborne over the Indian Ocean on the stroke of midnight,' Lukas continues. 'Prices are a fraction of what they usually are so they're headed to Australia to see a terminally ill relative. They can't afford to worry about potential systems failure—'

'If we're going to do that, can we at least talk to a pilot too?' Jonny interrupts again. 'They're the ones who actually need to keep the planes in the air. What if computer systems malfunction to the point they lose control of the aircraft?'

Lukas's clipped South African accent turns distinctly brusque. 'As I said, the planning department has been working overtime. We're also interviewing both a pilot and a spokesman for British Airways.'

'Well we already know exactly what they're going to say. The airlines are just trying to sell as many tickets as they have seats.'

Finally Lukas pauses, turning to the news editor seated directly next to him, a neat blonde woman whose sharp black jacket and crisp white shirt look at odds with the crumpled, resigned expression on her face.

'You can take it from here, Lisa. Jonny and I will be in my office.'

He points the rolled-up magazine at Jonny before flicking it in the direction of his office in the newsroom's far corner and stalking away. Loose newspapers flutter in their wake like tumbleweed as Jonny follows. He knows he's about to get schooled – and he deserves it. Lukas was doing him a favour by sending him on that course, and Jonny blew it.

'Close the door,' Lukas snaps. Jonny tries and fails not to bang it shut.

'What the fuck is your problem, man? Is this all because of what happened on the course last week?'

'I'm sorry,' Jonny begins, but Lukas is still shouting.

'Don't *ever* speak to me in public like that again.'

Jonny has to look away. 'I just ... Listen, it came out wrong.'

'And how exactly was it supposed to come out? Like you weren't questioning my editorial authority? Or openly shitcanning the work of your colleagues? Or making your disdain for the top news story around the world as plain as your disdain for the way in which we're covering it?'

'I'm sorry,' he repeats. 'I'm just tired—'

'Tired? We're all wrecked! Planning Millennium Eve is mincing everyone. What makes you special? You've even had a week off kicking back on a farm telling war stories.'

'Don't remind me.' Jonny shifts uncomfortably on the spot, finally choosing to drop into an armchair. A beat of uneasy silence passes between them before Lukas sits down too.

'Why don't you tell me what's really eating you?' Lukas asks. 'Is this all still because of failing some stupid test?'

'It can't be that stupid if I have to pass it to do any more frontline work, despite all the experience I've had already.'

'I'm well aware of how you feel about it, Jonny.'

Silence. The truth is Jonny knows exactly how Lukas feels about the course too. They were the only two punters left in the bar the night before he left when Lukas had finally admitted to feeling as dubious about their new training requirements as Jonny. He can't help thinking that if Lukas had schooled him to take the whole thing more seriously then he wouldn't have gone on to track Paloma down in the small hours and spill his guts to her. But he says none of this. Instead he just apologises again. 'Like I said. I'm just tired. It isn't all that surprising.'

'Ja, I suppose not. What are you, twenty-four? Twenty-five? Still a child. Just a child who's also a senior reporter at a major international newspaper.'

Thinking of the story that resulted in this promotion almost exactly a year ago makes Jonny feel even worse. He would never have got it into the paper without Lukas, who was the architect of Jonny and Paloma's arrival in London after their investigation into human-rights abuses in Argentina provoked riots on the ground there. Jonny owes Lukas a lot more than just his loyalty.

'So what are you saying – that I need to act my age? Apparently I already am.'

Lukas's tone softens. 'Just that you gotta be able to play the corporate game better than this. It's hard, I know. You've already achieved more than some reporters achieve in a lifetime of trying. I know you just want to get back at it. But the new millennium is the only story in town right now. And the fact all our computer systems might implode right as it starts is the most interesting angle by far. Some people are losing their minds over it. They think the whole world is going to flame out. Did your girlfriend tell you about the panic room we found on a shoot in a bank last week?'

Jonny tries and fails not to smart at the reference to his relationship with Paloma. 'She's not my girlfriend.'

Lukas waves a hand. 'Ja, I forgot. You two are still dancing around that idea.'

'It's complicated,' Jonny mutters. 'I guess it just bothers me more than I thought it would … The story, not Paloma,' he adds hurriedly.

Lukas leans forward. 'Listen, man. You know how the news business works. Determining what's in the public interest is also about what the public is interested *in*. And short of nuclear war – which, by the way—'

'—some people think might actually happen by accident as a

result of catastrophic systems failure on the stroke of midnight...'
Jonny finishes for him. 'Yep, I know. I've done that story as well.'

Now Lukas's eyes are boring into him, rimmed red with
exhaustion. 'Do you need more time off? Is that it? I need you
pumped and ready for the big day and night tomorrow. Don't
think I didn't notice – and appreciate, by the way – that you were
kicking your heels in here on Christmas Day with the rest of us.'

'Definitely not.' Jonny shakes his head a little too vigorously.
'I'm not that tired. I'd need a personality transplant to want to go
sales shopping. And believe it or not, I actually like microwave
turkey dinners.'

Lukas stares at him for so long Jonny has to turn away. No one
to spend Christmas with other than colleagues – again. Finally
hitting his stride in journalism, Jonny hadn't expected his personal
life to remain quite so spectacularly pitiful. Taken into care after
his single mother killed herself when he was nine. Discovering it
was because he once had a twin sister kidnapped by his abusive
father while they were both still babies. Spending every quiet
moment that followed wondering where this fabled twin sister is
now and whether finding her would ease the crippling fear of
abandonment he's been living with ever since. He peers at the
patterned carpet like it's some kind of Picasso until Lukas finally
says something else.

'Tell you what. I can live without a byline piece from you today.
Most reporters never turn down a byline, but on this occasion I'm
guessing you'll be OK with it.' Jonny looks up to find him waving
a sheet of paper from the printer behind him. 'Here. Have a read
of this.'

'"Essex police are investigating the death of a child on
Blackwater Island",' Jonny reads under his breath. '"Authorities are
appealing for the child's family to come forward. Anyone with any
information is urged to call Essex police." That's it? What is this?
A news wire? And where exactly is Blackwater Island?'

'You tell me,' Lukas replies with a half-smile. 'You've got until this time tomorrow to find out. No child should die without explanation, not in this day and age. Not in any age...' He trails off into a yawn, rubbing his eyes. 'Look, just call it a day off. No one needs to know you elected not to spend it in the pub except me.'

Jonny leaves a pause before saying, 'You're asking me to investigate something other than the potential consequences of a computer error?'

Finally Lukas grins, standing up and making for the door. 'Ja. Turns out that sometimes I'm not so great at playing the corporate game either.'

Chapter Four

Shoving the piece of paper into his pocket, Jonny is hurrying out of the newsroom via a side door before Lukas has even made it back to the newsdesk. The trip home to his tiny studio flat – chosen for its position a ten-minute walk away from the *Trib* newsroom – passes in a windy, wet squall. He'd live directly above the newsroom if he could. Better still, spend his life on the road. Asking the tough questions, holding power to account, never turning away. The mantras of journalism sound hollow as they rattle through his head but he doesn't care. Too much time alone in the empty silence of his flat takes his mind to places he doesn't want it to go. Unlocking his front door, he has to remind himself that he's only going to get his stuff and get out again.

Inside, he's shouldering his bag with one hand while rifling through the piles of maps on his bookshelf with the other. *Essex police are investigating the death of a child on Blackwater Island.* And where exactly is that? Shaking open a map of South-East England, he scrutinises the grid squares of Essex county, quickly registering the Blackwater river and an unlabelled island in the middle just a few clicks north of the wide blue mouth of the Thames. Not so far away after all, he thinks, swapping the map for the news wire folded in his pocket and absorbing its little information again with increasing incredulity. Why aren't police calling this investigation a murder inquiry? And how did the child die? If there is a killer of the worst kind on the loose, shouldn't a massive manhunt be under way? *Authorities are appealing for the child's family to come forward...* So the victim's identity remains unknown. No local children were previously reported missing? *Anyone with any information is urged to call Essex police.*

Finally Jonny pauses for a moment. He's cut his news reporting teeth in places where bodies turn up without explanation all the time. But they are almost never children. And when they are, they are never unidentified for long. There are always families going crazy with grief, screaming for news. Or a missing-persons file with a name and face to match. Reading between the few lines of this police report, Jonny knows exactly how much information has been left out. He tucks both the piece of paper and the map of Essex back into a pocket of his cargo pants before heading back out on to the street.

Outside, the rain is intensifying. But Bill's familiar black minivan is already idling at the kerb. Giving the driver a grateful smile, Jonny pulls open the passenger door.

'A new record,' Bill observes from the driver's seat, windscreen wipers thumping.

Jonny laughs as he slides inside, stuffing his rucksack into the back through the gap between the front seats. 'When did you get the call?'

'Twelve minutes ago.' Bill swaps hazard lights for a single indicator, pulling out smoothly into the traffic. 'From Lukas himself. Something about you needing an escort to Essex. There's a joke in there somewhere, but I'm not the man to make it.'

Jonny brightens further. The *Trib* has a fleet of drivers on retainer, ready to transport reporters and photographers at a moment's notice, but none come close to Bill. A flash of his distinctive white ponytail against his immaculately pressed black suit and matching shirt in the driver's seat gets every journey off to a hopeful start, no matter where it is due to end up. He's everyone's favourite. And Lukas has assigned him to Jonny.

'So ... ten minutes for the walk back over here,' Bill continues. 'Unless you ran? No cheating, now.'

Jonny shakes his head. 'I walked the usual way. Straight up the main road. So I was only upstairs for two minutes?'

'And nineteen seconds. Not bad. You don't even have a flight to catch. You've done it inside three minutes before, but only just.'

'I already had a bag packed.' Jonny gestures into the back of the van. 'I've been staring at it longingly every night for months.'

'I don't doubt it. You news reporters always want to be somewhere you're not.' Bill squints at the rucksack in the rear-view mirror. 'Hang on, you've got a sleeping bag too?'

'Yep. It's ultra-lightweight. Dead easy to carry.'

'You're camping in Essex? What on earth has Lukas got you doing this time?'

'Honestly, I'm not sure yet,' Jonny answers, frowning as the traffic thickens. 'But I thought it was a good idea in case I get stuck—'

'In Essex?' Bill laughs. 'It's barely fifty miles away, son. And they have hotels, I hear. Although it's going to take us a good while if the traffic is already this bad. Where exactly are we going?'

'Have you ever heard of a place called Blackwater Island?' Jonny reaches back through the gap between the seats and takes the map from the top pocket of his rucksack.

'No.' Bill changes lanes, indicator thumping through the van. 'And if I haven't heard of it, that usually means it doesn't exist. Nearly fifty years on the road will do that to a man.'

'Well, usually, I'd agree with you.' Jonny opens the map, folding it back on itself to leave the coastal section uppermost. 'But according to Essex police it definitely exists, and I can only assume it's this island in the middle of the Blackwater river.'

'Have you got a nearby village for me, or anything like that?'

'Eastwood,' Jonny answers, squinting at the map. 'According to this, we drive past the town of Maldon, and then Eastwood is right on the water.'

'Maldon.' Bill's face brightens. 'Now you're talking. I know exactly where Maldon is. It even came up on the radio just now.'

Jonny frowns. 'Really? So the news is already out?'

Bill looks quizzically at him in the rear-view mirror. 'Poncey cooks talking about fancy salt is news? Don't tell me you lot are falling for the stuff being different just because it comes as flakes in a box.'

'Oh...' Jonny realises what Bill is talking about. 'You mean Maldon sea salt.'

'Right. They want five pound a box. Salt is salt. And where else would it come from other than the sea?' He bangs a hand on the steering wheel. 'Please tell me that's not the news you're talking about.'

'Definitely not.' Jonny gazes at the map. 'Essex police investigating the death of a child on Blackwater Island is about all I know so far.'

Bill whistles. 'That's terrible. A kid?'

Jonny nods. 'Apparently. I haven't spoken to the police myself yet. I probably should have called first. But Lukas has given me a day out of the office. I didn't want to waste any time sitting on the phone.'

Bill sighs. 'You need to watch yourself, son.'

Jonny pauses. 'Watch myself? What do you mean?'

'You know what I mean. Burning out long before you're thirty is going to get you nowhere fast.'

Jonny shifts around in his seat. 'I'm hardly burning out. I'm just a bit bored. All I've been doing since I started reporting from London is writing up different angles on some computer virus that no one even knows is real. At least when I was freelance—'

'Ah yes.' Bill cuts him off. 'That old chestnut. You preferred being your own boss with no idea where your next pay cheque was coming from to being named senior reporter because of a scoop that most correspondents with decades more experience than you are still dreaming about? ... And don't look at me like that. I read the paper too, you know.'

Jonny hangs his head. 'I know I probably expected too much. I just thought I'd be out and about a bit more than I have been since, is all.' He leaves the rest of it unsaid. No family, no friends other than colleagues, no real possessions, unless he counts the rucksack and sleeping bag in the back of the van. No one of any real meaning in his life except Paloma. Who at least shares his purpose, if nothing else.

'Plenty of time for that,' Bill demurs, accelerating into a gap in the traffic. 'You've got years left in you to save the world.'

'I don't know about that,' Jonny mutters. 'But thanks. I probably don't say it enough.'

'For what? Doing my job?'

'That, and for always having deodorant and toothpaste in the back. You make it easier to do mine.'

'All part of the service,' Bill replies, tipping a hand to his forehead.

'Mind if I put the radio on? I need to know if anyone else has picked up the story.' *And got there before me*, he adds silently.

'Of course not.' Bill waves a hand. 'Unless it's those chefs again. I'd rather listen to the shipping forecast. I rather like the shipping forecast, truth be told...'

But Jonny is already back in the zone. The siren call of breaking news is the only real purpose he has. A child has been found dead on an unmapped island barely fifty miles outside the city of London. Not a single family member has come forward to claim the body since. All Jonny really knows is that he's got less than twenty-four hours to find out enough to keep the story alive.

Chapter Five

'We're here.' Bill's voice jerks Jonny awake. He swipes at the sweat beading on his forehead.

'How ... how long was I out?'

'What's the last thing you remember?'

Jonny fidgets in the passenger seat, squinting out of the window. Water. Lots of it. Covered in haze. Hard to tell where the water starts and the land ends. Or the sky – the same blank white as the haze. Or is that the water? 'I ... I don't know. I just...'

'I know, son. I know.' Bill taps a gentle finger on the gearstick. 'The motion gets most people.'

Jonny nods back a little too vigorously. 'Yes. That's it. Especially with the heating on.' He gestures pointlessly at the vents in the van's central console.

'And the way I drive too, right?' Bill cocks his head towards him rather than look Jonny in the eye.

'Exactly,' Jonny affirms gratefully. Bill is giving him an out. He can hardly admit that the only time he can sleep properly is in broad daylight. The vacant dark of a silent night invites visits by way too many ghosts from his past. Bill pulls up at the end of a dirt track, before turning to point at the flat, featureless land behind him.

'I didn't see much of a village back there so I kept on driving,' he explains. 'Eastwood, was it?'

'Apparently.' Jonny scrabbles for the map, now stuck between his leg and the passenger door. 'And I'm guessing that Blackwater Island is here.' He points to the unlabelled island in the middle of the river.

Bill pulls the map into his own lap, putting on the glasses hanging on a thin chain around his neck.

'This says it's a nature reserve,' he remarks, pointing between the island and the map's key in the corner.

'Something else the police neglected to mention in their report,' Jonny mutters to himself, looking at the tiny indicative symbols ranged in a neat box at the edge of the page. Bill traces the route back through Eastwood with his finger.

'Looks about right,' he says after another moment. 'I drove past a couple of buildings. That was pretty much it.'

Together, they squint through the windscreen ahead.

'So technically, straight ahead of us should be an island,' Jonny says, peering into the river and then turning to look out to sea. He can see nothing other than mist and, in the distance, the unmistakable hulk of a container ship chugging determinedly north across the mouth of the estuary.

'Technically, there should be a causeway, too,' Bill adds. He points out a thin line across the blue water on the map that Jonny hadn't seen before. 'When the tide is right, I'm guessing the riverbed is exposed enough that you can drive across.' He frowns. 'If you've got the right tyres, that is. Which, before you ask, I haven't.'

'Let me look around for a second.' The passenger door rattles as Jonny slides it open.

'Take your time,' Bill calls after him, but Jonny is too busy coughing to reply. The air is so thick with salt that it sticks in his throat almost immediately. Bill leans over to slide the door shut, turning off the engine.

What Jonny assumed was a dead end to the dirt track is actually just the rise of a river bank, covered in gritty reeds. Edging closer, Jonny can see the high-tide mark, written in the line of salty residue deposited just below the lip of the bank. Saltmarsh, Jonny thinks, squinting through the thick sea mist swirling in the middle of the estuary, blocking any view of the opposite shore. He looks up and down the river, and spots a second container ship steaming past in the opposite direction to the first. He briefly wonders why before he remembers that the Thames and its gateway to London is only a few miles to the south.

'You're right,' he says to Bill after heaving the passenger door open again. 'I guess it must be possible to drive – or at least walk – on to the riverbed at certain times. I could see the high-tide mark. The reeds are rimmed with salt.'

'Eastwood should be looking a whole lot smarter if they really are selling the stuff at five pound a box,' Bill remarks. 'I knew something didn't smell right. Want to go back? Ask around there.'

'In a second,' Jonny replies, pausing at the open door for another look into the mist. 'I'm sure this should still be a crime scene. Or at least there should be evidence that there was one nearby very recently. Especially if police are still investigating.'

Bill shrugs. 'Hard to stick hazard tape on the water.'

Jonny searches the length of the deserted river bank, finds nothing except reeds and haze. 'But there's not even a footprint or tyre track – nothing to suggest anyone has been near here recently. Unless you count the container ships steaming around the place,' he adds, into the distant blare of a horn.

'Well there's probably all sorts of rules if it's a nature reserve,' Bill says, gesturing into the haze.

'Yes, but...' Jonny trails off as he wonders. 'Never mind. Let's go back to Eastwood.'

Barely a minute later, Bill is slowing and waving at a cluster of buildings through the windscreen. 'This is it. See why I didn't stop? Hardly much of a village. Where next?'

'Drive through as if we're just passing,' Jonny answers. He'd have preferred not to draw attention to himself by having Bill drive a shiny black minivan with tinted windows back and forth through an area that's probably never seen a similar vehicle stop for long, but it was too late now. 'I'll walk back in alone when we've worked out where you can sit and wait for me for a bit.'

'Ah.' Bill nods. 'Sorry. Did I blow your cover?'

'Of course not,' Jonny answers just a little too quickly. 'We're in Essex. We're not on the moon.' Still he finds himself hunching down until they're far enough past the buildings that they are no longer visible in the rear-view mirror. 'Let me out here,' he says, pointing to the side of the road. 'I actually think it's probably best that you drive back to London rather than hang around. I don't know how long I'm going to be—'

'What?' Bill cuts him off. 'I thought you only had a day to look into this?'

'Lukas said twenty-four hours,' Jonny answers. 'So I've got a night as well.'

'You sure?' Bill pulls over. 'I can wait here for a bit, no bother. I don't want to have to turn around to come and get you as soon as I get back to the office.'

'Well at least you won't have been sitting around in the middle of a field the whole time. Your car radio probably doesn't even work properly out here.'

'We're in Essex. We're not on the moon, Jonny. Isn't that what you just said?'

Jonny reaches for the doorhandle, trying to keep the irritation out of his voice. The truth is he wants to string this fishing expedition out as long as possible. He doesn't need a quick route back to the place he'd rather not spend any longer in than absolutely necessary.

'OK, fine, so the radio works. I just think I'm better off on my own here. And I might be a while running this down. There's a lot of information missing from the police report.'

Bill frowns, but seems to decide against arguing any further.

'Alright then. Be off with you. I hope you don't have to use that sleeping bag.'

'So do I,' he replies, thinking the exact opposite as he gets out. 'Thanks. Hope the traffic isn't too bad on the way back.'

Chapter Six

Muddy fields spread flat and wide to his either side as Jonny walks quickly back down the road to Eastwood. A thick white sky hangs low overhead, every step bringing another layer of sticky damp to his clothes. Pausing just before he reaches the hamlet's cluster of buildings, he debates his next steps. What's his legend going to be this time? Are locals more likely to answer his questions if he poses as a clueless traveller looking for a bed for the night? Or is he an environmentalist on a research expedition to a nature reserve? If he is, why doesn't he already know how and when he might be able to access the river's tidal islands? Maybe he is best off as himself – a journalist looking into the mysterious death of a child. No locals will take issue with that – unless they've got something to hide.

Jonny walks on, still undecided. Past a post office, a general store, a few unmarked buildings and a pub, obviously. Named The Saxon. The only one of the buildings showing any sign of life, despite the fact it is barely lunchtime. Jonny pauses again, eyeing the pub's grimy façade. For a public house its small, darkened windows look decidedly private.

A voice calls from somewhere. 'You after a pint?'

Jonny stills on the spot.

'A pint,' the voice repeats, followed by the rattle of steel on steel. An elderly woman is stepping out from The Saxon's open doorway, heaving the remains of an iron security grille over her head.

'Sure,' Jonny replies after a moment, taking in the grubby Saint

George's Cross flag being unfolded and hung from a pole jutting out over the doorway.

'Can't help you, then.' The woman stands back to admire her handiwork. 'Need a new barrel. But I've got plenty of English Spirit.'

'English Spirit?' Jonny parrots, staring at the red cross fluttering on its white background, pointedly absent of the additional stripes that would turn it into a Union Jack.

'Never had any, have you. I can already tell.'

'I don't seem English enough for you?' Jonny replies lightly, eyeing the woman's slightly hunched back through her frayed grey housecoat.

'Well you're not from round here.' The woman's back is still turned. 'You'd know what English Spirit were if you was.'

Jonny is momentarily wrongfooted by her grammar. 'I suppose so,' he says hurriedly. 'Is there anywhere else around here open for a pint before lunch? I've had a long journey.'

The woman turns, appraising Jonny with a gaze as harsh and grey as flint. 'You better come in. The Sax is the best you're going to get.'

Jonny ducks below the flag, already hanging limp with damp, and follows her inside. He takes in the small saloon. Wooden stools and a couple of lumpy brown armchairs. A small Christmas tree that already looks dead. Low lights mounted on nicotine-stained walls. Dark carpet, pattern indistinguishable from stains. An ancient-looking dog bowl rimmed with limescale left just inside the door.

'Here.' A shot glass full to the brim lands on the grimy bar.

Jonny eyes the bead of clear liquid trickling over the rim of the glass. 'I'm guessing English Spirit is the local tipple of choice.'

The woman nods approvingly. 'Essex's finest. Far more refreshing than any pint. Make it myself, out back. Have done for fifty years. The first sip's always the best. And the very first? Well. That's the best of all.'

Jonny contemplates the glass in front of him, painting on a smile as he catches sight of his slightly pained expression in the smoked glass mirror hanging behind the small bar.

'Go on.' The woman nudges the glass towards him with a wiry finger. 'Set you up right for the day, it will. And there's plenty more where that came from.'

Jonny downs the shot, mercifully without coughing, feeling strangely proud of himself. Maybe those long lonely nights in the pub avoiding the empty silence of his flat have been worth something after all. Throwing his reflection another smile, he squints at the picture frame hanging beside the mirror, looking decidedly out of place underneath a row of tired optics. A fine pencil illustration of what looks like the angriest mermaid he's ever seen. And a single word – Inka – stencilled along the bottom in thick, angry black letters. Replacing the glass on the bar, the woman is already reaching for the bottle to fill it up.

'Two in a row,' she says. 'That's what you need. Can't do it in a bigger glass, mind. Need a minute to savour the flavour.'

'Yeah, I see...' Jonny plays along, distracted by the picture. He grapples to identify something other than the reek of pure ethanol. 'Is that juniper? Or raspberry?'

The woman replaces the bottle on the bar with a pointed clunk. 'This look like raspberry to you?'

'I can definitely taste something fruity,' Jonny answers, avoiding looking at the demonstrably clear liquid inside the bottle.

'Fruity.' The woman snorts. 'That's a new one. Go on, down the hatch. On the house. Always enjoy giving someone their first taste of proper English Spirit. Especially a young lad like you.'

Jonny grimaces, slugging down the second shot and willing his eyes not to water.

'Right you are,' he says pointlessly, swallowing hard. 'I feel fortified ... yes. I feel fortified with English Spirit!'

'Fortified,' the woman echoes slowly, as if she's rolling each syllable around in her mouth. 'Another new one. Must be something special you got to do today.'

There go those eyes again, sharp as the moonshine swilling uncomfortably in Jonny's empty stomach.

'Do you do any food to go with your English Spirit? Or know anywhere that does?'

The woman replies like he's asked the world's stupidest question. 'Oysters. By the dozen. No sauce.'

Jonny blanches at the thought of adding raw mollusc to raw alcohol. But the woman is already disappearing into the dark corridor behind her. Bending to empty what's left in his shot glass on to the floor, he spots the dog bowl again and the faded name *Monty* handwritten along its yellowing side. The thought of a dog snuffling around the place instantly makes the tired saloon feel more forgiving. There's a clunk as the woman returns and puts a plate on the countertop. Sitting up, Jonny is immediately stymied by the sight of a bed of ice covered in a hefty pile of oyster shells, gnarled and silver as the veins on the woman's hands.

'Thanks,' he says, opting to gesture at the bowl by the door rather than try his luck with the oysters straight away. 'Is Monty your dog? What kind?'

The woman looks pained, ignoring the question as she reaches under the bar. Jonny starts gabbling, further unsettled by the sight of the penknife in her calloused hand. 'I love dogs. I had one for years, her name was Hero. She was a terrier of some sort, maybe with a bit of greyhound or whippet in the mix. Came to us from a shelter when she was just gone three, wouldn't even let me stroke her at first...'

He trails off as the woman snaps open a fat blade and deftly shucks open an oyster for him. 'There. Get that down you. You can do the rest yourself. Only way to learn.'

Jonny tries not to wince, casting around for something else to say that will delay actually having to eat anything. 'Do you ... do you have any salt?'

The woman snorts. There's an unmistakable twinkle in her grey eyes as she regards him. 'You're a one. Go stick your plate in the river if salt is what you're after.'

Emboldened, he slurps down the first oyster, feeling distinctly like he's about to pass a test. The woman responds in kind. 'That's the spirit.'

A curious combination of salt, alcohol and the anticipation that he's about to be taken into someone's confidence starts to fizz through Jonny's veins. He reaches for the blade to shuck himself another oyster, but the woman stops him, reaching over to do it herself.

'Give over. Don't want you bleeding like a stuck pig over my bar.'

'Thanks,' Jonny says. 'Is it really that obvious I don't know what I'm doing?'

She passes him another oyster. 'As the nose on your face.'

Jonny slurps down a couple more in quick succession, finding them oddly satisfying.

'These are really good,' he mumbles, swallowing. 'Really, really good.'

'That they are. Wish I could say people come from far and wide to enjoy them. But they don't. We don't get nothing out here. Have to make our own luck.'

Jonny eyes the English flags pinned up like posters all over the stained walls. They're the only decoration save for the framed pencil drawing behind the bar. 'How long have you been in business?'

'Business,' the woman echoes bitterly. 'That's a laugh. The Sax is a family pub. I'm all that's left of the family, mind. Place dates back to the Vikings.'

'Does it,' Jonny prompts, toying with an empty shell.

'Don't know your history either, I see. That why you're here? Come to learn something?'

'You could say that. I didn't think I'd need to go back to the Dark Ages though.'

'For what?' The woman's eyes narrow.

Jonny holds her gaze for a second before digging around in his rucksack. Pulling out the map, he points out the island in the middle of the river.

'Is this Blackwater Island?'

'Depends who's asking.' He notes the woman looking away rather than at the map. 'You a Viking or a Saxon?'

'I guess I'm a Saxon,' Jonny replies after a moment, watching her carefully. 'Since the Saxons won in the end, didn't they?'

'Only after the Vikings raped and pillaged everything in sight,' the woman answers, still resolutely looking elsewhere. 'Hid on Blackwater for years, they did. No better place to hide than right offshore. Came up the causeway when they fancied having a go. Regrouped whenever the river closed around them. Took an age for the Saxons to finally win out.'

'So this is a causeway?' Jonny points at the line drawn in the river itself, trying to get her to actually look at the map. 'And this is Blackwater Island? There is dry land between the two when the tide goes out?'

The woman hesitates like she's given something away. 'Mud,' she finally answers, turning back to him with a sigh. 'Black mud. It's the reason they called the river Blackwater.'

'Must say I'm surprised you don't get more visitors,' Jonny continues, eyeing her tired and resigned expression. 'It sounds like a fascinating place.'

'Blackwater's closed to visitors. Has been for years. Only things there are plants. All kinds of plants. Magical apparently. Not that I'd know. Don't believe in fairy tales.' She opens up her cash register with a clang.

'Sorry,' Jonny says hurriedly, folding up his map. 'How much do I owe you?' He passes over a twenty-pound note without waiting for a reply.

'That'll do.' The woman takes it with a small nod. 'Don't got no more oysters due in today. So you best not come back looking for anything else.'

She disappears into the dark corridor behind her without another word.

Chapter Seven

Jonny gets to his feet. A nauseating combination of oysters and alcohol is churning in his stomach. Outside The Saxon, he finds the smattering of other buildings that make up the lonely hamlet of Eastwood still deserted. He swaps the map for the news wire folded into his rucksack's top pocket. 'Essex police' he reads from the top line for the umpteenth time, scanning the empty street for a local cop shop. Coming up blank, he heads back down the dirt track towards the river bank, but his view of the water is still completely blocked by thick, swirling cloud.

Staring into the mist, Jonny starts to feel distinctly like a victim of an ill-conceived practical joke. He can't see any evidence of a nearby crime scene, much less evidence that an island in the middle of the river even exists. Why didn't he call Essex police before haring back to his flat to get his stuff? Why did Lukas let him rush out without confirming the most basic of details about this news story first? Was it just to get Jonny out from under his feet and teach him a lesson in the process? He pulls the map out of his pocket again, scans the surrounding area with a sigh. The local police station must be back in Maldon.

Stepping off the track and into the reeds, he decides to trudge along the river bank for a bit, see if the mist is clearing a little further down. He can see the beginnings of a pontoon jutting out into the river. And another container ship motoring past the mouth of the estuary in the distance. And – he catches his breath with a satisfied chuff – a telephone box. Traffic-light red and set back from the lip of the bank a few hundred yards ahead.

Breaking into a jog, Jonny checks his pockets for change, feeling like his luck might be about to turn. He squeezes into the booth and slots coins into the box, gabbling his questions to Directory Enquiries. An automated service at the local police station immediately confirms its location in Maldon town centre and promises pressing zero will reach an operator. But all that actually awaits is the relentless blare of dial tone. Replacing the receiver, Jonny spots graffiti scrawled above the coinbox, a drawing that feels strangely familiar. Waves and curls of a woman's hair, diamond-shaped eyes, body shaped like a fish tail. Loopy writing that he can't quite make out in the gloom.

Tracing a finger over the drawing, Jonny realises it is scratched into the telephone mount itself rather than just scrawled on top. Where has he seen it before? Reaching for his notebook, he lays a blank page on the top of the image, rubbing a coin over the surface so a rough copy is imprinted on the back of the sheet. Pleased with himself, he considers the pontoon further down the shoreline, briefly wonders whether he can commandeer himself a boat. That is until he registers a figure emerging from the gloom.

And as she approaches he sees the woman is clad in the unmistakable blue and white of a police uniform.

'Afternoon,' the officer calls to him as she hurries along the river bank.

'Is it?' Jonny stashes his notebook, checks his watch, plays for time. The officer arrives slightly out of breath, her cap slipping askew on top of her dirty-blonde hair.

'Detective Inspector Gillian Peters,' she says, flashing an official police badge along with a pair of snappy winter-blue eyes. 'Lost, are you? No one comes down here unless they know where they're going. Where exactly are you headed?'

Jonny is wrongfooted. He wasn't expecting to be put on the spot so quickly. 'Sorry, officer. I was just using the phone.'

Peters folds her arms. 'I heard there was a stranger in town asking about Blackwater Island. Wouldn't be you, by any chance?'

Jonny is floored. The Saxon's flinty landlady must have called the police the moment he left. Why? He eyes the handcuffs dangling freely next to the radio clipped to Peters' belt and reaches for a business card of his own along with his notebook.

'Yes. My name is Jonny Murphy. I'm a journalist with the *International Tribune*. I was just trying to call the police myself, actually.'

'Were you.'

A statement, not a question. Jonny gives her his best smile – full beam. 'Yes. So it's great to meet you on the scene. Saves me a trip to Maldon. I understand you're investigating the death of a child on Blackwater Island. I assume that's why you're here too? Since no one comes down here unless they know exactly where they're going?'

'Christ,' Peters mumbles, glaring at him. 'A smartarse, too. As if I don't already have enough to deal with.'

Jonny holds her gaze even though it is having the, presumably desired, effect of making him feel guilty even though he hasn't done anything wrong. He keeps up the smile for good measure. 'Are you? Investigating the death of a child on Blackwater Island?'

Peters stares him down until he puts the notebook away.

'Off the record,' he adds. 'I see you've put out a press release calling for anyone with information to get in touch with Essex police.'

'Let me be clear.' She unfolds her arms only to put her hands commandingly on her hips. 'Anyone trespassing – or suspected of intent to trespass – on Blackwater Island will be arrested and fined immediately. And also risks being charged with tampering with a police investigation. Blackwater Island is a protected nature reserve. There are acres of paperwork in the public domain that attest to it.'

'That must make finding the body of a child there all the more disturbing. Your press statement doesn't mention a murder inquiry, though.' Jonny gestures into the mist hanging low over the river. 'Is that why this whole area is no longer a crime scene?'

Peters ignores the question, replying through gritted teeth. 'I thought I'd made myself perfectly clear. Suspicion of intent to trespass is a criminal offence—'

'How can you prove intent to trespass? Surely a journalist is entitled to ask questions of the police when the body of a child is found? Doesn't the public have a right to know if a child killer is on the loose?'

Peters advances on Jonny, scowling. 'Lecture me on matters in the public interest again and I'll have you in a cell overnight. Some of this land is private property. How do you know you aren't already trespassing?'

Jonny holds up his hands. 'I apologise if I am. I didn't think a public phone box would be on private land. Covered in graffiti, too. I'm obviously not the first person to have used it.'

At that Peters' expression changes, so fleetingly that Jonny can't read it. He keeps his hands in the air as she pushes past to check for herself. Returning to his side with a sigh, she extends a hand. 'Let's start again, shall we? I'm Gill. You're—'

'Jonny,' he replies, returning the gesture with a decisive grip. 'I'm not trying to get in your way, I promise. I hadn't even heard of Blackwater Island before I read your police report.'

'That's just it,' Gill replies with a grim shake of her head, finally taking a moment to adjust her cap. 'Hardly anyone has. And until we found the victim, we didn't think anyone had set foot on the place for years.'

'So what happened?' Jonny asks.

Gill sighs again. 'You best come with me.'

Chapter Eight

Gill motions Jonny into the front seat of a battered yellow Volvo overflowing with the detritus of a life spent on the road. She slams the door, sending litter showering into his lap.

'Everything I'm about to tell you is off the record,' she says, quickly putting the car into gear. 'I'm only trusting you because I have to.'

He peers gingerly over his shoulder as she reverses back up the dirt track at speed. Two battered children's car seats are flying from side to side across the backseat, along with a grubby pillow and blanket. An open washbag is spilling makeup, toothpaste and a small can of deodorant into the footwell.

'Cases involving children must be so hard,' he says, still eyeing the car seats and personal effects bouncing around all over the place. 'I appreciate you telling me more about it. I should have said so earlier.'

Gill purses her lips, accelerating. 'Indeed. I got the call before dawn on Christmas Day. Not the sort of thing you're ever really prepared to hear, even in this line of work. Someone left an anonymous message on the answering service at the station. By the time I got to the phone they'd hung up. And they must have used some new-fangled software to make the call as it's been impossible to trace. All I know is it came from a woman.'

Jonny doesn't need to ask what she was doing at her police station in the middle of the night. Probably more comfortable than the backseat of this car. 'What exactly did the message say?'

'Just that an innocent child was dead. And that not only would

I find the body on Blackwater Island, I'd find it in the middle of the wilderness in the centre. That's the reason the island has protected status. Its wilderness is thought to be almost completely untouched. *Was* thought to be, I mean,' she adds.

He looks over his shoulder again to peer through the rear windscreen at the river behind them. All he can see is mist. 'Then surely this whole area should still be roped off for investigation?'

'It should,' Gill agrees. 'Except it's not. Because as you correctly spotted in my press release, this isn't a murder inquiry. The cause of death has already been established as natural. We just don't have an identity yet. So we're back to the tired old status quo around here. Which is me, myself and I.'

Jonny frowns. 'You've already had a post-mortem?'

'Yes. I don't have the exact details. The pathologist'll have her official report ready by tomorrow.'

'And that's it? You're the only one left working the case?'

'Yes. Even though children don't routinely turn up dead in places thought to be uninhabited and closed to visitors. But look around you.' She gestures at the empty landscape to their either side, lying under a heavy sky quilted in grey. 'Does this look like an area overflowing with investment?'

'It doesn't seem particularly developed, if that's what you mean,' Jonny answers. He stops short of saying it looks like the definition of an abandoned, neglected backwater.

'Exactly. The same goes for the police out here.' She roots around in a pocket for her badge before tossing it into his lap. 'I'm a detective inspector. Going by rank, I should have a sergeant or constable on the team, preferably both. But instead I'm told to handle this district by myself because I'm apparently senior enough and experienced enough to manage alone. And I'm expected to be happy to do it because I grew up around here. Told it's a great gig because I'll be my own boss and I'll get reinforcements when I really need them. Well, it's been nearly five years, and I can tell you it is absolutely none of those things. It's actually like everyone wants to turn the other way when things happen around here. Especially now.'

'Why now?' Jonny asks, almost sure he already knows the answer.

'Millennium Eve. No one's seen a security operation like it before. It's unprecedented. Everyone is terrified of what might happen if that stupid computer bug takes hold.'

Jonny turns her badge over and over in his fingers, shaking his head. 'Are you honestly telling me that a child has died in demonstrably dodgy circumstances and the police are abandoning the investigation because of a giant New Year's Eve party?'

Gill bangs a hand on the steering wheel. 'Unbelievable, right? That's why I need help. I can't keep working this on my own.' She gestures at the car's squalid interior. 'You'd think I'd drive an official patrol car, but I don't even have that.'

'The child's family still hasn't come forward?'

'Nope. And I'm not holding my breath on that one, either.'

'Why not? Grief-stricken relatives don't usually stay quiet.'

But Gill just shakes her head rather than answer him directly. 'He was just a boy. Can't have been more than two years old.'

Jonny flips open his notebook, mentally noting to press her more on the child's family after she's finished telling him about the body rather than interrupt her flow now.

'And he was wearing the most curious outfit.'

Jonny's pencil stills. 'Outfit?'

'That's the only word for it. He was dressed like a Victorian street kid, is the truth. Looked as half-starved as one, too. Just not as dirty. Flat cap, shirt, waistcoat, those weird long shorts—'

'—pantaloons,' Jonny mutters, but Gill is still talking.

'Who dresses a child like that? Some kind of statement, I suppose ... Just a statement someone like me will never understand.'

'And you don't know exactly how he died yet because the post-mortem still isn't official?'

Gill nods. 'Right. And like you said, there are no relatives screaming and crying, or beating down the door for the details. Isn't neglect murder of a sort? The fact is that the only person who seems to care about what happened to this kid is me.'

'And me,' Jonny is quick to add, still wondering why she seems so sure about this.

But when Gill continues, she sounds anything but mollified. 'Which is why you're going to help me out. I need some more attention on this. And you're going to help me get it.'

Chapter Nine

Jonny frowns, thinking fast. Being taken into a police officer's confidence so quickly doesn't always mean being told the truth. And everything that Gill has said about the way this case has been handled so far sounds more than a little suspicious.

'Where are we going?'

'To the station,' Gill replies grimly, speeding through a red traffic light.

Jonny keeps trying to defuse the tension. 'What's back at the station?'

'Evidence. You'll see what I'm up against when I show it to you.'

Another red light flashes past in a blur. Low industrial buildings start to appear on either side of the road. A length of broken guttering swings dolefully in the wind. 'I take it you're the only traffic cop around here too,' he adds before he can think better of it.

Gill snorts. 'People around here get away with all sorts when I'm not looking.'

'Presumably that includes you too.'

She replies with another burst of acceleration. 'Just wait till you've seen the evidence. I know what you journalists are like. You need to see it for yourselves to believe it.'

Jonny can feel himself relaxing slightly at the prospect. 'That is true,' he says wryly, gazing out of the window at the outskirts of the town of Maldon taking shape – neat rows of prefab houses, wrought-iron streetlamps, a few sleepy shop fronts. 'I'm still finding it hard to believe that you're the only police officer permanently stationed out here. Isn't it standard practice to respond to emergencies in twos, for starters?'

Gill taps an irritable finger on the steering wheel. 'That's what I mean about people around here getting away with all sorts when I'm not looking. I'm not supposed to attend emergencies alone. Of course I do, because I can't ignore an emergency call. But then my version of events can always be called into question. And I can't be in two places at once, either. So what do I do? A bit of this and a bit of that. The job is half done all the time. The only other person officially affiliated to the police out here is the local pathologist. She's the one who had to come with me to Blackwater. Believe me, it took a lot for me to call her, but I needed someone fast and she had at least dealt with a body before.'

'But that level of staffing – or lack of it, I mean – is crazy for a district barely fifty miles from London,' Jonny says, wondering why calling the local pathologist was such a big ask. Surely Gill must speak to her all the time if she's the only officer within range. 'It'd be crazy for any police operation other than somewhere seriously remote. And it can't be sustainable in the long run?'

Gill pulls on to a gravel forecourt in front of a nondescript low-rise building. 'Well I've sustained it for plenty long enough. Come inside and you'll see.'

Jonny stares up at the building's grimy façade. The only sign it has anything to do with the police is a faded blue insignia mounted above a glass-fronted noticeboard. Gill is already halfway to the entrance as he opens the passenger door, showering more litter on to the gravel. He scoops up as much as he can with both hands and heads for the rubbish bins.

Gill pauses. 'Don't bother. Those bins will just get tipped over later. Kids round here have got nothing better to do. That's why my car is so full of crap. It just ends up on the street if I throw it away.'

Jonny puts it in the bin regardless. He can't bring himself to dump it back inside her car. The squalor was already suffocating.

Following her towards the building, he pauses at the sight of a pinboard by the door, its glass cover smeared with something that looks distinctly like bird shit. *Welcome to Maldon Police Station*, he reads off a notice set next to an ancient-looking missing-persons' poster – a picture of a small boy holding an ice cream, half hidden by the top of the poster curling wearily away from the pinboard itself. He squints at it, murky winter daylight already fading. And along with it, he realises, any chance of making it on to Blackwater Island before he's expected back in the newsroom tomorrow.

Inside the station, Gill heads through an internal set of doors into an unremarkable reception area. Plastic bucket chairs, raised check-in desk, harsh strip lights. An iron grille separates a single dank holding cell from the rest of the room. Already behind the desk, she flicks on an electric kettle in the corner and shakes instant coffee into two white china mugs. Jonny leans on the desk, peering into the recesses in time to see her stirring the contents of each cup with the end of a pen she pulls out from behind her ear.

'I'm out of milk,' she says, walking over to him with a steaming cup. He tries not to grimace at the greasy sheen on the surface.

'Thanks,' he says reluctantly. 'So. Evidence, you said? Of what, exactly? How the child died?'

Gill motions that he sit down. 'How long have you got?'

'As long as it takes. Especially if I'm the only journalist you're talking to.'

She answers after a meditative sip. 'You might be. It depends.'

'On what? Have you already spoken to other reporters?'

Gill shakes her head. 'No, but I might if you're no good to me. You might leave me with no choice.'

He frowns. 'How might I do that?'

She turns and walks over to a metal filing cabinet. Opening a drawer, she lifts the entire thing clean out of its aluminium housing and carries it back over to Jonny.

'There's plenty more where that came from too,' she says, dumping the drawer on the desk between them. 'Every cabinet you can see in here is stuffed full. Read any file you want and you'll find the same thing.'

Jonny stares at the reams of paper poking out of the drawer. He had been expecting crime-scene photographs and plastic evidence bags. Samples harvested from Blackwater's rare undergrowth. Transcripts of statements from potential witnesses.

'This is the evidence you've been talking about? Where can I find photographs of the crime scene?' He reaches over to take out some papers before pausing – he doesn't want to contaminate anything. 'Surely this filing cabinet isn't where you're keeping everything you bagged and tagged?'

Gill glares at him. 'You don't get it, do you. I don't have anything to show you. That's the whole point. A kid is dead and nearly a week later I've got nothing except this. A mountain of unfinished paperwork.' She gestures angrily at the overflowing drawer. 'This is what I'm up against. Every single one of these pieces of paper will prove it to you. I'm completely alone out here. I've got no resources, no support, no oversight – no nothing. No one cares what happens out here except me. All of these files are incomplete.'

She pauses to rifle out some folders before walking from behind the desk to sit down next to him. 'Here. Take a look at this picture-perfect snapshot of a consenting relationship.'

Jonny is silenced by the sight of the bruises and bite marks on the face in the photograph that Gill is placing delicately in his lap. It's almost as if she's taking care to handle it in a way that won't risk causing the victim any more pain.

'Now, that apparently consenting adult's emergency call got interrupted,' Gill continues. 'Don't ask me how. I'm sure you can guess. A blow to the head, probably. Or a mortal threat to the child watching. By the time I arrived, the husband had the story all straightened out. There was nothing I could do about it except take the picture. And here's another one.' She slots the photo carefully away before passing him a different folder. 'Be grateful I'm not showing you the photos this time. But feel free to have a browse. There's plenty there. I just can't close these cases without more help.'

Jonny fingers the file in his lap but can't bring himself to open it. He pictures the ancient missing-persons' poster drooping away from the noticeboard on the wall outside the entrance, only held in place by a glass cover smeared in bird shit. He couldn't even see the missing person's name.

'You join the force with a dream.' Gill's voice suddenly sounds very small. 'It's not about power, or control – or even about right and wrong. It's about community. All people really want is to feel like they belong somewhere safe. To feel like they are part of a team that always has their backs. And police officers are no different.'

Something clicks deep inside Jonny's mind then, in one of the dark corners where he tries to never linger. The news business is a tribe of a sort. And it's the closest thing Jonny has to a family. He can suddenly feel Gill's despair at being sold out by her tribe as viscerally as if it were his.

'This is the evidence you wanted to show me? And none of it has anything to do with the child found dead on Blackwater Island?'

'Right.' Gill meets his eye with a gaze full of conviction. 'But here's the thing. If you report that I'm investigating a murder, then we might actually be able to find some that does.'

Chapter Ten

Jonny stares back at her. 'But didn't you say the pathologist has already determined the cause of death as natural?'

'Yes. But I'm not convinced. I haven't read her official report yet, for starters.'

'So you don't trust her headline judgement? I thought she was with you when you found the body.'

'It's not as simple as that. Do you believe everything you read?'

'I thought you said you hadn't read her official report yet,' Jonny replies, putting a laugh into his voice.

'You know that's not what I meant.'

Gill's hackles are rising, but Jonny knows better than to let his rise too. He won't make progress by getting into an argument. 'I'm just interested to know what's stopping you believing her straight off.'

'It's not that I don't believe her. I just think there's a lot more to this case than some medical determination. Like how did the body end up there in the first place? There were no signs of recent disturbance. No footprints of any kind, not even teeny-weeny ones. A child thrashing around and dying in the reeds would leave footprints. So someone must have got rid of them.'

Jonny shrugs. 'Maybe it rained. It doesn't take much to wash away a footprint. Especially if they're small.'

She waves a hand. 'Rain. Fine. Whatever. But then explain to me how I'm tipped off to the exact location of the body without others being somehow involved. I think the boy died somewhere else and was moved deliberately to hide the evidence.'

'Makes sense,' Jonny agrees, choosing his next words carefully. 'Wouldn't there have been a trail of some sort, then? You said there were no signs of recent disturbance. But the vegetation in a nature reserve must be pretty thick and unwieldy. Actual footprints can be disappeared relatively easily but plants don't all immediately bounce back if they are stamped on and damaged.'

Gill gathers the files in her lap together and stands, bitter blue eyes blazing at him. 'Look, you don't believe this was some random accident any more than I do.'

He stays seated, nodding for good measure. 'You're right, I don't. But we're just speculating about it, aren't we? Unless you're sitting on some solid evidence that suggests otherwise? I don't have to get into the specifics on the record, of course. The last thing I want is to risk prejudicing any criminal trial. But I also can't report anything that wouldn't stand up in court.'

'Well if you won't do it then I'll find another reporter who will. I'll fix it so that they have to.'

Jonny holds up his hands in a last attempt to de-escalate things. He spotted where this conversation was headed long ago. Gill wants him to lie to help her case. She's not going to incriminate herself by asking him directly – so he won't do himself any favours by calling her out. But she's clearly desperate enough to hint at it. He can't risk her panicking further and doing something even more counter-productive, like planting evidence.

'Look, no one will be brought to justice if the crime scene is tampered with. I know that's not what you want to happen here.'

'What does a kid like you know about crime scenes? Think you've already been around the block for long enough? I took an oath—'

'—to discharge your duties according to the law,' he interrupts, he can't help himself. A child has died. Justice must be done. 'If either of us lie about this, then we're breaking it.'

Finally Gill pauses, covering her face for a moment. 'Christ. A kid is dead and here I am being lectured on the law by another kid who could actually help me do something about it. I should have a sergeant, a constable – hell, even two fucking constables to police a town this size. It's not right. Can you imagine what it's like for me, day in, day out, knowing I've been set up to fail at every turn? Now I have a tragedy on my hands that I can't investigate properly because some jobsworth won't give me even half the resources I need because it doesn't tick a box. I'm desperate, OK?'

Jonny watches her collapse back into her chair. He suddenly recalls the box-ticking training exercise that he was engaged in himself a few days earlier. She continues without looking at him.

'You think you know my oath. Well, I know a whole lot about yours, too. To make a difference, to give voice to the voiceless, to speak truth to power. Every journalist I've ever met wears their sacred vows like a fucking halo. So go ahead and write your story about the criminal levels of inattention our government pays to rural policing. See what kind of a difference that makes. And then come back and tell me what you think about what I'm really trying to do here.'

The sight of her shrinking into herself makes Jonny feel even more uncomfortable. 'Look, I can see what you're up against. And I understand your frustration a lot better than you think I do. But why are you being so openly set up to fail? No manager, not even a really crap one, can expect you to handle cases like these on your own.' He waves at the overflowing drawer. 'There must be more to it. So I can promise you I'm definitely not going to drop the story. But you know I can't just make stuff up. It won't help either of us. And it definitely won't help the victim.'

'I do,' Gill answers in a small voice, still staring at the grimy floor. 'I just thought...' she trails off into a sigh. 'I put the initial police report out right after we found the body. You're the only journalist to show up here since. I just thought—'

'—that I might be as desperate as you?'

'For a story, or something like that, anyway. I don't really know what I thought, is the truth. I'm so tired. Tired of it all.'

Jonny thinks about the squalid confines of her car, pictures the pitiful bedding strewn over the tiny backseat.

'It must take a toll. Especially at Christmas.'

'Don't remind me,' she mutters. 'I've barely seen my own kids. Proved their father right again with how absent and neglectful I can be.'

Something suddenly occurs to Jonny as he wonders about the occupants of those two child seats sitting on top of the bedding in her filthy car.

'You were very clear about this not being a murder inquiry while we were driving over here. Why didn't you tell me that it was from the outset?'

'Lying doesn't come all that easily to me either. I needed you to understand.'

'And I want to. I know it feels like you're the only one who cares, but you're not. I'm still here, aren't I? But you'll have to let me do it my way if you want me to stay.'

'Your way,' Gill echoes bitterly. 'What way's that, then?'

'Take me to Blackwater. Let me see the official post-mortem report. Show me how difficult it is to be part of a safely functioning community anywhere outside of the capital. Give me grounds to demand your superiors explain exactly why you're so isolated out here.'

'And you'll write about it all?'

'I will,' Jonny replies recklessly, pushing away the thought that writing about it doesn't always guarantee it will end up in the actual paper. 'Can we get going now?'

Gill lets out a brittle little laugh. 'No chance. There's no electricity on Blackwater. It'll be pitch-dark by the time we get there. I'll meet you on the pontoon at first light.' She raises an eyebrow at him. 'If you stick around that long, that is.'

Jonny tries not to look as crestfallen as he feels. He already knows there is a lot more to this story than a single body. But how is he going to justify more time off the millennium clock to the *Trib* when currently there's no evidence to suggest there's a child killer on the loose?

'I really do know how you feel,' he mumbles under his breath. 'I'll see you there,' he adds, more loudly. But Gill is already disappearing back out to her car.

'You can see yourself out,' she calls over her shoulder.

Chapter Eleven

On the desolate forecourt outside the tiny police station, twilight is rapidly turning to dusk. Jonny plods back down the road towards Eastwood, weighed down by a lot more than just the rucksack on his back. A child is found dead in an uninhabited nature reserve and barely a week later there's only one police officer still looking into it? That alone is enough for Jonny to keep at it. He knows what it is to be a child alone in the world. He isn't going to stand by and allow other children to just disappear, as if they never existed in the first place. He's so absorbed in his thoughts that the sound of an approaching vehicle makes him flinch. A black minivan with tinted windows is pulling up alongside him.

'Wotcha,' a familiar voice drawls. The window rolls down to reveal Bill's trademark white ponytail.

Jonny pauses. He should feel heartened at the sight of a friendly face. But ruminating on his past is still making him edgy. 'Hey. I thought you went back to London.'

'I did,' Bill replies with a smirk. 'Bet you're glad to see me again now, though.'

Jonny finds himself smiling back. The man's spirit is infectious. 'Why, because I need a lift? You don't even know where I'm going.'

'No,' he answers, turning off the engine to call over his shoulder into the back. 'You sure you want to walk, love? It's a good mile or so from here.'

Love? Jonny hesitates as the passenger door slides open. But then realises who is emerging from inside.

'Yes,' Paloma says, grabbing her camera case from the backseat. 'The longer I have to look around while it's still light, the better.' She grins at Jonny. 'Hello.'

'Hello,' he replies, trying and failing to sound nonchalant, and noting with more than a degree of trepidation that Paloma is also retrieving an overnight bag from the back of the van. 'What are you doing here?'

'Lukas figured you could use the company,' she answers, slinging the camera case over her shoulder. 'And it's beautiful out here, apparently. Bill was telling me all about it on the way over. Lots of unusual wildlife. Guess I'll believe it when I see it.' She gestures into the fading light with a wry hand, before heaving the door shut.

'Sure you don't want a ride the rest of the way?' Bill asks, tapping a finger on the steering wheel.

'Honestly, we're fine to walk,' she insists. Jonny is still busy feigning composure. 'It's always useful to see how the light changes things.'

'Amen,' Bill replies with another smirk. 'I'll leave you to it, then.' Closing his window, he drives away before Jonny has a chance to say anything else. Paloma regards him with an expression akin to pity.

'I didn't say goodbye to Bill,' he explains pointlessly.

'He'll forgive you, don't worry.'

'I just wasn't expecting him. Or you. I thought everyone was too busy for anything without the word "millennium" in it. I haven't even called in to tell Lukas how I'm getting on down here yet.'

Paloma cocks her head. 'And how are you getting on?'

'Fine,' he lies. 'I mean, I'm fine. But there's definitely something more than a little dodgy going on here. Blackwater Island is allegedly a protected nature reserve in the middle of the river. Which makes finding the body of a small boy there a whole lot more suspicious than, say, finding it in some filthy squat surrounded by evidence of abject neglect.'

Paloma looks suddenly mystified. 'What are you talking about?'

Jonny pauses again. 'You don't know? Didn't Lukas explain what I'm doing here?'

'No. I told you. He just figured we could use each other's company on a day like today so told Bill to bring me down to join you. I was hanging out in the crew room and I think he took pity on me when he realised I had nowhere else to go.'

'On a day like today,' Jonny echoes, stumped. He checks his watch, notes the date, it's unremarkable save for the fact it's almost the end of a millennium. A hurt expression crosses Paloma's face.

'Yes. It's exactly a year since we got here,' she says, reddening.

Jonny is instantly transported back to the turmoil of their evacuation from Argentina. Their reporting rewrote that country's history – and not for the better. Lukas had to move mountains to get them out in one piece. It was the kind of professional achievement that most journalists dream about. But it also cost Paloma her personal life. Unlike her, Jonny had nothing to lose on that front to start with.

'He remembered,' he murmurs. 'That's ... I wasn't expecting that. I've just been so caught up. I'm sorry. I should have remembered, too. For what it's worth, I think about how we ended up here all the time. I'm constantly trying to live up to the work we did in Argentina. It's why I've found covering the millennium bug all the time so frustrating. Lukas has a far bigger heart than I realised,' he adds, trying to make light of it. 'I suppose we should be grateful. We can't all get by on hearts of stone.'

'I think about it all the time, too,' she answers, avoiding his eye. 'Just not in the same way that you do, I guess. I'm just happy to have settled down somewhere new. I might feel differently if I had bad memories of this place to start with.'

'They aren't all bad,' Jonny replies, not trusting himself to say much more. Paloma knows the worst of his personal history. But they've never openly discussed it beyond establishing the facts. He's alone in the world. He's been alone in the world for years. This country is where his life fell apart. He was repeatedly lied to and finally abandoned aged nine by the one person he should have been able to trust above all.

Paloma roots around in her pocket for her familiar tin of tobacco. 'So what *is* going on down here? Lukas just said you were looking into a news wire and were due back in the office tomorrow.'

'I suppose he would say that,' Jonny says, mercifully relieved their conversation is back to business as usual. 'The news wire wasn't exactly detailed and I haven't had a chance to update him yet. Police found the body of a small boy on Blackwater Island on Christmas Day. It's an apparently uninhabited nature reserve in the middle of the river here. It's so uninhabited that it's not even labelled on the map. And the body is still unidentified. Not a single family member has come forward since. I've just had the only police officer looking into the case suggest I publicly lie about it so she gets the resources she needs to investigate properly—'

Paloma's exclamation echoes back at them over the water.

'I know, right? But she says her commanders won't commit any more officers to the case because the cause of death has been ruled as natural. And that she's been operating alone without support out here for years. A child turning up dead on an uninhabited island isn't suspicious enough for further investigation? The only concrete information I have is that there isn't any – which is even more suspicious. Now it's dark and apparently impossible to get on to the island to have a look around myself. She said she'd meet me down by the river at first light tomorrow. I tried to get her to take me today but she said it'd be pitch-dark by the time we arrived and there's apparently no electricity out there.'

'Just as there are apparently no people out there, too.'

'Right. She also tried threatening me with the charge of *intent* to trespass.'

'How can she prove *intent*?'

'That's what I said.'

Paloma snorts. 'So naturally we're going to try and go anyway?'

'Yes, but...' He trails off, something snagging in his mind at the discussion of Detective Inspector Gillian Peters. 'Actually, there's somewhere else worth going first.'

'And where's that?'

Jonny pauses for another moment, thinking of the drawing he saw in the phone box on the shoreline opposite Blackwater and the framed picture hanging on the wall behind the bar in The Saxon.

'I think I know where we might find someone who can help us.'

Chapter Twelve

Jonny pauses just before they reach The Saxon. Orange light is glowing from its grimy windows, the low hum of activity drifting from the open doorway.

Paloma lights herself another cigarette with a doubtful frown. 'This is where you think we'll find someone who might help us get to Blackwater?'

'Maybe. I've remembered a picture I saw in here that I also saw a version of in some graffiti nearby. I think they might be connected and I want to ask the landlady about it. It'll make better sense if I show you what I mean instead of trying to explain it.'

'You've already been in here once today? It doesn't look all that.'

He swallows reflexively at the thought of the oysters he ate earlier. 'It does certain things well. Just follow my lead, OK? I met the owner this morning. She wasn't exactly forthcoming so I'm going to have to try something different.'

She looks dubious, eyeing The Saxon's drab exterior. Heading inside, Jonny nods to the few punters he sees. No one smiles back. The dog bowl by the door is still empty and crusted with dust. Walking over to the bar, he pulls out two stools and sits down, motioning that Paloma follow. He is about to point out the drawing on the wall when The Saxon's flinty landlady materialises with a scowl.

'Thought I told you not to come back looking for anything else.'

'I found myself in need of more English Spirit,' Jonny replies, painting on a smile. 'She'd like some, too.' He nods at Paloma beside him, trying not to be distracted by the sight of her in the mirror behind the bar.

The woman looks sceptical. 'Don't usually get strangers turning up round here, specially not twice in one day.'

Jonny hesitates. He's not ready to show his full hand yet but pretending they're just tourists isn't going to get them anywhere fast either. 'We're journalists,' he finally says. 'We've been working flat out ahead of the new millennium and needed a change of scene from London.'

An unexpected spark of interest flares in the woman's eyes. She dumps a pair of shot glasses on the bar. 'So I s'pose you'll be needing somewhere to stay n'all.'

'Maybe so, yes. Anywhere you'd recommend?'

The woman fills their glasses. 'Mine's the only spare room in town.' She gestures into the dark corridor behind her. 'Blue door at the top of the stairs. Bathroom's opposite. No bath, mind.' She takes a brass key off a hook by the doorframe and pushes it towards them.

'Right, OK,' Jonny replies, sipping carefully at his drink before turning to Paloma. 'What do you think? I told you it was delicious,' he adds, willing that she play along.

Paloma takes the smallest sip possible from her glass, swallowing hard. 'It's definitely original. I've never tasted anything like it before.'

Jonny keeps improvising. 'What's it made of? Nettles, maybe?'

The woman looks at him with a small smile. 'That'd be telling. Recipe goes back generations. But you're close. I'll give you that.'

Grimacing, Paloma swaps her glass for the key.

Jonny casts around for other flavour options. 'Bullrushes? Marsh grass?'

But Paloma is already turning to him with an approximation of a yawn. 'I don't mean to be a drag, but since we're stopping here now, mind if I go and freshen up? The traffic was awful on the way over. I feel like I was stuck in the van for ages.'

'Sure,' Jonny says, downing the rest of his shot, suddenly far more unnerved by the prospect of sharing a bedroom with her than by any measure of alcohol. He'll have to find another opportunity to show her the drawing. She leaves the rest of her drink untouched and disappears with her bags.

'Americans,' the woman says, leaning forward with a conspiratorial grin. 'They think they can handle the hard stuff like us, but they can't. Especially not homebrew like this.'

'Too right,' he replies, willing her not to pour him any more. 'Hope you don't mind me asking, but I was wondering about that picture you have up there.' He points to the drawing on the wall and is relieved to see the woman putting her bottle of moonshine down to turn around. 'I'm sure I've seen it somewhere before.'

She frowns, reaching for the frame hanging next to the mirror. 'This?'

'Yes.' Jonny peers at the woman in the picture. Close up, he notices a small pistol sketched close to her body just above the point where it changes to a mermaid's tail. 'Who is it supposed to be?'

'Why d'you ask?'

Jonny hesitates, still not sure how far to go. 'I ... I like it. That's all.'

'And you think you've seen it before.'

Jonny pictures the graffiti he'd found earlier in the phone box on the shoreline. 'A version of it, yes. Is it significant in some way?'

'To what?'

'I just wondered if it was a local legend, or a symbol of some kind. I was just surprised to see the same drawing twice in one day. Was it done by a local artist?'

They are interrupted by a sudden snort. Jonny hadn't noticed the elderly man hobbling over to join him at the bar. 'Judith done that,' the man continues, banging his hand into his chest to clear a cough. 'Always used to have a pencil about her. Ain't that right, Judith?'

He taps his empty glass on the bar. She answers by drawing him a fresh pint. The man chuckles approvingly before shuffling away again.

Jonny stares at the picture, trying to compute its significance. Save for the fact he's seen two versions of it, it is otherwise unremarkable. He can't imagine why anyone would frame and display it.

'It's really good,' he tries again, but she is already turning away to hang it up again on the wall behind her. 'I was just interested in learning more about it.'

Judith pauses with a hand on the frame. 'You was askin' about Blackwater earlier.'

Jonny squints into the mirror but it is too clouded for him to make out her expression. 'Yes. I asked you to point it out to me on the map. You told me it was closed to visitors. Thing is...' He trails off as she turns around with eyes hard as stones.

'Blackwater is bad for business,' she hisses, gesturing angrily at the picture. 'And this here is why.'

'But isn't that just a drawing of yours? Why is it still hanging up if it's bad for business?'

She leans towards him. 'Because it ain't just a drawing. It's a ghost.'

Chapter Thirteen

Jonny lets out a nervous laugh. 'I'll need to drink a lot more of your English Spirit before I start believing in ghosts, thanks.'

Judith glares at him. 'She'll get to you in the end. She gets to everyone, round here. That's why the place is in such a state. The ghost of Blackwater, haunting us all until the end of time.'

Now a creeping feeling is tingling up the back of Jonny's neck. Being haunted by ghosts of the past until the end of time is a subject he does everything he can to avoid. He reminds himself of the real reason he started this conversation.

'Did you know that the police found the body of a child on Blackwater Island last week?'

A flicker of pain crosses Judith's face before her expression hardens again. 'Tragic. I told the coppers that n'all. But like I said, the ghost of Blackwater gets to everyone round here. Legend says she's been haunting us since the Dark Ages. The Vikings sent her over from Iceland to finish the fight against the Saxons. Name was Inka. Wild silver hair, spear made from diamonds. Swam like a mermaid. You get the picture.'

Jonny gazes past her to the drawing she's just described, re-reading the word 'Inka' along the bottom. 'So you've spoken to police about what's just happened?'

She nods. 'I told them the whole Inka story. Well, except for the mermaid part,' she adds. 'But Inka is out there. The Saxons beat the Vikings in the end, but not Inka. She's never left. Blackwater's her own. We just can't see her because of the mist. Never clears over the wilderness. Folks say it's something to do with all the special plants. They say nowhere else in the country has plants like the ones on Blackwater. But I know it's because of Inka.' She pauses for a moment, gaze becoming distant. 'And when you stop and think about it, you realise that anything could be happening inside that mist.'

Jonny broods over his glass for a moment. Ghost stories were definitely not what he was expecting to hear in response to a direct question about a dead child.

He tries a different tack. 'You grew up here, right? You've lived in this pub all your life?'

'Too right I have. The Sax has been in my family for generations. But it's just me now.'

'And to the best of your knowledge, Blackwater has been uninhabited all that time?'

'More than just uninhabited. Visiting's been forbidden for years.'

'Really? Do you know who made that rule?'

She shrugs, so he presses further.

'I suppose if it's because of the special plants, then environmentalists must have visited at some point to establish the nature of its ecosystem, to decide whether to give it protected status.'

Silence, then a small nod. 'I s'pose they must've.'

'Do you remember when?'

She shakes her head. 'Why would I?'

Jonny gestures at the dog bowl by the door with what he hopes is a winning grin. 'Well you probably walk Monty along the river bank at least twice a day, right? You must see all sorts out there.'

Judith suddenly looks stricken. 'You don't understand.'

Jonny is taken aback by the glimmer in her flinty grey eyes. 'I don't, but I'm trying to. A child has just died on that island, and no one from round here has come forward with any information yet. I just want to find out what happened to that poor boy.'

'I told you,' Judith parrots, sounding increasingly desperate. 'It's her. She's out there. Inka gets to everyone in the end. That's why I had to tell the coppers.'

Jonny gets off his stool. Detective Inspector Gillian Peters' frustration is starting to feel more and more justified.

'I'm sure they're grateful that at least one person from around here is telling them something,' he says lamely, trying to sound like he means it. 'Thanks for the drinks. I better get going now.' He makes for the dark corridor behind the bar. 'Top of the stairs, you said?'

Judith suddenly looks utterly crestfallen. 'The blue door,' she finally answers in a small voice.

Jonny edges past, eyeing her forlorn grey head. He hadn't meant to upset her. But was he the problem or was it this fucking ghost? Her ridiculous story is just making him think that something real and genuinely malign has been present on that island for quite some time.

Climbing the narrow staircase, he finds three doors arrayed around a tiny landing and knocks cautiously on the one painted blue. Paloma opens it almost immediately, ushering him into a surprisingly well-equipped attic bedroom. Quaint dressing table, two plump armchairs, small double bed, matching sets of clean towels neatly folded on top of a fleecy bedspread. A bedroom made up for a couple. Instantly Jonny feels hot and uncomfortable. He quickly makes for an armchair rather than look Paloma in the eye.

She leans against the closed door. 'Well?'

'Well, what? We don't have to share. Not if you don't want to, anyway.' He feels even hotter now.

Paloma walks over to the bed, only to hover beside it, fiddling with the covers. 'Well, you said you wanted to show me something. I'm guessing it's not in this room?' She gives the fleecy bedspread a sharp tug.

Jonny eyes her fidgeting. She seems as uncomfortable as he is.

'It was the drawing hanging up behind the bar. You probably didn't clock it. I only did because I was there for long enough the first time and it made a change from all the flags draped everywhere else.'

But Paloma is still distracted, muttering to herself. 'These hotel comforters are so gross. They don't get laundered between guests like the sheets do. Who the hell knows how many people have slept under this one.' She gives it another yank, sending a pile of towels flying at Jonny.

She apologises, and he pulls the towels off himself with a light laugh. 'Don't worry,' he says. 'It's not like we're actually going to sleep under it.' Instantly he realises his words could be interpreted in a number of ways and almost stuffs his fist in his mouth. 'Sorry, I didn't mean—'

'It's OK, I know what you meant. And even if we were, I'd take the comforter off first. To go to sleep, I mean.' She picks up the towels and starts to fold them in a flurry. 'Look, do you want to talk about this?'

'About what? The drawing?'

Paloma pauses, staring at her towels. 'No.'

Jonny realises what she means with a flood of mortification. 'Oh, right. No, I really don't.'

'Because we're going to need to be in rooms alone together without it being weird.'

'It isn't weird.'

But Paloma is still lingering. 'It's just after everything you said last week…' She trails off, leaving the rest hanging in the silence stretching between them.

'Forget about it,' Jonny finally says, willing for all the world that the bed's stupid fleecy cover might just spontaneously combust and end this appalling conversation. 'I didn't mean to make everything awkward.'

She turns to him. 'I never feel awkward around you.'

His breath stills in his throat. Didn't she just say that she did? And now she's leaning towards him, brushing his lips with hers, long eyelashes fanning out against her cheek. His own eyes flutter closed as he kisses her back, mind emptying of everything except the feather-light sensation of her mouth on his.

'Sorry if I made you feel like I do,' she murmurs, before kissing him again and pulling away, tucking a loose dark curl behind her ear.

Jonny runs an unconscious finger across his bottom lip. What just happened? And what does it mean? Paloma is back to folding towels as if it means nothing at all. The coral-pink flush staining her cheeks is the only evidence she stopped folding them in the first place. What exactly is she expecting him to do now? A neat square of towel lands on the bed, then another. She even starts humming to herself.

'So what's the drawing?' she finally says, all faux-brightness.

Jonny has to take another beat before he can reply. 'It's a picture of a very angry-looking mermaid,' he starts, wondering how he can possibly be talking about a random pencil drawing hanging on a wall in the arse end of nowhere when, contrary to all his expectations, she's just kissed him for the first time. He has to suppress an almost irresistible urge to laugh before he can continue. 'Lots of crazy silver hair, holding a spear of some kind. I only gave it a second thought because I saw an almost identical version of it in some graffiti down by the shoreline, directly opposite where I think the island is.'

'So you saw the drawing in the pub, then you saw the graffiti, realised they were the same, thought there might be a connection to Blackwater based on its location?'

'Exactly,' he says, resolve strengthening with every word back on topic. 'I thought the picture might be a symbol of some kind, or maybe even a call sign – graffiti is usually done in protest at something, or to make a statement of some kind, right? Or to draw attention to something or someone. And that drawing is literally the only thing hanging on the walls of this pub other than the cross of St George. But it's a dead end.'

She turns her gaze back on him and Jonny is unnerved all over again. 'Why?' she asks.

'Because it's apparently a picture of a ghost that's been haunting Blackwater since the Dark Ages. Our landlady told me some mad story about a mythical Icelandic warrior named Inka with a diamond-tipped spear and a mermaid's tail.'

'Do you mean that old woman behind the bar?'

'Yes. Her name's Judith. She drew the picture herself. I know it sounds ridiculous. It wasn't exactly what I was expecting when I brought us here.' He pauses for a moment as he remembers something else. 'Now I think of it, this warrior also had a gun sketched on her hip. Like there were tons of those around during the Dark Ages.'

'And how similar was the graffiti you saw?'

'Close enough that I clocked the resemblance immediately. There was some writing too that I couldn't read at the time but could easily have said "Inka" – it's written on the drawing in this really loopy script that I think was the same. In fact I made a copy.'

'How did you manage that? Can I see it?'

He roots around in his rucksack. 'Don't hold your breath. All I could do was trace the outline.'

He passes over his notebook. She runs a meditative finger over the crude imprint on the page tucked inside. 'Do you think the two drawings are similar enough that the person who did the original must also be the one who did the graffiti? And if they are, what would make an old woman angry enough to deface public property like some petulant teenager?'

Jonny tries to picture both drawings. 'I don't know. She said it's bad for business.'

Paloma stares at him. 'What is?'

'Inka,' he replies. 'The ghost of Blackwater. She gets to everyone, apparently.'

'And where exactly is this graffiti?'

'Inside a phone box, out on the shoreline at the spot on the map opposite the island in the middle. I only went inside to try and call Essex police. It was a punt more than anything else. Like I say, there's usually a message of some sort in graffiti. I just wasn't expecting it to be some supernatural bollocks.'

'What if it's not?'

'Are you saying you believe in ghosts?' He raises his eyebrow comically with a grin.

'No,' she answers, reaching for the jacket draped over the end of the bed. 'And you don't either. So there's nothing stopping us going to have a closer look by ourselves and in the dark. You're right, there's usually some kind of message in graffiti. We just need to find out exactly what this one is.'

Chapter Fourteen

Jonny digs around in his rucksack for a compass and a torch, suddenly smiling so hard his face feels alien. She kissed him. It happened. Does it matter what it means? Not right now. She obviously wanted to do it. She was the one who made the move. And now they're in this investigation together, looking into something that actually matters.

'I'm not sure we need to bother looking at the graffiti again,' he says, trying to control his grin. Thankfully she isn't looking at him.

'You're right – we don't. But we can try to get over to Blackwater. We just need to find ourselves a boat. Ideally one that isn't going to be missed for a few hours and doesn't make a lot of noise.' She pulls a small black case from a side pocket of her camera bag.

'Only if the tide is still high,' he replies, jamming a beanie on to his head. 'Apparently, you can drive across to Blackwater when the tide is out. There's a causeway marked on the map. Bill pointed it out to me. Said he could do it with the right tyres.'

'So we might be able to walk across?'

'Technically, yes. If the tide is right. Although I'm not sure it's a good idea to try without knowing when the tide is expected to come back in. I don't much fancy getting stuck in the middle of the river.'

'Calling it an island is a bit of a stretch if you can walk over from the mainland twice a day,' she remarks, unzipping the case and extracting a small digital camera. 'Check this out. It's brand-new. And it's waterproof too, how about that?'

But Jonny is still stuck on her earlier sentence. 'You're right,' he says. 'Blackwater is actually far more accessible than it sounds if you don't always need a boat to get there. It seemed like a million miles from anywhere when I first got here. But now I think about it, I saw at least three container ships steaming past in the distance within the same five minutes. It's nowhere near as isolated as it seems.'

'Right. And you said it's officially closed to visitors. But how is that enforceable once the tide is out?'

'I don't know,' Jonny wonders. 'I suppose we're about to find out.'

Paloma zips the camera back into its case and tucks it into her coat pocket before pulling on a pair of gloves and reaching for the brass key on the dressing table. 'Come on, let's go. At least we can lock all our stuff away in here. Getting this room was a great idea.'

Jonny's heart lurches. A goofy grin is back on his face before he can calm it down. He fumbles around zipping up his pockets and adjusting the lip of his hat before finally opening the door. Paloma locks it behind them, and they thread their way down the stairs, round the bar and back out through the pub in silence. Jonny casts a few furtive glances around the smoky interior. Judith is nowhere to be seen.

They quicken their step as soon as they are outside. The glow from Eastwood's few streetlamps dwindles out behind them in seconds, casting a cloak of darkness so intense that he can hear rather than see Paloma by his side. Twigs start to crack underfoot as the road becomes the dirt track leading down to the water.

'Is this the only way down to the river?' she asks, breathlessness captured in clouds.

'That I've found so far, yes. The track runs some way along the bank itself. I saw a pontoon earlier, a few hundred yards past the phone box. I imagine there must be loads of others along the estuary.'

Paloma shivers. 'It is crazy how dark it is out here.'

'There's probably never much of a moon, either.' Jonny looks out across the river, the ever-present haze making it almost impossible to distinguish where the water starts and the night sky ends. 'Apparently the mist never lifts over Blackwater Island itself. Something else Judith attributed to ghosts and ghoulies.'

'Convenient,' Paloma muses. 'Although I expect it's true.'

'That there's some magic fog as well as a ghost living on Blackwater?'

'No, that the mist never lifts. If the island has been designated a wildlife reserve because of its unique ecology then maybe it has a micro-climate all of its own.'

Jonny considers this. 'She said something along those lines. Now that I'm thinking about it she actually opened up quite a lot.'

'When did she do that?'

'This morning. Her pub was the only place open when I arrived. I was fishing around for locals to talk to. She intercepted me with her vicious homebrew. I was trying to get on her good side so I actually had to drink some. Which, now I think about it, worked a lot better than I thought.'

'I thought you said she tried to get rid of you.'

'She did. But that was after she invited me in.'

'Probably to figure out exactly who you were and what you were doing, sniffing around somewhere so obviously off the main drag.'

'So why not just ask me outright? She answered plenty of my questions, without once asking why I am so interested. It was only when we came back and I told her we were journalists that she started to look slightly less pissed off. Now I think she must have been gearing up to try and tell me something all along rather than warning me off – and became even more sure about doing it when she found out I was a reporter.'

'Is this your phone box?' Paloma gestures into the dark ahead.

'I think so.' Jonny peers at the murky shapes in the gloom. 'There's the pontoon beyond it.'

Paloma picks up her pace. Jonny keeps step before stumbling on something awkward underfoot and falling hard into the undergrowth.

'Hey, are you OK? Did you trip on something?' Now Paloma is kneeling beside him, feeling around on the path with a gloved hand. 'Aha!'

'What is it?' he asks, thanking the stars that it's too dark for her to see him sprawled in a heap.

She answers by way of a sharp clank. He can see some loops of chain dangling from her hand as she stands and starts following them down the river bank. The soft gurgle of water against wood comes a moment later. The tide is high, he thinks to himself.

A small beam of light flicks on below. 'Here,' Paloma calls over in a raspy whisper. 'Don't get up. Just slide down the bank in this direction.'

Pushing off the slippery reeds, Jonny tracks the beam from his feet to the gleaming wet edge of a boat nudging gently against the lip of the bank.

'Nicely done,' Paloma whispers, clicking off her torch and leaning forward to examine the boat rocking gently from side to side in the water. 'A rowing boat,' she murmurs, running a hand along the wet wooden edge. 'It's perfect. Super quiet and unlikely to be missed for a few hours.'

Jonny nods even though she can't see him. 'Right. I don't see whoever owns it pitching up for a midnight scull the night before the biggest New Year's Eve party in history.'

Climbing on board with a soft splash, they quickly locate the pair of oars stashed inside. Paloma starts reeling in the loose chain.

Jonny frowns. 'Surely that's tethered to something?'

Loose links continue piling up on the floor of the boat. 'It doesn't seem so,' she says, continuing to pull until something hits the underside of the boat with a dull clunk.

'Must be an anchor,' Jonny mutters, disheartened. 'We should have predicted that.'

Paloma passes him the length of chain. 'Hold on to this so I can have a look.'

The boat starts to yaw from side to side as she reaches gingerly over the edge. Jonny gives the chain a tug at the same time. A large, heavily barnacled object suddenly comes flying into the boat, along with a cold slop of river water.

'Strange,' Jonny wonders, oblivious to the water soaking into his boots. He reaches out to inspect the object between them – a rectangular cage of some kind, thickly encrusted with salt and seaweed. 'Why would anyone tether a boat to something like this?' He lifts a corner of the cage off the bottom of the boat with nothing more than a fingertip. 'It's not remotely heavy, either.'

Paloma shakes her wet hand in the air. 'It's not tethered to the boat. It's tethered to the chain—'

'Which is just as strange,' Jonny finishes. 'Right? The chain runs all the way up the river bank. You'd think as a means to secure the boat. But instead it's to secure this.'

'What is it?'

Jonny considers the wire basket between them. 'Some sort of crab pot, I guess. Or oyster rack—'

'Oysters? Round here? Really?'

'I didn't think so either. But oysters were all that was on the menu at the pub today, believe it or not.' Jonny probes the edges of the cage, tries to find a hinge of some kind.

'What are you doing?'

'Trying to open it.'

'Why?' Paloma starts gathering up the loops of chain. 'Just chuck it back over the side and we can get going. I'll stack these up on the bank.'

'Hang on a second.' Jonny manages to lever the top open an inch. 'I just want to see what's inside. It must be important if someone's bothering to secure it at the expense of an actual boat.'

'Make it quick, then.' Paloma leans past him to dump a pile of dripping wet chain links on the shore.

Jonny manages to dig his finger inside the cage, and comes up against a smooth, thick knot of some kind and the rough edge of what feels distinctly like plastic.

'Well?' Paloma asks.

Jonny winces as he removes his finger. 'I can't really tell. It must just be for oyster farming. Or crabbing. I still don't understand why someone would tether it in place. But I don't know much about either enterprise.' He considers the plate of surprisingly delicious oysters he demolished for lunch at The Saxon. 'Judith said Blackwater was bad for business. Maybe that's the kind of business she meant.'

Paloma manoeuvres the cage back over the side of the boat as gently as she can, trying to muffle its splash. Jonny grabs an oar, staring out across the river into the implacable darkness. It's only once they've pushed off that he starts to consider what other kinds of businesses Judith might have been referring to.

Chapter Fifteen

The night tightens around them with every stroke of the oars.

'Do you have any idea how wide this river is?' Paloma whispers.

Jonny shakes his head. 'No,' he adds. 'And Judith clammed up when I asked her whether the unlabelled island on the map was Blackwater.'

'Didn't you ask the police officer you spoke to?'

'No. I should have done, I know. I was too keen to see this so-called evidence she was going to show me. For what it's worth she intercepted me almost exactly where we found this boat. I was trying to work out where Blackwater was, and I think she was heading there herself when I met her and only turned around because she wasn't going to let me follow her or try and go over by myself.'

'So what more did she actually tell you?'

'That the boy died of natural causes. And he was found dressed in some curious Victorian outfit. Flat cap, shirt, waistcoat, long shorts. Like a costume from a hundred years ago. As if the fact he was discovered on an allegedly uninhabited island wasn't weird enough to start with.'

'How did the police find out he was there in the first place?'

'An anonymous message was left on the answering service at the station in Maldon. It's apparently been impossible to trace. The only thing this officer said she's sure of is it came from a woman. She claims she's been left to handle the investigation alone since the cause of death was established. And that she's largely overlooked by her superiors – she's been operating on her own here since she arrived five years ago. The main thing I got out of her is how angry she is about it all.'

'I'm not surprised,' Paloma muses. 'And where's this poor kid's family? Why hasn't he been identified yet?'

'Right,' Jonny agrees. 'Kids don't just disappear without at least one person making a fuss. There are usually relatives screaming from the rooftops. Or missing-persons' photos plastered on every lamp-post and milk carton within a ten-mile radius,' he adds, remembering the yellowing poster he saw curling away from the wall outside Maldon police station. 'Christmas or not, there should be multiple lines of inquiry under way. Instead there is just some angry detective inspector being blanked every time she calls for assistance.'

'That's why you think she tried to get you to juice up your reporting?'

'Yes. She said if I told the whole country she's actually investigating a murder then resources would follow. She's obviously desperate. If someone actually agreed to lie on her behalf, they'd be discredited the minute the pathologist piped up with their official post-mortem report. And so would she.'

'Did she give you any more details from this autopsy itself? Like whether there were any underlying health issues that might explain dying so young?'

'No. Finding and interviewing the pathologist is on my list for tomorrow—' Jonny stops abruptly as his oar catches on something underwater.

Paloma pauses. 'What is it?'

Jonny probes around with his oar, squinting into the dark ahead. 'Can you see that? That ... that shape.' He gestures into the shadows. 'We must be coming up on Blackwater. I think my oar just scraped the riverbed.'

Paloma prods her own oar into the water. 'You're right. It's suddenly super shallow.' She peers around blindly. 'Unless this is just the tide going out.'

'We better hurry up, then. The last thing we need is to run aground.'

'At least then we could walk back,' Paloma replies doubtfully, starting to row again.

Jonny shivers at the thought of chancing a journey on foot across a marshy causeway with no idea when the tide is going to rush back in.

They are barely a few feet further on before their oars start dragging in the mud.

'Bollocks,' Jonny mutters, frustrated.

'We can just wade the last bit,' Paloma says, unlacing her boots. 'Come on.'

Heaving his oar into the boat, Jonny pulls off his own boots and socks.

Paloma is already climbing over the side, a little gasp escaping at the cold. 'Wow,' she says, splashing as she flails around. 'The riverbed is like quicksand.'

Jonny sticks a foot into the water and finds himself immobilised almost immediately. 'It's black mud. It's apparently the reason the river is called Blackwater.'

'Feels more like cement,' she replies, huffing with the effort it is taking to move.

Together they manage to heave the boat on until it is firmly stuck in a combination of thick bullrushes and glistening black sludge.

'Let's just leave it here,' Jonny pants. 'It can't go anywhere fast.'

'Unless the tide's actually coming in,' Paloma warns, holding on to his arm for support as she retrieves her boots from the boat. Suddenly Jonny feels a lot better about being dragged down by the mud.

'We'll just have to chance it,' he answers with renewed conviction, wrapping an arm around her.

They half walk, half drag each other through the bullrushes

until the ground solidifies enough for them to stop and put their shoes back on. Turning, Jonny checks the boat is still where they left it. In the dark, its chunky silhouette looks like a beached whale.

Beside him, Paloma is still lacing up her boots. 'What now?' she asks, bent over.

'Wait here for a second.' Jonny tramples ahead, climbing the hillside rising up in front of him. He can see the dim outline of something solid even further up.

He turns and calls back to Paloma. 'I think there's—'

But then the rest of his sentence evaporates into a gasp at the grip of something cold, determined and unmistakable curling around his ankle.

Chapter Sixteen

Instantly Jonny is laid out flat on his back, head smacking into the ground. Damp marsh grass towers to his either side, sharp with encrusted salt. He's so disorientated that he can't even yell out before he's yanked down into a hole of some kind. Tumbling on to a dirt floor, he instinctively clamps his eyes shut against a sudden, harsh flare of light. There's a decisive crash overhead. The heavy tread of someone else's boots. And then ... a voice. Full of the same cold, hard determination as the grip previously wrapped around his ankle.

'Scream all you like. No one is going to hear you.'

Jonny cracks an eye open into more light – dazzlingly bright, unmistakably electric and accompanied by a menacing low hum. In an underground cave on an uninhabited swamp island? Shock takes hold. He fights not to tremble as he tries to make sense of it.

'But don't worry,' the voice continues. 'No one else is going to get hurt around here.'

No one else is going to get hurt around here? Instantly Jonny is visualising the discovery of the body of a child somewhere nearby a few days earlier. His eyes fly open to find a woman planted stock and steady before him. A heavily muscled warrior of a woman with a wild mane of silver hair.

Jonny turns cold. He recalls Judith's detailed pencil drawing of the angriest mermaid he's ever seen. Inka, the Vikings' secret weapon in their fight against the Saxons. The ghost of Blackwater, as ancient as the war itself, haunting everyone and everything she encounters. Except the woman before him looks as real as anyone

Jonny has ever met. And she's standing in a decidedly fortified underground bunker, spotlit by a naked light bulb dangling overhead.

She holds up her hands, making her muscles bulge from her upper arms, silver curls trailing like ivy over her broad shoulders.

'I'm not going to harm you. That isn't what this is about.'

'This?' Jonny echoes weakly. 'What the hell *is* this? What do you want?'

'Want,' the woman repeats, dropping her arms. 'How long have you got?'

'From ... from me, I mean. What do you want from me?'

The woman stares steadily back at him. He takes in the sight all over again. Shock of unkempt silver hair. Glittering dark eyes. Lined and determined pale face. Fitted military-issue undershirt, lumpy utility belt, faded cargo pants.

'I'd have thought the better question is what you want from me. You're still in here, after all. Haven't tried to peg it like most normal people would.'

She pauses and turns to a dark opening in the corner of the wall behind her.

'Go get the girl,' she commands of someone lurking in the shadows, her tone as unflinching as stone.

Adrenaline suddenly surges through Jonny like an electrical current. This woman better not be referring to Paloma. 'No,' he shouts, launching himself forward, his arms pinwheeling around in the air, mind emptying of anything other than the absolute need to protect her.

Instantly the woman shoots out a powerful hand and palms him hard to the floor.

Seconds later, another woman steps out from the shadows to join her.

'Go get the girl, Arwen,' his assailant repeats. 'He came here with her. So I want her down here, too.'

Jonny is momentarily encouraged to see this second woman shrink into herself rather than jump to attention. He is further emboldened by her appearance. Thin as a rake, dressed in torn rags, skin so sallow she looks yellow. Bare feet crusted in black mud. Tangled hair so thin that Jonny can see her scalp shining ghostly white under the harsh light. Not a figure who looks like they could take on anyone in a fight and win.

But then she catches his eye. The terror in her gaze is unmistakable. It is the unhinged look of someone so broken they will do whatever is asked of them, no matter what it is.

He holds up his hands, looking between both women. 'I came here alone. Whichever girl you mean, she isn't with me.'

'Nice try,' his assailant replies menacingly. 'You heard me, Arwen. Go get her. Now.'

'No,' Jonny shouts again as the second woman turns like an automaton back towards the dark hollow in the wall.

Hurling himself towards his assailant, he manages to wrap a hand around her ankle before a boot thunders into his wrist. A hot pain courses down his forearm, but he can barely feel it. All that matters is stopping either of these women from getting to Paloma. Clinging on to her leg, he propels his body towards the second woman with as much force as he can muster. But Arwen has already vanished. His boot hits the stone wall with a sickening thud. Frustration overwhelms the waves of pain throbbing in both his wrist and foot.

'Let go of me,' his assailant commands from above. 'I don't want to have to kick you again. I told you, no one else is going to get hurt around here.'

But Jonny is still bent on doing whatever it takes to protect Paloma.

'No,' he hisses, digging his nails into her leg. 'Call your lackey off. Arwen. Whatever her fucking name is.'

The woman leans down and calmly unfastens his hand from

her ankle with fingers of steel. His grip is so weak from her previous kick to his wrist that there is absolutely nothing he can do to stop her. He shouts in vain, picturing Paloma above ground and able to hear him. 'Paloma. Palomaaaa! Run! Hide!'

Now the woman's laugh is echoing dully around the bunker. Jonny's rage is suddenly so implacable he can barely contain it. He looks around wildly, searching for an exit. They're in a surprisingly large stone cave with a closed steel trapdoor overhead. Two dark hollows in both back corners are emanating the low hum and whirr of equipment. Thick black tangles of electrical cables are snaking all over the floor. A load of oyster baskets are randomly piled up next to a plastic tank of clear liquid. Water? Instantly Jonny is picturing the last plastic tank of liquid he saw on his warzone training course and assuming its contents were going to be used to build a bomb.

'Save your breath,' the woman says. 'She can't hear you. No one can now, except me. These bunkers were built to last. And she'll be down here with you soon, anyway. You've got nothing to worry about. I keep telling you that no one else is going to get hurt around here.'

Jonny tries to leap up but is hobbled by his gammy foot. 'Then why have you taken me prisoner?'

The woman jerks her head at the trapdoor overhead. 'You can leave if you want. Go on. Feel free. But then you might miss your friend. And you don't want that, do you?'

Jonny swears under his breath. He's somehow managed to trap himself just by trying to get out and protect the person he cares about most of all.

'No,' he says quietly, fighting to stay calm. 'But if you didn't want anyone else to get hurt around here, then explain to me why you almost broke my wrist.'

That laugh again. 'If I'd wanted to break any of your bones, you'd be looking at tiny little pieces of your skeleton scattered all over the floor right now. For the last time, I'm not going to hurt you or your friend. Take this if you don't believe me.'

She reaches into her lumpy utility belt before holding out her hand. Jonny instantly regrets goading her until he registers the item dangling from her calloused fingers. A pistol – small, black, deadly as a venomous spider. And not just any old pistol. A kind of pistol Jonny is certain he has seen before. He reaches out and grabs it. The solid heft of steel in his palm is unmistakable. Just like its conspicuous lack of a manual safety catch. He looks at the woman in front of him like he's seeing her for the first time.

'Who are you?'

'Not Inka, if that's your next question.'

His eyes narrow. 'How do you know about Inka?'

'Well it's a good story, isn't it. The mermaid's tail – nice touch. Almost makes me wish I really could swim like a fish. But you don't look like someone who read a lot of fairy tales as a kid. I bet you thought that story was a load of supernatural bollocks.'

Something snags in Jonny's mind. Didn't he use those exact words while he was talking to Paloma upstairs in The Saxon?

'How do you know that?'

'How do I know everything, is the better question. How is it that I already know the legend of Inka, if I'm not actually Inka myself? What am I doing down here in this hole if I'm not a ghost?'

'You tell me. I thought this island was a nature reserve.'

There goes that laugh again, ringing around the bunker. 'That's another good story too. And makes the place sound so poetic. Really tugs on the old heartstrings.'

'You mean it's not?'

'Of course it's not,' she shoots back. 'How does a kid turn up dead on it if it is? That's my point. Which, if I'm not mistaken, is exactly your point too. It's why you've bothered to come and check this wretched place out for yourself.'

Jonny's grip tenses on the pistol at the mention of the dead child. 'And I take it you expect me to believe that the person with a gun hiding out by the crime scene has nothing to do with the crime itself?'

The most unexpected expression suddenly crosses the woman's face. Resentment, shame – Jonny might even say it contained a little bit of fear.

'Easy now,' she warns, lifting her hands in the air again. 'We're on the same side here. I even gave you my gun to prove it. I just want to talk.'

'To me? Why? You don't even know me.'

'I know you're a journalist. I know you're here because police found a body in the wilderness. And I know you care about what happened to that boy because you wouldn't be grubbing about in the pitch-dark otherwise.'

By now Jonny is unsurprised that this woman knows exactly who he is. But he no longer cares all that much about why. Because he's holding a gun in his hand and Paloma still hasn't materialised. Which means she's still being pursued somewhere on this fucking island by someone looking deranged enough to do whatever it takes to satisfy the woman standing in front of him.

He looks at the pistol, its black shine glinting in the harsh light, more lessons from his training course flashing through his mind. And then into the dark opening in the wall a few feet away.

Fight for your life.

Jonny takes his chance, levelling the gun at her as he dives into the dark.

Chapter Seventeen

Jonny hurtles down the passageway. He knows he could still be taken down at any moment. The tunnel quickly opens out into a second bunker and more dazzlingly harsh artificial light. But there's no time to consider why it's full of computer monitors blaring white static into the spotlight. The bunker leads to a smaller, more twisty tunnel, then around a corner into some kind of living quarters. A sleeping bag, a folding table, a couple of camping chairs. More oyster baskets, one used so recently it is leaking murky water on to the ground. The menacing glint of more weapons lined up and leaning against the wall. Beyond, into another passage that starts to slope upward. Jonny has to hunch as the ceiling lowers, yet another improbably bright light bulb glancing hot off the side of his head. Then the bulbs run out. Shadows close in with every step. Darkness approaches fast.

Blackness descends. Something soft catches underfoot. Stumbling, Jonny rebounds off a stone wall into the horrifying sensation of suddenly being in the presence of another human being – a clutch of fabric, a length of bone beneath, a puff of hot breath. Strands of hair whip past his face – unmistakable, like the frayed ends of a lash. Another acrid bolt of air and the smell of sweat so ingrained it lingers like musk. A scuffle ensues. Jonny bellows like a bull cornered in the dark, thrashing around until he is caught out underfoot again and falls. Shadows quiver in the fading glow behind him before disappearing in a thunder of footsteps.

Scrambling to his feet, he careens on. Tries to anchor himself against the passageway walls. Steps diagonally side to side. The atmosphere becomes increasingly foul. More hot pockets of air. The unmistakable rasp of terrified panting. Is it his own? He slows, pressing himself up against a wall, inching forward. One step, then another. Another soft wad on the ground sends him lurching into the dark.

Then – his ears explode in a burst of sound. So intense it feels like the whole tunnel should collapse with it. The pistol clatters from his hand, but Jonny can't hear a thing. Just an unbearable keening, a cacophony of confusion and terror. From somewhere deep in the fug, his brain surfaces the only logical explanation.

The gun he was carrying must have been fully loaded.

And he's just accidentally fired a shot.

Jonny levers himself on to all fours, fighting to stay calm. *Has he shot someone?* He reaches out blindly in the dark. *Where is the gun?* Another few inches forward and he finds more curious wads of fabric or padding, dropping everything he touches for fear it might explode in his hands.

Until – something inescapably solid. A stone wall of some kind. Strung with evenly spaced pieces of metal – footholds? Jonny is suddenly grabbing at them, hauling himself up and up until he gasps into a distinct change in the air. Cold, damp, fresh. Redolent of open space. He claws to his either side, finds nothing but more air. Flopping out on to cool, hard stone, he rolls away until he hits something – another wall. There he pauses, listening with his entire body, straining every muscle for evidence of predators on his tail. A gentle wind whispers to him, swishing through the nearby reeds, the soft call of an undisturbed night.

Staying low, Jonny finally takes a beat to assess his new surroundings. A stone floor. A wall at his back. Patches of dim light filtering into the dark on either side. Windows? Has he climbed out into a building of some kind? He lifts his face to the sky, to the unmistakable sensation of open air. Standing, he strikes out towards a patch of light and quickly crashes into a heavy stone ledge, falling over into a thick tangle of undergrowth.

Jonny drops and rolls again, revelling in the salty bullrushes crackling beneath him. He's made it outside in one piece. And it doesn't seem like he's been followed. Overhead, the clouds warp and shift, the ghostly eye of the moon beaming shafts of silver light through the dark. Jonny squints into the shadows, searching desperately for any sign of Paloma. There is still someone out here bent on dragging her down into those tunnels.

Then he hears his name.

And realises there is only one person who could possibly be calling it.

'Paloma,' he rasps, trying to keep his voice low. 'Where are you?'

'Over here,' she calls back. 'At the bottom of the slope.'

Jonny wills that she stay quiet until he finds her. Staring wildly around, shapes start to emerge from the shadows – bushes, trees, some random rocky outcrops, the outline of the low building he's left behind.

'Here,' Paloma calls again, closer this time.

Launching himself towards the sound of her voice, he crashes down the slope through the bullrushes until he almost knocks her off her feet.

'It's OK, it's me,' he rasps again, staggering as he tries to steady himself. They grapple with each other in the dark. His legs feel suddenly empty. 'Don't say anything else. We need to stay quiet. She sent someone out here to catch you.'

'She? Who? What are you talking about?'

'Never mind. We just need to get out of here, and fast. She's got a gun—'

'What?' Paloma's voice trembles. 'The bang I just heard was a gunshot?'

'Yes. Let's move. Come on.'

They cling to each other as they hurry out into the shallows, panting with the effort it takes to drag themselves through the mud.

'Are you OK?' Paloma whispers between gasps. 'What happened? Where have you been?'

'There's a woman hiding out here who looks almost exactly like that mad drawing on the wall of the pub. Inka isn't a ghost. But I wasn't necessarily expecting her to be flesh and blood either. Nor armed to the fucking teeth, or living in a bunker full of computers.'

'Why? Who is she?'

'I don't know. She yanked me into her bunker. There was another woman somewhere down there with her too. The Inka woman sent her outside to grab you. Are you alright?'

'I'm fine. Unless you count panicking about you disappearing into thin air.'

'You're not hurt? You've been alone this whole time?'

She nods. 'Yes. I've just been trying to find you, and when I heard that bang…' She trails off into a sigh. 'Are you sure you're OK?'

'For now, yes.' Jonny looks over his shoulder. The shadow of the island is still hulking too close for comfort behind them. 'She actually gave her gun to me—'

'What?' Paloma pulls up short with a small splash. 'Why would she do that?'

'To prove she wasn't going to hurt me – or you. That's what she said, anyway. Come on, we need to keep moving.'

'So when I heard a gunshot, it was—'

'—me that fired it, yes. It was an accident. I was running with the gun in my hand, slipped and fell in the dark and it went off. I had to keep going, I was trying to get out and find you before anyone else did.'

'So some mad woman drags you into a hole, only to give you a loaded gun. Then you run away anyway—'

'—to find you,' he interrupts, frustration threatening to get the better of him. 'I tried telling her I was alone, but she wasn't having any of it. I told you, she put some other lunatic woman on your tail. She's still out there looking for you, by the way.'

Paloma looks around in the dark. 'But how did she know we were coming?'

'Because she's not working alone out here,' he replies, muddy hand stealing into hers. 'She knew I was a journalist. She knew why we came to Blackwater. She knew so much that it wouldn't surprise me if she already knew my name.'

Chapter Eighteen

They flounder the moment they try and run, the gunshot Jonny accidentally fired still ringing around in his mind. Did it hit someone? Fighting to stay calm, he casts around for something to help them move faster.

'Wait here a second. Just let me see if I can find a stick or something to help us get through this mud.'

'Don't go too far, OK?' Paloma's voice trembles.

But Jonny is already squelching backward to drier land, looking for anything solid and large enough to work. How did any marauding Viking army stage successful assaults out of this swamp? He grabs at some reeds further up the bank, salt showering from his hands, feeling increasingly hopeless until he remembers how they got themselves to Blackwater in the first place.

He wades back over to Paloma. 'Where did we leave the boat?'

'Back that way.' She gestures vaguely into the dark.

He grabs her hand, pulling her back towards the island. 'Come on. We need the oars. We can move much faster if we can lever ourselves along.'

A shaft of moonlight illuminates the ghostly silhouette of the boat in the distance. Paloma's eyes gleam through the dark with renewed determination. Back on drier ground they are finally able to speed up.

'I don't understand,' she mutters as they hurry. 'There surely can't be any phones out here. The place is waterlogged. So how the hell does anyone get a message to that woman in time to warn her that we're on our way?'

'Well there's apparently no electricity out here either, but I've just seen light bulbs blazing underground. So I think we can safely assume that the place is definitely not what it seems. And one thing I am sure of is that it was Judith who sent the message.'

'That old landlady at The Saxon?' Paloma is incredulous.

'Yes. She was quick to tell me her ridiculous story about the ghost of Blackwater when I arrived. Then it comes up again, practically word for word, even the bit about the mermaid's tail, when I'm ambushed by some woman bearing more than just a passing resemblance to this fucking ghost.'

'But you said it yourself: that story is just a load of supernatural bollocks—'

'Which is something *else* she already knew. She used those exact words. Told me I thought the whole story was just a load of supernatural bollocks. How else would she know that's exactly what I'd said to you back at The Saxon unless she'd been told by someone who was listening in? Someone was spying on us at the pub. It's the only explanation.'

Paloma falls silent for a moment. 'But why would Judith voluntarily tell you some crazy story about a ghost in a location where a dead body has just been found if she's actually in league with this so-called ghost herself?'

'I don't know,' Jonny replies. 'I can only think she's under duress of some kind. She could have said nothing. Maintained total deniability. Instead she draws a picture of this ghost, complete with a pistol on her hip, and displays it proudly on her wall. When asked about it by a total stranger she goes into florid detail. Then even volunteers that she's told police the same tale. Like you said, a dead body has just shown up here, for fuck's sake. So don't tell ghost stories. Tell everyone about the woman hiding in a bunker nearby with a loaded gun.'

'Unless she can't,' Paloma agrees. 'I think you might be right. That story – and the graffiti – feel more like they're designed to make people more curious about Blackwater than warn them off.'

'Exactly,' Jonny says. 'It's pretty desperate stuff, though.'

'Same as handing you a loaded gun with the safety off,' Paloma replies. 'We have to get out of here.'

Jonny wavers with the reference to the gun. He can't get past the possibility that he might have accidentally shot someone. Even if it was the woman who violently ambushed him, he is suddenly poleaxed by the thought. Does she need help? Should they turn back? But Paloma is already splashing through the last bit of mud to the boat, grabbing the oars and shoving one towards him. She quickly strides back out on to the riverbed.

'You said the police already searched the island, right? After the body was found?'

'Not exactly.' Jonny hurries to catch up, trying to remember his exact exchange with Detective Inspector Gillian Peters. 'Apparently there's a lot more that needs doing but there's no money or manpower to spare. I would say that explains why the bunkers and tunnels have managed to remain hidden for so long except that I just came out of one directly into a building. I don't see how you miss that. And I don't see how you get all the computers I saw in the bunkers on and off an island unnoticed either.'

'You don't,' Paloma answers, panting. 'That much is obvious. Some people are going to pretty extreme lengths to hide everything. The question is why? And how does it connect to the dead kid?'

'I don't know,' he mutters, not daring to voice his even more pressing concern. He squints into the dark at the mainland coming closer. They struggle on in silence until they are staggering up the river bank.

Paloma flops down into the bullrushes, breathing hard. 'Finally.'

Jonny peers into the surrounding shadows. No sign of the path along the ridge. Nor the phone box that he'd tried to use earlier. Just reeds. And trees. He turns to look back out across the mudflats but the island's silhouette has already disappeared in the dark.

'We must be on the opposite shore,' he says, dropping to his knees. 'Unless we've just come out a bit further down the coast.'

He casts around in the boggy dirt for anything that might confirm they are close to where they started. Nothing other than reeds, slippery with mud and sharp with salt until—

'Strange,' he murmurs, tracing the outline of a solid object with his fingers. 'I think I've found another oyster basket. Except it's not in the river. So it can't be collecting oysters. It's just ... here.'

Paloma rolls on to her side. 'Is it tethered to anything, like the last one we found?'

Jonny ferrets around in the reeds before trying to open it. 'I don't think so. I think this one is stuffed with plastic too. I also saw a load of them inside the bunkers...' He trails off as he manages to poke his hand inside and comes up with something even more unexpected. 'I actually think there's a plug in here.' He presses his fingers against the plug's pins to confirm it to himself. 'It must be a power pack of some kind; it's attached to a cable. There are some other smaller packets in here as well.'

He manages to pull one out – a few fabric items wrapped in more plastic. It's too dark to see what they are.

Paloma levers herself a few feet further up the bank. 'Like a power pack is any good to anyone in a soaking marsh. It must be junk. Just leave it.' She points to something further away along the ridge. 'There's a jetty over there. At least I think there is. Look at that shape. It's right by the water.'

Jonny reluctantly lets the basket drop to crawl over to her. They pause together at the top of the bank. He can see the shadow she's pointing at – an incongruous dark oblong.

'I think that's actually a low building,' he says, considering it. 'It's too far away from the water to be a jetty.'

Paloma agrees. 'We're definitely not back where we started.'

Jonny wriggles a little closer, staring so hard into the dark at the shape that his peripheral vision starts to flicker. Wind whispers softly through the reeds.

Paloma tugs on his arm, pulling herself forward too. 'What is it?'

More flickers in the corner of his eye. 'Hang on,' he starts to say. And then a dark mass moves, unmistakably, out of the shadows ahead.

Chapter Nineteen

Jonny flattens himself into the ground, willing that Paloma follow his lead. A volley of cracks and snaps ripples through the silence – the unmistakable sounds of someone or something moving at speed. Towards them? Paloma's hand closes around his – clammy, terrified.

Footsteps now, the heavy tread of a human rather than the rapid patter of an animal. He grips Paloma's hand, giving it a firm shake. They need to be ready to move.

Then he hears a cry – ragged and low. A cry of pain.

Paloma's hand twitches in his. He doesn't dare speak. Too consumed by his fight on Blackwater to assume anything other than this sound is malign. His survival instincts were already primed. He has to trust that hers will follow.

Another low moan – heavy with undisguised panic. More movement ahead, and a shadow rippling closer in front of them. Jonny raises into a crouch, pulling Paloma along with him, every muscle tensed for action. Then he whispers, 'Run.'

They start to move inland, low to the ground. Footsteps crackle behind them through reeds splintering like shattering glass. Paloma speeds up, squeezing Jonny's hand in kind. More human sounds now – frayed breathing, agonised sobs. Jonny slows through a slick of mud, Paloma's hand slipping from his. She grabs at him, flailing in a patch of bogland.

'I'm here, I'm here,' he manages to say. They are barely steady on their feet before they start running again, thundering along the river bank. Plump hedges rise up on the inland side, blocking their route like silent sentries in the dark. Jonny wavers again at the sound of a dull splash. Is someone heading out on to the riverbed? A series of wet thumps follows – one-two, one-two, before ebbing away into the rustle of their own flight.

Then a light flicks on in the shadows ahead, shining ghostly yellow through the dark. The low building, Jonny realises, with a burst of adrenaline. Paloma sees it in the same moment. He pulls her off the path into the hedges, breathing hard, holding a finger to his lips. There they pause, motionless and silent.

A minute passes. Jonny listens with every fibre of his body. The distant caw of a raven. The soft flap of an owl's wing. The glint of a pair of beady dark eyes – a fox? A blink and they're gone. Thick silence descends, so heavy Jonny can practically feel it.

Finally he feels safe to whisper. 'There's someone in there.' He points at the yellow square of light ahead. 'They might be able to help us get back to Eastwood.'

'Or not,' Paloma rasps back, shaking her head. 'Whoever that is has a permanent view of the island and everything that goes on there. Doesn't exactly fill me with confidence.'

Jonny assesses the hedgerow with a cautious hand – dense, sturdy and thick. 'We have to get past that building no matter what we do. There's no way through these hedges. And we can't go back the way we came. We still don't know if we were being chased or not.'

He feels her flinch. He thinks about the sounds they've just heard. Snatches of someone else's fear, pain and panic.

'We also still don't know exactly where we are,' he adds. 'Unless we knock and ask. Better still, get someone to give us ride.'

Paloma's reply becomes even sharper. 'That is not why you want to knock. I know you, Jonny. You want to talk to whoever lives in that building because you just found an armed fugitive hiding out near a crime scene that they've been staring at this whole time.'

Jonny looks between the light and the blackness in the middle of the riverbed. An unmistakable line of sight. Blackwater's fabled wilderness mist isn't hiding anything. It's the people on all sides that are choosing to look away – both the senior commanders that have left Gillian Peters to police this district alone and the locals with a view of the island itself.

'All we need to say is that we're lost,' he finally replies. 'We're just going to ask for a lift. It's an innocent enough question.'

'I don't think anyone is particularly innocent around here, and neither do you. That's why you won't stop asking questions, as usual.'

Another slice of light flicks on – enough to illuminate the distinct outline of a bungalow and a wooden picket fence, which is blocking their path ahead.

'There's no other way,' Jonny says, pointing at the fence. Beyond it he can also see the dull smudge of a white transit van. He takes her hand. 'Come on.'

They move slowly down the path, Paloma running her free hand along the hedges. Searching for a different route out, Jonny thinks, instinctively trying to speed up. They pause at the edge of the fence – shoulder-height, sturdy, recently painted with smooth gloss – all the features you'd expect from a fence designed to keep out intruders – except there's a shiny set of keys hanging from a hook mounted on one of the posts nearest the path.

'Is there a gate?' Paloma whispers. 'There must be a way in for the van at least. Maybe that's what the keys are for?'

'Not that I can see,' he answers, running a hand along the wooden grid – smooth, uninterrupted. 'We're going to have to climb over.'

He gives Paloma a leg up before pocketing the set of keys and hauling himself over. Gives them an excuse to knock on the door and ask whether they were left there accidentally, he reasons. Beyond the fence, the undergrowth gives way to gravel. Jonny touches the van's metal exterior on their way past. Cold and dark.

Definitely not driven recently. Reaching the doorway, he senses Paloma hesitating so he knocks before she can object. The door creaks open almost immediately. Light floods out, along with a puff of warm air. Followed by the bulky figure of a bald man in a red fleece dressing gown and slippers, expression caught somewhere between shock and confusion.

Jonny pauses. The air is suddenly thick with tension. This man opened his door so quickly he must have been expecting someone. But judging from the look on his face, it definitely isn't them. So who is it? The person they heard struggling, panting and flailing on the river bank? He starts gabbling before he can think better of it.

'I'm so sorry to disturb you, but we need help. We were out on the water when the tide went out, and we got stuck in the mud and now we're stranded. We need to get back to Eastwood. I know it's a lot to ask but we were hoping to find someone here who could give us a lift? I don't think either of us are capable of walking all the way back and we've also completely lost our bearings...'

He trails off as the man looks between them. 'Not from round here, I see,' he finally answers, putting his hands into the pockets of his dressing gown and appraising them.

'No,' Jonny answers with his best approximation of a clueless grin. 'I guess you must be sick of tourists turning up on your doorstep after misjudging the tide.'

'Tourists,' the man repeats thoughtfully. 'That's what you two are, then?'

'We are,' Paloma jumps in, correctly anticipating a use for her American accent. 'And again, we're so sorry to disturb you. We should have known to get moving too when we saw other boats heading back.'

'There weren't no other boats out on the water.' The man folds his arms, suddenly regarding them both with a far more suspicious look. 'You've been sniffing around somewhere you shouldn't. And now you're stuck. That about right?'

Jonny pulls the bunch of keys from his pocket, quietly pleased with himself for having the foresight to swipe them.

'We're sorry to have bothered you,' he replies lightly. 'If you don't mind pointing us in the right direction, we'll get going. We found these outside, by the way. Thought they might be yours.'

The man's face pales. He quickly reaches out and grabs the keys, tucking them into the pocket of his dressing gown. 'Thanks,' he says after a moment, shifting from foot to foot. 'Didn't realise I'd lost them.'

'They were hanging on a hook on the other side of your fence,' Jonny adds, watching him carefully. 'Someone else must have left them there for you.'

The man lets out a nervous laugh. 'Lucky they did,' he says, turning and swapping the keys for a different set on the hall table behind him. 'I can run you back to Eastwood. It ain't far. And getting lost around here can be dangerous.'

'Really?' Jonny tries not to sound too interested. 'Why's that?'

The man's shoulders slump. 'Never mind. Come on. My car's round the side.'

He gestures behind the bungalow, stepping out and closing the door behind him. They follow him towards the corner of the house. Overhead, the clouds have cleared, a bright moon beaming its iridescent shine on to every surface it catches. The effect is magical. The leaves on the trees swaying gently in the wind are suddenly dancing like silver fireflies in the dark. The glimmering discs of water slowly puddling on the causeway look like they could be portals to another world. For the briefest of moments Jonny feels as if the landscape itself is trying to tell him something.

'Thank you again,' he says hurriedly, staying a step behind. 'We really appreciate it. It's a lovely spot you have here. You must have a great view of Blackwater Island.'

'Mist never clears for long enough,' the man grunts back. 'Place is haunted. Some say that's what the mist really is. Ghosts. All of them dead Vikings burning and crying in hell.'

'Ah yes. Someone told us the legend of Inka earlier today,' Jonny says. 'Certainly sounds like one reason why it might be dangerous to get lost around here.'

He is unsurprised to watch the man visibly tense. Rounding the corner, they pause in front of a small and tired-looking hatchback, which is parked opposite a break in the fence.

Shaking the bunch of keys between his fingers, the man lets out an ostentatious sigh. 'Give us a tick. Brought the wrong keys. These are for the van.' He quickly turns around and walks back the way they came.

'I don't like this,' Paloma whispers almost immediately. 'He opened the door practically before you finished knocking. Was he warned that we were coming too?'

'I reckon he was expecting someone else,' Jonny answers, thinking fast. 'And the keys on the fence might have something to do with it. He certainly wasn't expecting us to have found them. Putting them on a hook on the fence feels deliberate, somehow.' He gestures at the break in the fence. 'Why hang the keys on a hook when you can just come round this way and knock on the door?'

'And then he suddenly said he'd give us a lift,' Paloma agrees. 'He probably wants us gone before whoever he's expecting actually arrives.'

'Yes, and he's even thrown in the local ghost story,' Jonny adds, bristling at the thought of the legend of Inka. Despite how magical the setting suddenly looks in the silver light of a full moon, he knows that woman is actual flesh and blood.

'Well he might actually believe it,' she cautions. 'We don't know whether he's got any other reasons for telling us how dangerous it is to get lost around here.'

Jonny clenches and unclenches the fist that fired a gun an hour earlier. 'I suppose so,' he says, still unconvinced. 'I just don't buy that anyone can live here and not know about that woman out there. Look at the moon.' He gestures at the bright sky and then out into the river. 'The whole place is practically floodlit. If I hear about that mist never clearing for long enough to see anything again, I swear I'm going to—'

He stops abruptly as the man returns, waving yet more keys.

'Sorry,' he says, unlocking the driver's door. 'Don't know why I got that wrong. Haven't driven the van for years. Used to be for work.' He gets in, leaning over to unlock the other doors. 'Car's a bit of a state, sorry. Don't drive this one much neither.'

Jonny opens the passenger door and instantly wishes he hadn't. The smell that assails him is almost overwhelmingly putrid.

'Sorry,' the man says again, hanging his head.

'It's ... it's OK,' Jonny replies, gingerly folding himself into the front seat and trying not to step on the items in the footwell. 'What do you do for work?'

'Electrician,' the man says shortly, jerking his head at Paloma. 'She coming or what?'

Paloma reluctantly reaches for the back doorhandle. The man reverses at speed through the break in the fence almost before her door is closed. Jonny doesn't need to turn around to know the backseat is as clogged with stuff as his footwell. He can hear items flying from side to side.

'Have to drive fast to get through the mud,' the man says, by way of explanation. 'You're lucky it's not too wet else we wouldn't get the car out.'

'I can imagine,' Jonny says, jolting around. 'How far away is Eastwood by road?'

'Fifteen miles on the tarmac. But we got three miles over the reeds first. Buckle up.'

The car accelerates forward, lurching and bouncing over the marsh grass. Jonny winces as his head glances off the car's ceiling.

'Getting to work every day must be a challenge. Though I suppose this terrain is less of a problem for a van.'

The man's only reply is another burst of acceleration.

Jonny tries a different tack. 'Honestly, we can't thank you enough for giving us a lift. Walking through the mud around here is like wading through cement. And it's so spooky when there's no moon. Do locals really think Blackwater is haunted, or is it just a story you tell your kids to stop them messing around on the causeway?'

The man's knuckles whiten on the wheel. 'Blackwater ain't a place to mess about, son.' A note of urgency sounds in his voice. 'Don't go trying your luck. It won't end well. And I should know.' He pauses, as if deciding how much more to say. 'This land's been in my family for generations,' he finally adds.

'Folks said the same about Blackwater in Eastwood,' Jonny replies, willing the man to tell them more. 'We got chatting to the owner of The Saxon.'

The man suddenly slams on the brakes, sending them all flying forward. Behind him, Jonny can hear Paloma fumbling for the doorhandle, readying to jump out and run.

'Sorry,' the man says, breathing hard. 'Foot slipped. Dodgy ankle, and that.'

Jonny lets out an awkward laugh. 'Do you ... do you know Judith?'

A sigh, long and deep, before the man shrugs in a gesture that looks decidedly like defeat. 'Everyone knows everyone around here. Should mean we all trust each other. But not me. I can't. Not after...' He trails off, gripping the steering wheel so hard it's as if he's hanging on to it. 'You shouldn't neither,' he finally adds.

Jonny holds his breath for more. But only silence follows. It's so uncomfortable that it starts to take on an almost physical quality, until a streetlamp appears on the horizon.

'There we go,' the man says brightly. 'Won't be bumping around much longer. The road's just up there by the light. It's quick as you like back to Eastwood after that.' He leans forward and flicks on the radio, and the car fills with tinny music.

Frustrated, Jonny stares out of the window, knowing his chance to get the man to open up any further is gone. He tries to relax as the streetlamp nears until it starts to illuminate more of the car's interior. And with it, the exact nature of the items strewn around inside.

Soft toys. Stray bottles. Packets of nappies. Pieces of clothing, all small sizes, old and stained. The unmistakable evidence of the presence of a child.

Chapter Twenty

Jonny's mind spins. Does this man have a child? Could that mean he knows something about the child found dead on Blackwater? He strains to pick out details from the items at his feet. Small vests. A teddy missing an eye. The trailing end of a miniature pair of tracksuit trousers. Then he spots the gilded edge of a photoframe, reaching down to grab it almost before he's fully realised what he's doing.

The man apologises for the mess again. Jonny's hand stills on the frame.

'It's no problem. I'm just worried I might have stepped on something and broken it.'

'Just leave it,' the man replies, but Jonny is already lifting the frame into his lap.

'Nope, it's fine. That's a relief. I was sure I felt something crack under my shoe.'

He runs a thumb over the glass covering the picture. The faded figure of a small boy holding an ice cream beams back at him for the briefest of seconds before the man snatches the frame away, tucking it roughly into the pocket of his dressing gown.

'Sorry,' Jonny says, struck by more than just the man's reaction. Even though he only glimpsed it, the picture in the frame looked strangely familiar. 'I didn't mean to pry. I just thought I'd broken it.'

But all the man does in response is grunt, swiping a finger angrily under one eye.

Jonny tries not to stare. Is this man fighting back tears? Is the boy in the picture his son? Jonny tries to remember what he looked like. Young. Smiley. No more than two or three years old, judging by the size of the cheeks. Apparently the same age as the boy found dead on Blackwater. But dressed in decidedly non-Victorian clothing, he remembers with relief, recalling Detective Inspector Gillian Peters' description of the body. The car begins to slow, pulling over to the side of the road.

'Best you get out here,' the man says gruffly, only coming to a stop once they are well past the glow of a streetlamp. 'It's not far to walk the rest of the way.'

Jonny pauses, trying to inventory the items in the footwell, but Paloma is already opening her door.

'Perfect, thank you so much,' she calls, getting out into the dark.

Another grunt. Jonny reluctantly opens his door. 'All the best,' he adds half-heartedly as he climbs out. It's only as the car turns around that he notices the man has turned his headlamps off.

Paloma sighs with relief as they start to walk. But Jonny is still too preoccupied by what he saw inside the car to relax at all. 'He wouldn't take us the whole way. He turned off his headlights to drive back. So it's obvious he doesn't want anyone to spot him. But he gave us a lift anyway...'

'And his car practically needed decontaminating,' Paloma finishes. 'There were old blankets, toys, clothes, all sorts in the back with me. I didn't poke around; he kept looking at me in the mirror. Were you trying to find out more about it when you were talking at the end? I couldn't really hear you over the radio.'

'I found a picture frame in the footwell. Pretended I thought I'd broken it so I could look at the photo in it. He grabbed it back almost immediately. I suppose I upset him by poking around. Could you see his face in the mirror then? There was a moment when I thought he was trying not to cry.'

'What, really? Why? What was in the picture?'

'A child. A young boy smiling and holding an ice cream. And I know it sounds crazy but I got the weirdest feeling that I'd already seen the picture somewhere before. I just can't figure out where. He snatched it back so quickly it obviously meant a lot to him.'

'His son?' Paloma wonders.

'That's what I thought at first, too. But judging by the smell a lot of the stuff in the car can't have been used for ages.'

'So maybe the kid is grown up now,' Paloma says, not sounding entirely convinced.

'Or maybe all that stuff is to do with a totally different child,' Jonny says, reflecting again on the inescapable line of sight between the man's bungalow and Blackwater Island. Something else suddenly occurs to him. 'I kept slipping on things as I ran out of the bunker. They felt like wads of fabric or something. Soft underfoot, almost like small cushions.'

Paloma's eyes widen. 'You don't think...?'

'That they were children's clothes or blankets? They certainly could have been. The child's body was found fully dressed in an outfit that would have taken more than a degree of planning.' He pauses for a moment as he remembers something else. 'And as well as the power pack there were these weird fabric items wrapped in plastic in the oyster basket that we just found on the bank by his house. It was too dark for me to see what they actually were. They could easily have been clothes or bedding.'

'But if that man had anything to do with the kid found dead on Blackwater, there's no way he would have voluntarily taken two complete strangers for a ride in a car full of potentially incriminating evidence.'

'Unless getting rid of us quickly was more important than showing us what was inside his car. He was definitely expecting someone when we arrived. So who was it? The person we heard scrabbling around in a panic in the reeds?'

Paloma looks around the deserted road in vain. 'Or a crazy

woman with a loaded gun. We need to find a phone and call the police. We should have asked to use his before we left.'

The mention of the gun pulls Jonny up short. 'Shit,' he mutters. 'My fingerprints are all over that fucking gun. In a location the police already warned me away from. I should never have touched the damn thing.' And I might have shot someone with it too, he thinks, a cold sweat breaking out down his back.

Paloma tries to placate him. 'Don't sweat it. I'd have grabbed it too. Anyone would, if it came down to having it pointed in their face otherwise. We need to call Lukas, too,' she adds, slowing as Eastwood's few buildings materialise up ahead and checking her watch. 'We've been out for ages. The Saxon might already be shut.'

'Another mistake,' Jonny mutters, still cross with himself.

'Let's go round the back. We can duck off the road here, look.'

Paloma steps into the undergrowth, threading her way towards the smattering of buildings. Before long they stumble upon a darkened gravel clearing, empty save for a couple of industrial-sized rubbish bins.

'Think we're behind The Saxon?'

Jonny eyes the back of the building beyond – dark, nondescript and quiet. He steps into the clearing, lifting the lid of one of the bins to check whether it is full of empties.

'Seems so,' he answers, about to close it on top of piles of cans and bottles. But something else catches his eye. 'Is that what I think it is?' He points to an object amongst the bottles, so large that some of them are sitting inside it. 'It looks like an oyster basket.'

Paloma joins him, peering into the bin. 'Another one?'

'Yes,' Jonny replies, picturing the sodden and barnacled wire container they'd hauled out of the water and the second similar object he'd found on the opposite shore.

'I guess,' she ventures, squinting. 'So what if it is? Didn't you say oysters were all you found to eat around here?'

Jonny lets the lid drop as he wonders to himself. 'There are just one too many weird things stacking up around us, that's all.'

'For sure. Come on, let's try the back door. You'd better knock first. We don't need to be charged with breaking and entering as well as misuse of an illegal firearm.' She pauses, eyebrow raised at him. 'Too soon?'

He grins back at her. 'I'll let you have that. Since it's you.'

They walk towards the door set into the back wall. A thin strip of light is emanating from underneath. He knocks once, then twice. Nothing. A gentle push, and he is unsurprised to find the door opening at the merest hint of force.

'So people round here chain up oyster baskets but don't lock their doors,' Paloma says wryly. 'More weird behaviour. I guess I'm not surprised.'

'And also apparently believe in ghosts,' he adds in agreement, before calling into the hallway, 'Judith? Are you there?'

Still nothing. He steps inside. He can see the shadowy interior of the bar beyond, the dark shapes of a couple of bottles left out on the counter.

Paloma clicks the door closed behind her. 'Do you know where the phone is?'

'Probably behind the bar,' he says, peering into the dark.

She looks up the stairs. 'And do we think Judith is asleep up there?'

'Maybe,' he says, reflexively checking whether the door is firmly shut. 'I mean, I suppose I'd be surprised if she went upstairs to bed with the back door open under normal circumstances. But everyone seems to be in on the same secret around here.'

Paloma squeezes past and heads for the bar. Jonny eyes the drawing as they go behind the counter. The phone is mounted on the wall just inside the doorframe. Paloma grabs the receiver and starts dialling.

'Hang on.' Jonny ferrets in a pocket for his notebook and

Gillian Peters' calling card. 'I've got a direct line to the police station in Maldon.'

But Paloma is still hanging on to the phone and frowning. Repeatedly cutting the call and dialling again.

He knows the minute she hands him the receiver, her eyes widening with trepidation.

The line is completely dead.

Chapter Twenty-One

Jonny traces the length of the telephone's curly wire back to its port on the box on the wall. All seems present and correct. 'There must be a problem with the outside line. None of these connections are damaged.'

Paloma looks past him back into the tiny hallway, her face furrowed with concern. 'Can you remember whether there is an extension in our room upstairs?'

'Even if there is it won't work either unless this place has multiple phone lines. Which, judging from the state of everything else around here, it almost certainly doesn't.' He fiddles with the wire again. 'Maybe Judith has unplugged it from the mains.'

'But why would she deliberately disconnect her phone?'

'I don't know.' Jonny walks back down the hallway and pauses at the foot of the stairs, peering up at the three doors arrayed around the tiny landing above.

'Where are you going?'

'She kept telling us the guest room had a blue door and the bathroom was opposite. The third door must be her room.' He climbs the first step, calling in a low voice. 'Judith? Are you there?'

'Wait,' Paloma says, but he's already heading up the stairs. She catches up to him a second later.

Pausing outside the third door, he knocks smartly before calling her name again. Nothing.

Paloma puts her ear to the wood. 'Is she inside, do you think?'

Jonny pauses, listening hard. He can't hear a sound other than their shallow breathing. No hint of anyone nervously hovering behind the door waiting for them to leave her alone. He cautiously tries the knob. A click and the door opens a crack into a dark, silent room.

'Wait,' Paloma repeats, but Jonny is already pushing it wider. The room has an unmistakably still and unoccupied air. He takes a step inside, immediately catching his foot against a stack of papers on the floor.

'Come on, Jonny,' Paloma implores him. 'We can't go through her things.'

But Jonny is already bending down to investigate. All he can make out in the dark is the outline of a photo printed in the centre of the top sheet of paper with some lettering around it. 'These look like posters of some kind.'

Paloma tugs at him. 'So what. We shouldn't be in here.'

'I know, I know.' Jonny lets the page drop before backing out of the room and pulling the door closed again. 'I just don't understand why she would rent out her spare room for the night only to unplug her phone and do a runner at closing time. Our room is immaculately kept. She obviously cares about that side of her business. And she must have left in a rush. She left the back door open when she usually has a security grille locked over the front of the pub after hours. I saw her opening it when I arrived this morning.'

'I hope she's alright,' Paloma says nervously, heading back down the stairs.

'Something must have spooked her,' Jonny adds, following her. 'She didn't even have time to turn the hallway light off.'

Paloma pauses at the foot of the stairs, hand on the back door, seemingly undecided whether to stay or go. 'So what do we do now?'

Jonny weighs their options. 'The only other phone box I know about round here doesn't work either. We're at least three miles' walk from Maldon. And we know for a fact that a child died around here last week and there's an armed and violent woman hiding out nearby. The detective I met earlier said she'd meet me at the pontoon at first light. I think the safest thing to do is to stay here and wait until then.'

Paloma shrinks into herself as she stares into the darkened bar.

'Look, I don't want to stay here overnight any more than you do,' he adds, trying to sound like he means it. The truth is he's perfectly happy to stay – especially if he's with her. The bigger question is whether she's happy to stay with him. And he's not sure he wants to know the answer to that. 'But we don't have much choice – unless you fancy walking all the way to Maldon in the pitch-dark. You can lock yourself in upstairs and I'll keep watch down here. One of us may as well get some rest.'

A beat passes between them. Jonny wills her to beg not to be left alone, to vow to stay up all night with him in this creepy and deserted bar. Or to lead him upstairs and willingly press herself into his arms. But all she does is stare at him with a pained expression on her face. The silence stretching out between them is so charged with expectation that it starts to feel almost electric.

She finally breaks it with a small nod. 'OK, then. If you're sure. Thanks, I guess.'

He nods back, mentally kicking himself. Why did he suggest she go upstairs on her own? What is he so afraid of? She actually kissed him earlier. What he's longed for since he met her actually happened. But what does it mean? That she's suddenly willing to take the next step – contrary to everything she said the night before he left for that stupid training course? If all it took to change her mind was being alone in a room above a pub in the arse end of nowhere, then why was she so convinced it was a bad idea in the first place? And how is he going to find out if he pushes her away?

But as usual he says none of this. Instead he just agrees: 'Yes. Of course. Neither of us will be able to sleep unless the other is awake. And there's no point in both of us sitting up down here.'

'Maybe we can take it in turns,' she ventures. 'I'll sleep for a bit, then you.'

'If you like,' he answers, the tiniest seed of warmth budding in his chest. 'I'll knock on the door in a few hours. How about that? Make sure you lock it, though.'

'I will,' she answers, digging around in her pocket for the key.

Jonny watches her glossy black hair falling about her face with ill-disguised longing. She slips past him without a backward glance, and he waits until he hears the creak on the stairs before grabbing the bottle left open on the bar. A quick swig of English Spirit later and the lumpy shadows of armchairs and tables beyond the counter instantly look more forgiving.

Jonny sinks into a seat, letting the alcohol slow his thoughts. Are unlocked doors and disconnected phones particularly suspicious in some tiny rural backwater? Only in the context of an armed assailant hiding out in a bunker on an island nearby, he thinks. And a bunch of locals pretending not to know or see a thing, other than a ghost, even after the body of a child was found in the same location.

Another glug to fortify himself against the thought of the woman who assaulted him. Aggressively muscular, whiplash reflexes, military-issue boots and clothes. Hiding out on an island, which, by rights, should still be a crime scene. Soon to become prime suspect number one when he's told police about her ... and with plenty of Jonny's DNA to use in her defence, courtesy of handing him a gun.

His palm prickles at the thought. That fucking gun. Then he rears up in his armchair as something else suddenly occurs to him.

The gun.

He knew he'd seen it before.

And now he knows exactly where.

Jonny grips the lumpy armchair, head suddenly spinning. The state-of-the-art weaponry demonstrated by those security officers on his training course last week. The pistol they gave him to handle just so he knew what features to look for in a crisis. *Play for time. Every second counts.* The barrel, the chamber, the smell – its powdery, oily, iron tang. The pistol he handled on the course was exactly the same as the pistol he fumbled with in the bunker. And one of the reasons he failed the course is the reason he accidentally fired the fucking thing too. He forgot it didn't have a manual safety catch.

Jonny is on his feet without thinking, pacing around in the dark, trying to connect what he knows. An unexplained death in a mysterious location. Ancient bunkers hiding modern military-issue weapons and electrical equipment. A desperate and inexplicably isolated police officer being stonewalled by her superiors – and that long before the body of a child was ever found. It smacks of a cover-up. But of what? Jonny pictures the woman in the bunker, tries to recall every word she said. She knew he was coming. She knew he wasn't alone. She gave him a gun. Why would she do that if she wanted him silenced? Then he considers the legend of Inka. Why would someone tell the story to any old stranger that will listen, and replicate it in graffiti that everyone can see? Judith must have been trying to tell him about the woman herself. And Jonny ran away from her before he found out why.

Jonny thinks about the self-appointed security officers that ran his warzone training course, all former elite soldiers in the special forces. Too young to retire, too old to serve. Then he runs over everything he already knows about covert military operations – the code words, the clandestine preparations, the complete communications blackout. Where better to conduct any of them than an apparently uninhabited island already fortified with ancient military bunkers barely fifty miles from command and control in the capital? What if there's still plenty of work available for ex-military types, without them needing to travel very far at all? What if he's stumbled upon the beating heart of British black ops, right here in the middle of the Blackwater river?

And if he has, could the operations taking place here have caused the death of a child? He almost reels at the thought. Now he's reliving every word of his conversation with Gillian Peters – apparently the only member of the police force who still cares about what really killed the small boy found dead on Christmas Day. The tip-off came in before dawn. An anonymous message left on the automated answering service at her tiny police station in Maldon. Delivered via some cutting-edge software that's made the connection impossible to trace. All she's sure of is it came from a woman. She's been left alone with the investigation since the cause of death was ruled as natural. She's been operating overlooked and isolated since she arrived in the district five years ago.

Jonny examines the facts he has from every possible angle. Whoever the woman who made the anonymous call was must have known enough about the local police to try and contact Gill directly rather than go through emergency services. Not the most natural choice when dealing with a child dying. But the logical choice if the caller already knows there are other players on the field – ones who will do what they can to keep the information from coming out. Which would also explain why Gill has been left in the cold since she arrived in Maldon. Senior authorities must be deliberately looking the other way. Most importantly, whoever made the call knew exactly where the body was. Jonny's back in the bunkers again, his assailant's calculated conviction suddenly as tangible as the English Spirit racing through his bloodstream, and he arrives at the only conclusion he can.

No one else is going to get hurt around here.

That woman must have made the call herself.

Chapter Twenty-Two

Jonny's head clears in an instant. The woman in the bunker wanted the body to be found. She chose to alert Gillian Peters because she already knew the detective wasn't party to hiding what might really be happening on Blackwater and would put out a public appeal for information. She did it anonymously because she knew she'd immediately become a suspect if she made herself and her location known. Which is why she went on to ambush Jonny rather than Gill herself – he's a journalist rather than a police officer in the pay of the state. She must have planned the whole thing. And she gave him a gun. She literally laid down her arms. She's an ally, not an enemy, he's convinced of it. She wanted to talk to him. He's just got to find out why.

He puts his bottle back on the bar before continuing silently into the corridor beyond. Glancing overhead, he pictures Paloma exhausted from their struggle through the mud and sound asleep, secure in the knowledge she's behind a locked door. How will she react if he interrupts her now? Assume he just wants to get into bed with her? Isn't that exactly what he wants? Once he's gone back out into the dark to find out what's really happening on Blackwater, that is. But what if she won't agree to move before they've spoken to the police? And what if she won't entertain the idea of spending time alone with him in a bedroom? He cannot reconcile himself with either outcome. Zipping up his jacket, he resolves to be back before she wakes and heads out into the night. He doesn't worry that he's leaving her alone. There's plenty Jonny hasn't worked out yet. But one thing he's sure of is any threat they're facing is coming from somewhere far beyond the middle of the Blackwater river.

He heads round the side of the building and out on to the street, retracing his steps along the dirt track to the river. The sky is still clear, casting his surroundings in a new light. With the tide a long way out, the causeway is fully exposed and glistening beguilingly under the bright moon. What was a high black river when they originally set off is now a damp and muddy expanse of solid ground with a dark mass rising at its heart. He walks a short distance along the river bank, tries to approximate where they first set off by searching for the oyster basket they found previously, chained up in the water. Dropping on to his knees, he ferrets around in the reeds until he finds a chain and traces it down into the mud on the riverbed. But there is no longer anything tied to its end.

Jonny pauses, crouching in the mud. He can't be sure he's in the right spot. But in the light of the moon he can see the dim shadow of the phone box a few hundred yards further along the bank. He knows they didn't walk as far as that the first time. So he must be pretty close to where they originally started their journey. He considers the loose end of the chain, rolling the cold links between his fingers. He can't see any objects lying nearby, the riverbed wide and empty of anything other than a few loose rocks and little glimmering pools of water. Is this the same chain as earlier? It certainly feels like it is. Has someone come to take possession of the basket and its contents? He knows it was no good for farming oysters. But it was obviously in use for something to have been tethered down in the first place. So what was inside? He pictures the basket he saw amongst the empties in The Saxon's dustbin. Could it have been the same one?

He reluctantly lets the chain drop and strikes out across the mud towards the black mass hulking in the middle of the river. It doesn't take him long to reach the thick clumps of bullrushes springing from its foot. He navigates his way through them, trying to make as little noise as possible. Being convinced there's an ally and not an enemy hiding in the bunkers is one thing. But being confident he won't encounter another malign presence on the island is quite another. He already knows that woman wasn't alone underground. And the crazed look he saw in the eyes of the lackey she sent out into the dark to catch Paloma is not something he's going to forget in a hurry. It was the look of someone completely out of control.

He clambers cautiously up the slope, wincing into every crackle and snap until the bullrushes level off to reveal the dim outline of something more solid up ahead. Pausing, he tenses in anticipation of someone knocking him off his feet and dragging him down into a hole. But the sounds of his own movement die away until he is left with nothing other than the wind swishing through the reeds again. He's become used to that sound by now. It calls to him like a warning.

Turning on the spot, he peers up the slope, tries to approximate how far up he was before being ambushed. He takes one step, then another. His foot catches on the third. Dropping to his knees, he finds a solid, square trapdoor. And then – a voice. Unmistakable, even in the pitch-dark. Cold and derisive, cutting through the shadows like a knife.

'Welcome back. I guess you weren't as scared as you looked the first time. Most people faint in shock when taken by surprise like that. They can't remember anything.'

Jonny's hands tense reflexively into fists. *Most people faint in shock.* His assailant has done this before. A lot.

'And you almost knocked me out, too,' he replies, standing up slowly. A shadow is hovering in the dark a few feet away, its upper half rippling with wild curly hair.

'Well I did give you my gun to make up for that. Then you nearly shot me with the damn thing.'

The gun Jonny fired sounds so loudly in his mind again he can practically hear it. Would he feel better if he'd actually hit her? Despite all the consequences that would have entailed it suddenly feels like he might.

'It was an accident. I wasn't deliberately trying to shoot you.'

'I know that. And it was loaded with blanks, anyway. I needed to get you to trust me, not kill me.'

Jonny pauses. Knowing that the gun he fired was in fact harmless isn't making him more confident. This woman is obviously always ten steps ahead of anyone she encounters.

'I suppose that's a relief,' he finally says. 'I'm just a journalist. I'm not used to feeling like I'm armed and dangerous.'

A snort. 'Really. You don't think information can be weaponised? Journalists have paymasters just like the rest of us. And they aren't all in service to the truth.'

'So who's paying you to hide in a bunker on a wilderness reserve? What are you really doing here?'

She moves closer, undergrowth rustling menacingly underfoot. 'Plenty of time for that. I need to know we're on the same side first before I tell you any more.'

He holds up his hands. 'Well, I'm only here because a child was found dead in this swamp last week.'

'I know. The only reason he was is because of me.'

A little of the tension leaves Jonny's chest. 'So you're the one who tipped off the police. And you didn't make yourself known because you'd immediately become a suspect?'

'Correct.'

He drops his arms, spreading his hands wide. 'So then why did you grab me? Don't you think I'll make your presence known?'

'You'd have done it by now if you were going to.'

'Except you conveniently managed to get me to plaster my fingerprints all over your weapon.'

'Indeed. I suppose you could call that insurance.'

'Against what? I don't believe you're the one who killed this child. I wouldn't be here if I did.'

'Why not? You don't think someone like me could do such a thing?'

'Not exactly,' he says cautiously. Even in the half-light her posture looks intimidating. 'I just don't think you would draw attention to it if you did. You only expose yourself in the process. So who are you? What are you really doing out here?'

The woman sighs, so long and deep Jonny can feel it. 'What *aren't* I doing is the better question. What did I stop doing years ago, only to find there was nothing left for me but exile and disgrace.'

'Exile,' Jonny echoes, confused. 'What kind of exile do you mean?'

'You think I'd be out here in this swamp if I had a choice? I've got nowhere else to go, is what I mean. And I'm not the only one.'

Chapter Twenty-Three

Instantly Jonny is picturing the second woman in the bunker and the deranged look in her eyes. He thinks about the presence he felt in the tunnels, the commotion he and Paloma witnessed on the opposite shore.

'Who are the others?' he asks. 'Where are they now?'

'Don't misunderstand me. We're not together.'

His eyes narrow. 'But you weren't alone in your bunker before.'

A snort. 'Arwen is not someone I would ever do business with.'

Jonny briefly reflects on Arwen's wasted appearance – so emaciated he could see her bones jutting through her rags, so much hair missing from her head that he could see her greasy white scalp. 'So why did you make her go and chase Paloma down?'

'Is that your friend?'

Jonny mentally kicks himself for giving away a personal detail, but he can't do anything about it now. 'Yes. Luckily she got away unharmed.'

'How many times do I have to tell you that no more innocent people are going to get hurt on my watch?'

'That's still kind of hard for me to believe. You ambushed me in the pitch-dark. Handed me a gun just to cover it with my fingerprints. And sent someone who didn't look particularly sane to grab Paloma.'

'I said no more innocent people are going to get hurt. I didn't say anything about sparing fucking deluded fools.'

A light flicks on and off again in the distance, so quickly Jonny wonders if he's imagining it.

'There they go again,' she goes on. 'Continuing with their stupid signals like nothing's gone wrong.'

Jonny squints in the direction of the light, trying to put it together. 'I don't understand. Was that flash a signal from the mainland? What have you all done that's left you nowhere to go other than some nature reserve in the middle of the river?'

A second light flicks on, stopping him in his tracks. Because this time it's up close, dim and red. Night vision, the kind of light used by the military during the most covert operations of all. The woman is wearing a special-ops head torch in her tangled silver hair.

'Isn't all that "nature reserve" garbage still kind of hard for you to believe too?'

Jonny is mesmerised for a moment by her dark eyes, glittering with conviction beneath the eerie torchlight.

'For sure,' he finally answers. 'But I don't believe this island is some benign hideaway either. You've got a state-of-the-art weapon in your arsenal and a load of computers in your bunker. If you're not a fully paid-up member of the military then I'll—'

The rest of his sentence dies in his throat as a hand suddenly closes around his neck.

'What? Eat your hat? Scream bloody murder?'

Jonny starts to flail, clawing at the hand clamped around his throat. Panic takes hold as the oxygen drains from his body. In the dim red light, the woman's expression warps from anger to frustration and finally settles on something akin to pity. When she lets him go, all he can do is gasp for breath, crumpling on to the trapdoor in the ground beneath them.

'Sorry,' she mutters, flexing her hand. 'You didn't deserve that.'

Jonny cradles his sore neck, panting with relief. Contrition – something else he wasn't expecting from this woman. First she risks exposing herself by tipping off the police to a crime. Then she snatches Jonny, only to give him her gun. Now she's apologising for trying to choke the life out of him. Why?

'You must have one hell of a guilty conscience,' he croaks. 'Are you going to tell me who you really are?'

The woman extends a hand, lumpy with callouses. 'You can call me Jane.'

'Jane?' Jonny parrots back, gingerly shaking her outstretched hand for the shortest time possible.

'Yes. Jane Doe, if you want a fuller version.'

'I'm guessing it's more than your life's worth to give me your real name.'

'Correct. And it doesn't matter anyway. I've been faceless and nameless for decades now. I suppose you could call it an occupational hazard.'

'In what occupation, exactly?'

She looks away into the dark. Jonny waits, rubbing his neck.

'You don't trust me,' she eventually says. 'I get it. I don't blame you. But you have to understand, this isn't easy for me. The only person I've had to answer to for years is myself. And the problem is I hate myself. I hate everything I've done. And now I need to make it right or else there's no point.'

Jonny shrinks into himself, wishing he'd never heard those words before. Suddenly he's nine years old again and wondering what someone taking their own life actually means. A social worker had to explain that his mother had killed herself. She couldn't live with herself after his abusive father absconded with his twin sister. It was guilt that killed her in the end. The night tightens around him, quivering with familiar ghosts.

'I still don't understand,' he says, trying and failing to keep the emotion from his voice. 'And believe me, I want to. Right now, I want to understand more than I want anything else in the world. That's why I came back to find you. A child has died out here. I can't just forget I found a heavily armed fugitive hiding in a bunker underneath the crime scene.'

'I'm not a fugitive.'

'Then why don't you have anywhere else to go?'

'Because I was a hired gun for thirty years and all it's left me with is blood on my hands. I made a living out of things the British government wasn't officially allowed to do and I've still been left with nothing. It's finally time to make some people pay for that.'

Jonny takes a sharp breath. His hunch about black ops was right. But this woman isn't a soldier. This woman is a mercenary. Hired off the books to complete the kinds of missions that even the most elite of special military forces can't officially carry out. He's suddenly scouring his mental world map for all the conflicts that Britain has been caught up in over the last thirty years. Then he realises it doesn't matter. There won't be any record of anything this woman has ever done.

'I see why calling you a fully paid-up member of the military really hit a nerve.'

'Indeed. And for what it's worth I haven't been fully paid-up since a mission went wrong. To think some idiots still call us soldiers of fortune. The truth is we're hostages to fortune. And these days all our fucking fortunes are paralysed by the prospect of the Doomsday bug. There's a totally different kind of arms race under way now that's putting people like me out of business. Don't you know how lucky you are to witness the dawn of a brand-new digital age?' she adds sarcastically.

Jonny stiffens at the reference. 'I know all about the Doomsday bug. Believe me, I find the whole thing as frustrating as you do. But honestly I'm not sure you're hostage to anything other than your conscience.'

Jane's voice suddenly sounds very small. 'You think I don't already know that? My conscience is all I've got left.'

'So what more can you tell me about the boy found dead here last week?'

'Come inside and I'll show you,' she answers, leaning down to lift the edge of the trapdoor embedded in the dirt between them.

Chapter Twenty-Four

A dazzling column of light beams straight into the dark sky as she heaves the trapdoor open, blinding Jonny for a moment. When his vision settles, Jane is already back inside her bunker, hand outstretched to help him down. He doesn't hesitate. He's on the edge of a breakthrough. And he's got himself out of this hole once already. He knows he can do it again. Gripping her hand, he jumps down beside her. She pulls the trapdoor closed with a decisive clunk.

Jonny turns on the spot as if he's seeing the inside of the bunker for the first time, eyeing the two dark openings in each corner of the far wall, the pile of oyster baskets, the plastic tank of clear liquid. The low stone ceiling immediately feels oppressive. He can still hear the low hum of electrical equipment whirring disconcertingly in the background. 'How did you know these bunkers existed? This island isn't even labelled on the map.'

Jane walks towards one of the tunnels, gesturing at the light bulbs dangling overhead. 'How do you think I knew? These bunkers have been used recently enough that they're still wired with comms and electricity. This place was, in actual fact, fortified to the eyeballs for marine training exercises during the Second World War. This is the place where it all fell apart for me.'

The mission that went wrong, Jonny thinks. It must have involved Blackwater. 'So this island was once a black site?'

She pauses at the tunnel opening. Jonny notes with a degree of trepidation that it's not the tunnel he used to escape last time. 'I suppose you could say that, yes,' she answers quietly. 'And all that protected-wilderness status and crap about ghosts and Vikings and ancient military conquests is just to give the place a different story.'

Jonny joins her at the tunnel entrance, peering into its murky depths. 'All it actually does is draw attention to it though. And I don't think all the locals around here believe those tales either. Which I am guessing is how you knew that I was on my way out here to investigate in the first place. Someone warned you.'

She starts walking again. Jonny follows a pace behind, feeling slightly more confident as the hum of equipment fades away.

'Right,' she says. 'So what does that tell you?'

'That there's at least one person on the mainland who knows a lot more about what's going on out here than they say they do,' he says, thinking about the flashes of light he saw coming from the shore a few moments ago. 'More than one, if I had to bet on it. And none of them are inclined to speak up now the body of a child has been found here too. You keep saying no more innocent people are going to get hurt on your watch. So how do you explain what happened here last week?'

The light dims as the tunnel starts to twist and slope downward.

'Because it's not just me out here. I told you. I'm not the only one shunning this allegedly civilised society of ours. At least I know why I'm doing it. But the others are just nutters. You'll see for yourself in a minute.'

'Who are the others? Are you talking about Arwen?' Jonny puzzles over the other woman's wretched appearance again, remembering Jane's earlier comment about never doing business with her. 'Did she have something to do with the boy's death?'

Jane visibly rankles. 'It's all her fault. Well, hers and that other fucking moron.'

Jonny slows. He thinks about the presence he felt in the dark during his way out of these bunkers the first time. 'There's someone else down here?'

'Yes. They're a couple. A man and a woman playing at being Adam and Eve in the Garden of Eden, if you can believe that. They hate everything about modern life and want nothing to do with it. Think they can turn back the clock just by pretending it's a hundred years ago.'

She ducks as she turns another corner. The passageway is becoming uncomfortably narrow and cramped. Jonny is suddenly picturing the Victorian outfit Gillian Peters had described on the child's body.

'What have you got to do with each other? Have you been helping them?'

'I already told you we're not together,' she replies, a warning note creeping into her voice. 'Those idiots had no idea I was here until recently. I know every inch of this island. I know exactly how to operate off grid. It was easy for me to stay hidden from them. And they didn't want to be found. I understood their motivation at first. I am one of the few people that actually knows what goes into maintaining the freedom and security you lot take for granted. I get why some folks don't want any part of a society like that, even if they have no idea what I know. The way they chose to live didn't bother me until they decided it was a good idea to have a kid.'

'Out here?' Jonny asks in horror.

'No,' she answers grimly, pausing and crouching. Jonny has to crane his neck over her to see what she is doing. There's a scrabbling noise before something heavy clumps dully on the stone floor of the tunnel.

'*In* here, to be precise,' she continues, rocking back on her heels.

There's a dark hole in front of her. A large slab of rock is leaning against the wall of the passageway. Jane has somehow lifted a piece of stone clean out of the floor.

'I don't understand,' Jonny says, trying not to breathe in a sudden draught of putrid air.

Jane lowers herself into the hole. 'I know you don't. It's very hard for anyone sane to understand. But it's true. This is where that boy was born and raised. Follow me and you'll see. It's a squeeze, but not for long.' She holds up her arms in order to wriggle her shoulders through the gap before disappearing.

Jonny peers into the hole, trying not to breathe deeply. The smell is getting worse. The air is almost humid with it. Below, Jane flicks her head torch back on, casting a dim red glow in front of her. He swings his legs into the hole and pauses, suddenly frozen with dread.

'Is there anyone else down there?'

A muffled snort. 'No. Not now.'

But Jonny still can't bring himself to move. 'How can you be sure of that?'

A note of menace creeps into her voice. 'Trust me. I'm sure. I know exactly where they are now. I've dealt with them myself.'

Jonny remembers the broken look in Arwen's eyes. A cold sweat starts to prickle down his back. But he's come this far. He's not going to stop now. And thinking too hard about what he's going to find next will get him nowhere. He just has to keep moving.

He begins to inch his body through the opening, holding his breath to stop the stone edges digging painfully into his sides. Dangling himself down with his arms outstretched, he finds his feet are already almost touching the floor.

The first thing he notices when he lands are dark marks on the ground and some crumpled piles of fabric stained with something that looks distinctly like dried blood. The smell is suddenly almost unbearable. He covers his mouth and nose with a hand, speaking through his fingers.

'What the hell is this place? Is it part of a second tunnel system?'

She nods. 'It was once known as the Deep State. Hard to get

in. Even harder to get out. I believe you journalists are also familiar with gallows humour.'

But Jonny can't even force a laugh. He looks around the dank hole, notes the opening to another passageway behind where Jane is standing and more bloodstained fabric wadded up against a wall. A horrifying thought suddenly occurs to him. 'Did that boy die in here?'

'No. He was born in here. That's what all this sheeting was for.'

The image of a woman voluntarily choosing to give birth to a child in the dark, on this cold stone floor, is almost too much for Jonny to bear. 'How do you know that?'

Jane points at the open hole overhead. 'Because I was listening. I heard the whole thing. And I already knew Arwen was pregnant. They wanted to have the kid out in the open. They'd already built some shrine out of rocks ready for their fantasy birthing ceremony. But Mother Nature had other ideas. They couldn't get outside in time. Arwen almost bled to death. She only survived because they had help from offshore. And after all that they still chose to keep living underground with that poor kid. Still seemed to think they could raise him safely. Some guff about having been blessed because he was born beneath the roots of a tree.' She turns to the opening in the wall behind her and sets off down the next tunnel. 'That's why they spent most of their time in here. These tunnels eventually come out on the west side of the island in the middle of a massive root system.'

Jonny follows behind, feeling faintly nauseous. The passage quickly opens out into another bunker containing basic essentials. Torches. Some dirty crockery. Bedding. A teddy bear with its arm hanging off. A small plastic crate filled with canned food. He reaches inside and pulls out a shiny tin of baked beans. Squinting in the dim light, he notes the best-before date printed on the side is well into the new millennium.

'They got hold of these beans pretty recently,' he murmurs to himself.

'I told you, they had help from offshore,' Jane answers. 'No one could survive for long out here without assistance – except someone like me, of course. They had a whole supply system in place. At least they used to have, before the boy died.'

Jonny pictures the house on the opposite shore and the man driving a car full of children's clothes, then relives the commotion he and Paloma overheard on the river bank. The cries of pain, the air of panic. The set of keys hung seemingly deliberately on the fence. 'And now he's gone, no one who helped these people will say a word, in case they're found guilty by association.'

'Correct. I should have tipped off that police officer the minute I knew the woman was pregnant. I wish I had. Like I said: no more innocent people are going to get hurt on my watch.'

Jonny looks around the dank space again in disbelief, trying not to picture a baby boy wriggling around helplessly in the dark, until he realises there is no obvious way out other than back the way they came.

'How did they get in and out of here? I thought you said this tunnel system opens out on the other side of the island.'

'It does. There's a turn of this last tunnel. It's easy to miss unless you know what you are looking for. They only found it because they came in the way we're about to head out. They've never had a clue about the access hole in the ceiling. It's almost invisible from the inside. Especially when you're only operating by torchlight. We deliberately didn't put any electricity in the Deep State.'

He quickly follows her down the passageway. There is a sharp turn lurking in the dark halfway down. The next passage starts to slope upward almost immediately. Jonny feels lighter with every step until he remembers he still doesn't know exactly what killed the child he can still picture toddling around in the fetid dark.

Jane stops suddenly as the passageway ends. Looking up, her

red torch illuminates a wide vertical shaft strung with metal footholds either side. As they start to climb, Jonny tries to imagine how a pregnant woman could possibly think she'd be able to do the same while in labour. Then he pictures how difficult it would be to get a baby or small child out safely too.

Before long Jane is climbing out between the thick, gnarled roots of a giant tree. He follows, gulping great draughts of cool, fresh night air.

'Watch your step,' she says, pulling herself to her feet. 'The salt in the mud around here makes everything really slippery.'

Jonny hauls himself out of the shaft, picking his way over the roots to where Jane is standing. She turns to him, folding her arms as she asks, 'So what are you going to do about all this?'

He is suddenly unnerved by the strange look in her eyes. Under the red light in her hair their fervour looks positively demonic.

'I'm certainly not going to drop the story, if that's what you mean,' he answers warily. 'But I'm not ready to report anything yet. I still don't know exactly how the boy died.'

She scoffs. 'Haven't you seen enough to work it out?'

'It definitely seems like something seriously messed-up has gone on here,' he says. 'But I can't just take your word for it. There's a post-mortem report being readied on the mainland, though. Presumably you already know that.'

She waves a hand. 'That report won't tell you anything.'

'Why do you say that?'

She looks away into the dark, pursing her lips. A creeping feeling starts to tingle up the back of Jonny's neck. He peers past her, trying to establish exactly where he is in relation to the shoreline. Then he remembers something else she said, and it unsettles him further.

'It would help if I could also speak to Arwen,' he ventures. 'Where is she now?'

'I told you. I've taken care of her and that other fucking moron.'

'The boy's father, you mean?'

'Yes. She called him Echo. I think you can safely assume that wasn't his given name.'

Much like yours, he thinks, with a jolt of adrenaline as he remembers why Jane is going to such lengths to hide who she really is.

'I know what you are thinking,' she continues, that menacing note back in her voice again. 'And I don't blame you. After all, how would someone like me go about taking care of people like that?'

Jonny tenses. The thought of one dead body somewhere in this swamp was bad enough. The prospect that there might be two more is chilling him to the bone.

'Thing is, I haven't done anything of the sort. And I certainly wouldn't be telling anyone about it if I had. Two more casualties out here wouldn't serve my purpose at all.'

'And what exactly is your purpose? I still don't understand what you're actually doing in this swamp.'

She pauses, as if sizing him up. 'I told you at the start,' she eventually says. 'I spent thirty years as a hired gun, and because of that I have blood on my hands. It's finally time to put that right. More bodies will only complicate matters. But a journalist going missing? That might just do the trick.'

Chapter Twenty-Five

Jonny holds up his hands. The air is suddenly thick with tension. 'What happened to no more innocent people getting hurt on your watch?'

'Who said anything about you getting hurt?'

He answers with as much conviction as he can muster. 'Well I don't plan on willingly becoming your prisoner. And besides,' he adds, picturing Paloma waiting back at The Saxon, 'I'm not alone. If I suddenly disappear it'll take no time for someone to raise the alarm and police will swarm all over this place again.'

'You think? A child was found dead out here last week. How many police officers have you found still looking into it?'

Jonny turns cold. He starts to back away, keeping his hands in the air. 'Well you can bet that plenty of officers will come back here once I've told them about the armed woman hiding out by the original crime scene. And I think that's actually exactly what you want to happen next. Why else would you give a journalist a guided tour of this wretched place? You tipped off police. You didn't make yourself known because you would have immediately become a suspect. But you also knew police would put out a public appeal for information and a reporter would turn up soon enough. You want justice for that boy as much as I do. You'll just make sure you're long gone by the time any more officers arrive. I'm more use to you off this island than tied up in one of your bunkers.'

'Smart,' Jane says, staying exactly where she is. 'You're good. I'll give you that.'

'So you're going to let me leave,' he replies, trying to make it sound like a statement and not a question. He looks around vainly in the dark. 'It would help if I knew which way to go.'

She points directly behind him. 'Turn sharp right in about two hundred yards. Then just keep walking. You've got time before the tide turns.'

Jonny nods back at her even though he can't be sure whether she can see him properly now. He's managed to put enough distance between them that all he can see of her is an eerie patch of red light. He tenses as the light starts to move before he realises it is fading away. Jane must be moving in the opposite direction to him.

Turning, he strides as quickly as he can through the undergrowth. The vegetation is tall and thick, sticky with damp and over his head in places. Thrashing around, he tries to keep walking in as straight of a line as possible. Before long the ground starts to gently slope downward, brambles and plants making way for thickening and sharp clumps of bullrushes. He speeds up, realising he must be at the edge of the island. The ground turns slick with mud a short while later. Then the causeway opens wide and glistening ahead.

Jonny is seized with relief. He makes a sharp turn to the right as Jane has instructed and immediately spots the shadowlands of the opposite shore a short distance away across the riverbed. Little pools and streaks of water glimmer alluringly in the mud, lighting up his path. A gentle breeze swishes past, rushing through his jacket, ruffling his hair. After the fetid dark of Blackwater's hidden bunkers and tunnels, he suddenly feels like he's being washed clean. He knows better than to think there is magic in the air but can't help feeling like nature itself is trying to tell him something again.

Striking out across the mud, he considers the hard facts of his discovery instead. A couple raising a baby in the wild barely fifty miles outside London. Living underground on a tidal island deliberately given protected-wilderness status to hide its former use as a secret black site. Enabled by locals, who, now the child has died, have gone to ground for fear of association with a crime. Exposed by a former mercenary furious at being left with nothing after a classified mission went wrong on the island in the past.

There Jonny's mind sticks. He hurries through the last bit of mud before the reeds on the river bank, working his way backward through Jane's information. She's 'taken care' of the child's parents. Arwen and the curiously named Echo. But not in the grisly way Jonny is imagining. She certainly wouldn't be telling anyone about it if she had.

So why tell Jonny about it at all?

He backs up a bit further. The mission that went wrong. On Blackwater, the place where it all fell apart for Jane. *No more innocent people are going to die on my watch.* Jonny still doesn't know exactly how this particular child died. Could the reason be connected to the original mission? He relives his conversation with Detective Inspector Gillian Peters in her deserted police station. *It's like everyone wants to turn the other way.* From what? Jonny wonders, fatigue taking hold as he reaches the darkened clearing behind The Saxon.

Pushing his way inside, the sight of the hallway light still burning and the blue bedroom door still firmly closed on the upstairs landing is enough to make him feel faint with exhaustion. He closes the back door, collapses in a heap at the foot of the stairs and almost instantly falls into a heavy, dreamless sleep.

Chapter Twenty-Six
31st December 1999

He rears up instantly at the slightest touch to his shoulder. Paloma is crouched on the step behind him. 'It's me. It's OK. It's just me.'

Jonny winces. His back feels like the rungs of a ladder have been imprinted into it.

'I can't believe you actually slept in this position,' she continues, sympathy welling in her dark eyes. 'You were going to switch places with me.'

'It wasn't too bad,' Jonny grunts, squinting. He's never been able to bring himself to tell Paloma he can only sleep properly with the lights on. 'What time is it?'

'Just after six.'

Jonny knuckles his eyes, dried mud falling off his hands, thinking of Gillian Peters' promise to meet at the pontoon at first light. 'The sun won't be up for ages yet.'

'I know,' Paloma agrees. 'At least we've got plenty of time to get hold of Lukas before we go. He's expecting us back for millennium coverage. Should we walk into Maldon? There must be a phone box on the road somewhere.'

Jonny levers himself upright. 'We can't risk missing Gill. Talking to the police as soon as possible is way more important. We've got to be at the pontoon on time. I figured out some unbelievably disturbing things last night while I was keeping watch...'

He trails off. He needs to tell Paloma what he knows. But he can't find the right words to explain why he chose to hare off without her.

'You could have watched the door from an armchair in the bar instead of from the bottom of the stairs, you know.' She gives his shoulder a sympathetic squeeze before stepping delicately around him. 'Go splash some water on your face or something. It'll make you feel better. In the meantime, I'll see if I can find us something to eat in the bar.'

He calls weakly after her but she's already disappeared into the saloon. Turning, he trudges up the stairs in search of the bathroom. She might be more inclined to go easy on him when he confesses to leaving her behind if he does what she says first.

Heading into the bar a couple of minutes later, Paloma has unearthed four packets of crisps from somewhere and filled a couple of pint glasses with water. Suddenly weak at the knees, having eaten nothing other than oysters since he arrived, Jonny rips open a packet and empties it directly into his mouth.

'Sorry,' he mumbles. 'I hardly ate anything yesterday.' He makes short work of a second packet.

Paloma eyes him with something akin to pity. 'So,' she begins. 'Do you think your police officer will actually show up to meet us?'

Jonny nods, swallowing. 'Definitely. She's desperate. She's says she's completely isolated here. And she's the one who found the child's body to start with. You don't forget something like that in a hurry.'

Paloma shivers in kind. 'In a civilised society like this, too. It's still hard to believe.'

'Not really,' he answers, bracing himself before quickly filling her in. Choosing to go back to Blackwater alone to find out why the woman there tipped off the police so he didn't put Paloma at unnecessary risk for a second time. Good thing too, because it turns out the place is a former black site. And that his assailant is a mercenary with a massive axe to grind after a classified mission went wrong there. Not to mention the horrifying account of Arwen and Echo, and the baby boy born in a bloodstained cave.

By the time he is finished, Paloma is propping herself against the bar in shock.

'The woman who snatched you is a hired gun?'

'Former hired gun,' Jonny corrects her, the relief that she's reacting to what he's told her rather than how he went about it so intense that he has to prop himself against the bar too. 'With thirty years of British black ops experience under her belt, apparently. She even told me to call her Jane Doe,' he adds, reflecting again on her pointed choice of alias.

'So what the hell is she still doing on Blackwater Island?'

'She's got a score to settle over the failed mission. Said even after these thirty years of experience she's been left with nothing, other than blood on her hands. I just don't know what she's planning to do about it. She kept saying that no more innocent people were going to get hurt on her watch.'

'Maybe children died in the original mission,' Paloma wonders.

Jonny nods back. 'Yes, and maybe the reason they did is the same reason that boy died last week. I can only think that's why she risked exposing herself by tipping the police off to the body in the first place. No one would have known about that kid otherwise. There must be a connection between what happened on Blackwater in the past and what Arwen and Echo have got themselves caught up in now. We've got to talk to the pathologist doing the post-mortem and find out more about this apparently "natural" cause of death.'

Paloma brightens. 'Well we should easily be able to negotiate access to the report in exchange for all this new intel. We're about to hand the police a prime suspect, as well as information about the boy's family.'

'Yes, but she'll be long gone by the time any officers get back there. She's no fool. She knows they'll come running as soon as we make her presence known. And the fact she said she'd already dealt with his parents is even more alarming.'

'Because you think we're going to find two more bodies?'

'I think we're actually going to find something even worse. We know the island hosted black ops at some point. So what kind of ops were they? We have to find out whether the reason the boy died involves something that is still on Blackwater.'

'And they're calling it a protected nature reserve,' Paloma adds wryly, checking her watch. 'We better go, come on.' She starts gathering up their discarded crisp packets, but Jonny is fixating on what she just said. He's suddenly back on his training course learning about all the kinds of natural bio-hazards that exist all over the world. Recasting Blackwater's unique tidal environment in an altogether more threatening and sinister light. The thought nags at him all the way back down to the river bank.

'That's her.' Jonny motions at the figure in the distance. The outline of a police cap is coming into focus in the pallid light of a winter dawn. 'Let me do the talking, OK?'

Paloma nods agreement, trailing a step behind as he skids down the last few feet of dirt track. Detective Inspector Gillian Peters is waving them over.

'Morning,' he says, extending a hand.

Gill frowns rather than returning the gesture. 'A rowing boat has been reported stolen from this exact spot. You wouldn't happen to know anything about that, would you?'

'No,' Jonny lies. He gestures at Paloma with his dismissed hand. 'This is my colleague, Paloma. She arrived last night. The paper usually deploys us in groups of two. Much like the police,' he adds, picturing her alone in her deserted station, hemmed in by towers of incomplete case files.

Gill's frown lines deepen as Paloma murmurs a greeting. Turning away, she walks down towards the pontoon and the police boat docked at the edge. He realises she must have travelled from Maldon by water.

'You best watch your step,' she calls over her shoulder. 'The salt in the mud around here makes everything a lot more slippery.'

'Don't I know it,' Jonny mutters, remembering that Jane had told him the exact same thing a few hours earlier. 'Listen, Gill. We've got some new information to share. You need to know what it is before we go any further.'

Gill pauses at the end of the pontoon, turning expectantly. 'Go on.'

'You said you needed reinforcements to investigate this properly,' he begins warily, mindful he's talking to someone who spent their last conversation trying to get him to lie to help her case. 'Well, I think I know how you can get some.'

Gill folds her arms, waiting. Jonny senses Paloma stiffen behind him.

'I have some information that could turn this case on its head. But I'll need some assurances from you first ... Is the post-mortem taking place in Maldon?'

'Yes. The pathologist was with me when we discovered the body. Why?'

'I'd like to speak to the pathologist myself – as soon as possible. Can you arrange that? Or pass on a contact if not?'

'Last time I looked, I was the one in charge here, not you.'

'And last time we talked, you were the one asking me to speculate to help you out.'

Fire blazes in Gill's flame-blue eyes. 'What do you want?'

'An interview with the pathologist. Full access to the post-mortem. And then further access to the island, when you're finished dealing with what I'm about to tell you.'

'Get to the point or I'll arrest you for obstructing a live investigation.'

Jonny suddenly wishes they were having this conversation somewhere other than the precipitous edge of a pontoon. 'We went to Blackwater overnight and I was ambushed by an armed woman. She said she wasn't alone. I know you didn't get the resources you needed to search everywhere you wanted, so it's not really a surprise she was missed.'

Gill pales. 'But Blackwater's uninhabited. It's a protected nature reserve. That's why I haven't been able to search it again. Access is tied up in red tape a mile long.'

'I think that's deliberate – and for a whole different set of reasons. You said it yourself – it's like everyone in authority wants to turn the other way when it comes to Blackwater. A child is found dead and still no one has much to say about it. And the two locals living within sight of the place are blaming a fucking ghost.'

'How do you know about that?'

'Because that's exactly what they told me, too. The legend of Inka. All of those dead Vikings crying and burning in hell, to be precise. But I actually think what one of them was trying to do was tip me off to what the island is hiding without incriminating themselves in the process. Their description of Inka bore more than a passing resemblance to the woman I actually met. Blackwater definitely isn't just a nature reserve. It's actually heavily fortified. She ambushed me almost as soon as we'd arrived and dragged me into an underground bunker full of guns and computers. I only managed to get away from her through a bunch of tunnels. There's a whole labyrinth of them under that swamp.'

'But if this woman was prepared to give herself away to you then why the hell didn't she make herself known to me?'

'You're a police officer investigating the death of a child. She'd immediately become a suspect—'

'And she doesn't think she'll immediately become a fucking suspect now?' Gill is suddenly furious, bearing down on Jonny. 'You need to come down to the station with me immediately. I need to do this by the book. I need a record of everything you're about to say so I can deal with a crime properly for once.'

He holds up his hands, trying to placate her. 'Last time I went to your police station all you could tell me was how badly doing things by the book was working out for you.'

'Don't tell me how to do my fucking job,' she shoots back, turning and climbing into her boat. 'I've spent long enough being failed by the system to know exactly what I need to do now to make it work for me.'

Jonny hurries on board behind her. 'But the system is the problem. That's what I'm trying to explain. It's Blackwater's officially protected status that's been keeping you away this entire time. I don't know exactly what's going on yet, but that place definitely isn't just some benign wildlife sanctuary. The woman I found isn't just some mad vagrant with an ancient hunting rifle. She says she's a former mercenary with thirty years' experience in British black ops until she was left with nothing after a mission went wrong there. There's a reason you feel like everyone always seems to be looking the other way where Blackwater is concerned. We have to find out more about what it is before you go in with both barrels...'

He stops as Paloma clambers in beside him, picking up the thread.

'We need to work together. Whoever you've asked for reinforcements in the past might be under orders from higher up to make sure Blackwater stays firmly off the books. If you knock on the same doors now, you could easily tip off the wrong people.'

'And you won't take this woman out with anything less than an elite tactical unit,' Jonny adds. 'You're going to need the kind of people this woman has worked with herself. And you need to be doubly sure of whose side they're really on.'

Gill yanks the starter cord. 'So what are you saying?' she shouts over the howl of the motor. 'That I've been played but I'm still supposed to sit around and do nothing? A kid has died on my watch—'

'But how?' Jonny yells back. 'That's why we need to talk to the pathologist. I think it might be something to do with what's happened on Blackwater in the past. We need to find out as much as we possibly can about that before we tell anyone else in authority around here. And then we can go and shake more out of everyone spouting that stupid ghost story.'

Gill's mouth sets in a grim line.

'Leave that to me,' she says, and they zoom away from the shore.

Chapter Twenty-Seven

The boat scythes out into the river. Black water foams against the sides, spraying salt into their faces. Jonny revels in the sting, eyes streaming. The feeling that they're on the edge of a breakthrough is tangible, even from deep inside the impenetrable estuary mist.

Gill guns the engine through the fog, and minutes later they are approaching Maldon. She steers expertly down a small channel cutting into the mainland and docks at a shabby pier reeking of fish. A couple of misshapen oyster baskets lie discarded and empty in the middle of the decking.

They climb out on to the jetty, pausing for Gill to retrieve her keys from the boat's ignition. Jonny spies a set of plastic-encased school photos clinking on the key chain – one in colour featuring two children, one in black and white featuring three. Something nags at him as he remembers the children's car seats in Gill's car but he can't quite surface it. They walk quickly away from the jetty and into a small alleyway.

'The morgue's this way,' Gill says without turning around. They hurry to catch her up, but she keeps powering ahead, breathing hard.

'Look, I know this is all coming as a bit of a shock,' he offers, wondering if their recent revelation isn't all that's unnerving her. 'But I am certain that whatever is really going on here has implications far beyond Blackwater river. You've been inexplicably isolated since you arrived in this district. And it looks like the island has been deliberately sealed off – to protect more than just its wilderness. Neither of those things can happen without a whole lot of executive-level decision making and paperwork. And so far my only source on the matter is an armed woman hiding in a bunker going by the name of Jane Doe—'

He stops abruptly as Gill turns and asks: 'That's what this woman is calling herself?'

'Yes. She says she's had so many different names over the years that she can't even remember them all. I suppose going by Jane Doe makes a certain kind of sense in that context.'

'A certain kind of sense?' Gill echoes disbelievingly. 'I found the body of a dead child in this so-called protected wilderness that no one around here seems to know hide nor hair of. Does that also make a certain kind of sense to this woman?'

'Definitely not. She kept saying no more innocent people were going to get hurt on her watch and that's why she tipped you off.'

'She's the one who left the message at the police station?' A little of the fight has left Gill's voice. 'Why?'

'Because this child apparently belonged to a man and woman, who have also been living in secret on Blackwater, allegedly because they wanted nothing to do with all the trappings of modern life. She said she tolerated them until they decided it was a good idea to try and raise a kid out there. The mother was hiding somewhere underground when Jane ambushed me the first time. She called her Arwen. I saw her for a second and she looked like a prisoner of war or something – skin and bone, loads of hair missing, a completely deranged look in her eyes.'

Gill covers her face with her hands, muttering from between her fingers. 'Oh God.'

'Jane also showed me where she said the baby was born,' he continues. 'It was in a different bunker, dug deep below the roots of a giant tree. Apparently they wanted to have the birth out in the open and had already built a ceremonial shrine out of rocks for the occasion, but in the end it all happened too quickly. There were still dried bloodstains on the floor. It was horrific, I could barely breathe in there.'

Gill sags against the alley wall. The suspicion that she's bothered by more than just his discovery of Jane Doe starts to harden in Jonny's mind.

'Where are this man and woman now?' she asks faintly.

'I don't know. Jane said she'd already dealt with them. Like I said, she kept repeating no more innocent people were going to get hurt on her watch. When I questioned her on Arwen's appearance she pointed out that she hadn't said anything about sparing fucking deluded fools. I didn't hang around for much longer after that. I reckon this boy's death must have something to do with that mission that went wrong for her.'

'This couple obviously had some help,' Paloma adds, eyeing Gill with a frown. The detective still looks visibly shaken. 'Jane told Jonny they had a whole supply line in place. We were so disorientated in the dark when we ran away from the island last night that we ended up on the opposite shore. There's a house right on the water.'

Gill pushes herself away from the wall with a shaky hand. 'But that's Marshall land. It's been privately owned since the dawn of time. Apparently, I can't set foot on it without contravening some ancient scroll of parchment. And even if I could, David Marshall wouldn't so much as look at me, let alone speak to me. Five years ago, he lost a little boy of his own too – Matthew. Toddled out on to the causeway and never came back. David's never trusted anyone since he lost him. Least of all the police. He was raising him alone, too. Word is his wife died of cancer not long after giving birth. Loads of missing-person posters went up around town about Matthew, but they just kept getting torn down. The Marshall case is the reason I was sent here to start with. The old team were moved out over their failings around it. I've kept a poster up on the noticeboard outside the station ever since. I haven't given up hope of finding out something. Even if it's just catching some yob red-handed in the act of vandalising the thing.'

Jonny's blood turns cold. 'Does David Marshall still live in that house?'

'Yes. He barely leaves. And he never went back to work. Thinks the community betrayed him.'

Jonny pictures the faded snapshot of a little boy holding an ice cream in the photoframe he'd found amongst the old baby clothes in David Marshall's car – and the missing persons' poster curling away from the noticeboard outside Gill's police station. He knew he'd seen the picture in the frame somewhere before.

'He's never found out what really happened to his son?'

'Like I said. No body has ever been found. No one saw a thing.'

'Or no one admitted to seeing a thing,' Jonny corrects her, sickened at the thought of posters of a still-missing child being deliberately torn down. 'I reckon David Marshall was part of this couple's supply line. He was very quick to open his door when we knocked in a panic. It was almost as if he was expecting someone else – and we definitely heard someone crashing around in the reeds while we were trying to find our way. I've been thinking about what it would take for someone to support people choosing to raise a child in such an extreme way. It would need to be someone who truly understood their motivation – in this case, someone who hated the local community as much as they did. Anyone else would be straight on the phone to the authorities.'

'And I guess the fact they had a baby boy spoke to him in a certain way too,' Paloma adds.

Gill slowly starts moving again. 'I suppose now she's identified herself, your Jane Doe expects us all to believe she wasn't involved either.'

'I think her goal is something far bigger than just exposing these people,' Jonny answers. 'Otherwise, why would she risk identifying herself to start with? She could easily have stayed hidden. She's had thirty years of practice in covert operations. Like I said, there were still old bloodstains on the floor of one of the bunkers. She knows neither police nor journalists are just going to take her explanation for them at face value. But I can't think what kind of black-ops mission could possibly have taken place in an environment like that.'

Gill shivers involuntarily as the alley opens out on to a damp, grey street. 'A black site within such close range of London does make a certain kind of operational sense. These waterways open out on to a very strategic area of the North Sea. Container ships motor past in both directions at all hours. It's where the big cargo freighters from Europe turn either north for the big ports or south towards London.'

Jonny remembers the container ships he's seen steaming past each other across the mouth of the Blackwater river. 'But on a swamp island in the middle of a river? It doesn't make sense unless the reason is connected to the environment itself – to this rare and endangered ecosystem we keep hearing so much about. The island's protected status may be a fudge. But the environment is definitely unique. I don't know anything about rare flora and fauna, do you?'

'No,' she replies thoughtfully. 'But the pathologist does. She was a microbiologist before she was a pathologist. She's big into trees and plants.'

Jonny brightens. 'Great. There could be something toxic out there, for example. Something you wouldn't routinely find on the mainland.'

Gill slows. 'You think the boy might have been poisoned?'

'I don't know what to think until we've asked the pathologist. This investigation started with one unidentified dead body. It's become about a whole lot more than that since Jane Doe got involved.'

Crossing on to the pavement, Gill pauses outside a wide, solid, brown wooden door, a small adjacent window covered with a heavy iron grille. She gives the button on the intercom mounted between them three short stabs followed by one long peal. A burst of static answers before the door clicks open by itself.

'At the end of the corridor.' She motions at the door. 'The name is Michelle Rogers.'

Jonny pauses. 'You're not coming in with us?'

Gill looks away, face still pale and stricken. 'No. Just tell Michelle I brought you here, but had somewhere else to be. She'll understand.'

Chapter Twenty Eight

Jonny watches Gill disappear down the wet street before eyeing the open door with suspicion. He runs a finger over the intercom, considers the conspicuous absence of a voice emanating from its speaker asking who they are.

'Why isn't she coming in with us? And who opens the door to a place like this remotely without checking exactly who is standing outside it first?'

'It's a small town,' Paloma says doubtfully. 'Is there a security camera?'

Jonny looks in vain up and down the building's façade. 'Doesn't seem so.' He gives the door a gentle push. Inside, the morgue's lobby is surprisingly wide and airy considering the heavy iron grille over its only window. Immaculately painted white walls. A console table housing a bowl of dried rose petals that smell of nothing at all. A sheaf of leaflets detailing the local funeral services. He picks one up just for something to do with his hands.

'Gill should be more interested in the results of this post-mortem than we are,' he muses. 'She's the one charged with finding out what really happened to this poor kid. She was so angry and frustrated about her lack of progress yesterday she basically asked me to publicly lie about it to help her. I'd understand her rushing off if it was to apprehend Jane, but she didn't seem to be in much of a hurry to do that either.'

'She actually just seemed like she needed to go and lie down in a dark room somewhere,' Paloma agrees. 'And what detective lets a pair of journalists question a crime scene officer without a police escort? Gill either already knows what Michelle is going to say or she doesn't care what it is.'

Jonny turns towards the pair of frosted-glass doors that form the back of the lobby. 'Which also makes no sense, because Gill spent all her time yesterday telling me she basically had nothing. So what's changed?' He puts the leaflet back, absently straightening the whole pile. 'And more to the point, when? We've only just finished telling her about Jane. So what did we say that suddenly made her lose interest in whatever Michelle might have to add?'

'Come on.' Paloma starts towards the doors. 'It must be this way.'

The doors glide open as they walk towards them, to reveal a corridor tiled in more medicinal white. Stepping over the threshold, Jonny shivers reflexively at the unmistakable hum of equipment. He is suddenly assailed by the desperate image of a child-sized body bag lying unclaimed and alone inside a giant steel fridge.

A voice calls from behind a door hanging open at the end of the corridor. 'Gill?'

A squeak, then a clang. Followed by a dirty-blonde head curling around the doorway. Jonny is floored. Save for her pristine-white coat and purple latex gloves, the woman walking out from behind the door towards them with her hands in the air is a carbon copy of Detective Inspector Gillian Peters, right down to the mole in the dead centre of her left cheek. Twins, he thinks, instantly wrongfooted by the thought of his missing sister. He's never known what she looked like as a baby, let alone what she might look like now. He's never seen a single photo, much less retained a memory. Jonny wouldn't know her if they came face to face in the street.

The woman peers behind him before appraising them both with a look caught somewhere between relief and disappointment. 'Can I help you?'

Jonny tries to collect himself, extending a hand. 'I'm Jonny Murphy, this is Paloma Glenn. We're both journalists with the *International Tribune*. You must be Michelle Rogers?'

She wiggles the ends of her purple fingers. 'Yes. You don't want to shake my hand though, trust me. I'll need to take these off first.'

Jonny lets out a nervous laugh as he realises exactly where her purple fingers may have just been. 'I'll take your word for it. Thanks for letting us in. We're in town looking into the child found dead on Blackwater Island last week. We were just speaking to Detective Inspector Peters. She said you were still finalising the post-mortem report.'

Michelle peers behind him again, frowning. 'She didn't come in with you, then.'

'Sorry, no. She told us to let you know she had somewhere else to be. Is talking to us without her present going to be a problem? And, can I ask...' He pauses for a moment before continuing. 'How did you know she came here with us?'

Michelle sighs, pulling off her latex gloves with a pop. 'She's the only person who rings the bell like that. This is family business. We figured out that little secret code when we were all kids. And in case it wasn't already obvious, Gill and I understand each other without having to say anything out loud sometimes.'

Jonny eyes her. The resemblance is so pronounced it is disconcerting. Dirty-blonde hair, china-blue eyes, quizzically direct expression. 'You're twins, right?'

A flicker of irritation crosses her face. 'Indeed we are. And I must admit I'm surprised she let you in without checking with me first. I like to respect the privacy of the dead that I work with. After all, it's not like they can defend themselves,' she adds with a grim smile. Jonny tries not to stare too hard. The similarities between the two women are still unnerving.

'We just gave her a load of new leads to deal with. I expect that's why she had to run. And she said you'd understand,' he adds, wondering if Michelle will add anything that further explains this. 'She didn't say why, though.'

Michelle's smile fades. 'New leads?'

'Yes. They might be of interest to you too, especially if you haven't completely finished the post-mortem yet. Would it be OK to stick around for just a few minutes? We won't take up too much of your time.'

Michelle answers with a reluctant nod. 'Let me close up in there first.' She gestures at the open door behind her. 'Then we can have a quick chat.'

Jonny catches himself before he grimaces, trying not to picture what she means by closing up. 'Of course. Thank you. Would you mind if we use the phone while we wait? It's just to call our news editor in London. We're due back this morning and need to let him know we're running behind.'

Another nod. 'There's a phone in the family room. I won't be long.'

She motions them into a small ante-room – well-worn brown sofa and armchair, plastic flowers arranged in a glass vase, box of tissues laid purposefully on a side table – before closing the door and vanishing down the corridor.

'Twins, huh,' Paloma remarks, perching on the edge of the sofa.

'Uncanny, isn't it.' Jonny tries to keep his tone light, turning to the black telephone unit mounted on the side wall. 'Even their voices sound the same. But they're obviously not in sync about everything. Michelle wasn't thrilled to find us down here unsupervised.'

'And yet she hasn't thrown us out,' Paloma muses. 'She's even shown us into her waiting room.'

'Because I told her we had new information,' he says, picking up the receiver, ready to call Lukas. 'She obviously wants to know what it is.'

But Paloma is still preoccupied. 'It shouldn't matter enough to her though to risk her professional career talking to the press. She's a pathologist doing a post-mortem on a body that hasn't been formally identified yet. She can't break patient confidentiality without the express permission of family members. We haven't told her what you found out about all that yet. We've only told Gill. As far as Michelle's concerned, this boy is still unidentified.'

The dial tone blaring out of the receiver suddenly sounds like an alarm. Jonny slams down the phone, forgetting all about calling the newsroom.

'Unless he isn't any more,' he mutters before turning back to her. 'We obviously told Gill something that really spooked her. Something that apparently Michelle will already understand. And something that accounts for Michelle no longer needing or caring about getting permission from the victim's family to speak to us. Gill can't have known anything about Jane. But what if she already knew something about Arwen?'

Paloma stands up, eyes alight. 'And Arwen and Echo can't have pitched up here as tourists,' she agrees. 'Blackwater Island isn't even labelled on the map. They must have been part of the community to start with and already known it was there. And Michelle just said this was family business...'

Jonny nods back. 'I think we're about to find out that Gill and Michelle aren't the only ones that are related around here,' he says, just as the heavy door flies open and dead-ends into his back.

'Ouch. Sorry about that.' Michelle Rogers peers round the doorframe, still in her white coat. 'Wasn't expecting to find you right up against the door.' She sweeps past and flops into an armchair. 'Do you mind if I sit? This isn't an easy story to tell.'

'Of course not,' Jonny answers, eyeing her fiddling with her hands. She is far less comfortable without her purple latex gloves. When she looks up, he is curiously unsurprised to see the faintest glimmer of tears in her eyes.

'It must be hard,' he ventures. 'Especially when a child is

involved. Even more so when no one has come forward to claim the body. It must feel even more like no one cares about what happened.'

'Actually it's sometimes easier that way,' she answers, blue eyes clouded with emotion. 'Dead bodies leave evidence of how a person lived as well as how they died. And sometimes you learn unbearable things. You don't always want to meet the families.'

Her stare becomes distant. Jonny tries not to think too hard about what she means. The cold, hard facts included in some news stories about people being abused to the point of death are often too much for him when simply printed in black and white. He cannot conceive of how it must feel to learn about them through flesh wounds and broken bones.

'No such luck this time, though,' she continues. 'There's going to be a reckoning.'

Jonny tenses, feeling Paloma stiffen beside him too. 'What do you mean?'

'The DNA test results just came through. Both mine and Gill's are on file for the purposes of omission. She's the only police officer in town and I'm the only pathologist. Any dead bodies that come through here have our fingerprints all over them. So there's really no doubt about it. No doubt at all. The evidence is conclusive.'

The silence that follows stretches out for so long that Jonny has to ask even though the answer is obvious:

'No doubt about what?'

'The boy, you see. The boy was our nephew.'

Chapter Twenty-Nine

Jonny only realises he was holding his breath when it all comes streaming out in one go. Meanwhile a range of different emotions are crossing Michelle's face. They end in the kind of resigned sadness he is so familiar with that he can feel it in his bones.

'But I thought Gill was still appealing for relatives to make themselves known to her.'

'She is. I haven't told her about the DNA results yet. We don't talk unless we have to. You might have already figured that out.'

Jonny remembers Gill's account of finding someone to accompany her to Blackwater in the first place. *Believe me, it took a lot for me to call her.*

'So you two have another sibling?'

A long, weary sigh. 'Indeed we do. Although we haven't been in the same room together for years.'

'Why not? What happened?'

A beat of awkward silence stretches between them before Michelle finally continues. 'Small towns are always cosy. Everyone knows each other. It's almost impossible to get any privacy. The stakes are even higher when you're an identical twin. Everyone's got questions for you. Do you feel each other's pain? Can you read each other's minds? What's it like talking to each other? You stick out a mile. And when you're a triplet ... you become the town attraction. The local freakshow.' She pauses, staring at her hands.

Jonny takes another sharp breath. 'You're a triplet?'

'See? People can't believe it even when they're told.'

Jonny tries to recover himself but can't seem to get his words out in the right order. He remembers the school photos he glimpsed for a second on Gill's keychain – one featuring two children, the other featuring three. 'But you're identical, though. You and your sister. Gill, I mean. Is there another sister?'

Michelle shakes her head. 'No. A brother. Josh. Obviously we started out as fraternal twins. One male and one female until the female egg split in two. Unusual, sure. But it happens. I came out first. Always lorded that over Gill. The midwives didn't half get a shock when a boy popped out after her. The lucky last. But he was trying to put distance between us from the word go.'

There she stops, seemingly lost in thought for a moment before she can continue.

'Gill took it personally. Like, why wouldn't he want to be associated with us? Aren't we the coolest kids on the block? She didn't mind all the attention herself, and always held it against him that he did. But I kind of understood it. It's weird enough seeing the mirror image of yourself walking around. But being known as the freak triplet brother? Josh didn't feel special, he just felt odd. And he was horribly bullied for it. For a while, I told him to pretend he was just our younger brother. After all, he did come out last. But like I say, it's a small town. Everyone knows each other. No one's business is private. Everyone would have known he was lying and gossiped about why. He was already gunning to leave long before he met *her*. And once he had, I didn't stand a chance of keeping him here.' She lifts and drops her hands in a gesture of complete defeat.

'Her?' Jonny prompts, picturing Arwen – wild-eyed, emaciated, practically bald.

Michelle sighs. 'He fell in love. She wasn't from around here. Thought we were a bunch of inbreds. And that was before she found out we were triplets. He was so scared of losing his ticket out of here that he upped and left with her before I could even try and change his mind. The irony was she wasn't exactly conventional herself. She was, in actual fact, the most unconventional person any of us had ever met. She was a druid. Believed in the power of nature over all. Called herself Arwen. Insisted on calling him Echo. Demanded he pray to Mother Earth and Father Sky. And he went along with the whole thing.'

She pauses to wipe away a tear brimming in the corner of one of her blue eyes.

'I suppose that's the part that actually does make some sense,' Jonny says gently, thinking about Blackwater's wilderness. 'You'd have to be unconventional to want to try and set up camp undetected in a nature reserve.'

Michelle's voice suddenly takes on a sharper edge. 'Or just totally delusional. She told him that he risked the integrity of their "cosmic belonging" if he didn't worship at her shrines of rocks and plants. That it would interrupt the energy of their sacred union if he continued to associate with us. Now, I was a microbiologist before I was a pathologist – I can get behind the nature part. But I was also in the womb with Josh. And so was Gill. If that's not cosmic belonging, then I don't know what is. Gill washed her hands of them after all that. But I didn't find it as easy. And the fact I've never been able to completely abandon Josh has always upset Gill almost as much. It's like I've betrayed her more than he has.'

'So you're the reason Josh ended up coming back here in the end?'

Michelle looks away. 'I wish I was,' she eventually says. 'But I think it was all about living out their little woodland fantasy on Blackwater. I only discovered they'd come back when it was already too late.'

Jonny is suddenly back in Blackwater's fetid bunkers, looking in horror at the dried blood still staining the ground. *Arwen almost bled to death. She only survived because they had help from offshore.*

'When did you find out they were back? Did you know they were doing something as extreme as trying to raise a child on Blackwater?'

By the time Michelle looks up at him, the tears are streaming freely down her face. 'Josh came to me when the boy was born. He was frantic, said he thought Arwen was going to die. I gave him antibiotics, some basic trauma kit, begged him to take me to her. But he ran away while I was looking for more supplies. And I had no way of finding him after that. I've been searching for him ever since. I never imagined that I'd finally work out where he was from the body of a small child showing up in my morgue.'

She swipes a hand across her face, drawing a juddering breath. Jonny watches her try and get her emotions under control, suddenly feeling like an interloper of the worst kind.

Paloma reaches a tentative hand out to rest gently on Michelle's shoulder.

'I'm very sorry for your loss,' he says softly. 'I can assure you we have no intention of reporting such intimate details about your family.'

Michelle smiles weakly at him. 'Thank you,' she says, with an unmistakable sigh of relief. 'I was hoping you'd say that. I thought if I didn't tell you everything you'd just keep digging and potentially misunderstand things. We've had years of being the local freakshow. It's going to be hard enough to deal with all this without becoming a national headline too.'

'I'm sure,' he says, choosing his next words carefully. 'I'm sorry to have to ask you another intrusive and potentially upsetting question, but I'm wondering if you have pinned down the exact cause of death yet? Gill said you thought it was natural but hadn't finished writing up the report. Exactly what kind of natural cause do you think it was?'

She reaches for a tissue. 'I suppose there's no harm in telling you if it isn't going to end up in the newspaper.'

'It won't,' Paloma answers, a little too quickly, but thankfully Michelle is blowing her nose so noisily that she doesn't notice. She spends another minute collecting herself. Jonny's eyes flick between the phone and his watch, trying not to betray his impatience.

Finally Michelle clears her throat and starts talking again. 'I found a pronounced cutaneous lesion on one leg and fatal levels of pulmonary swelling and oedema in the chest. Taken together in the absence of any other troubling abnormalities – such as bruising around the neck, for example – it is clear that the boy died from a catastrophic reaction to either an allergen or toxin.'

'You mean he just stopped breathing?' Paloma asks. 'Why?'

'Like I said,' Michelle replies, composure visibly returning now she's back on professional ground. 'Because of a catastrophic reaction to either an allergen or a toxin. The cutaneous lesion – that's an obviously fresh mark or scar on the skin – suggests he was either bitten by something like a spider or similar biting insect, or that a naturally occurring toxin entered his body through a pre-existing wound.'

'Such as?' Jonny prompts, desperate to get to the point.

'I don't know. Blackwater's tidal environment is very rare. But one thing I am sure of is that access to modern medicine would have bought more than enough time to save him. There are hundreds of poisons and allergens to be found in nature. We'd have to analyse the composition of the entire island to find out exactly which one was the culprit in this case. It would require bucketloads of time and money. And that kind of investment is non-existent around here.'

'I bet,' Jonny answers, thinking about an altogether different set of reasons for why that kind of investment would be so hard to come by.

'I suppose I should be grateful,' she adds, still blissfully ignorant of his alternative perspective. 'I could speculate for hours about the root cause – like I said before, I was a microbiologist before I went into pathology. Those sorts of tests used to be my bread and butter. But that kind of money would only attract more attention. And this is a private matter.'

Jonny takes a deep breath before he replies. 'That's the thing,' he says. 'We're afraid that's not entirely true.'

Chapter Thirty

Michelle pales again. 'What do you mean? I thought I could trust you not to print any of this. No one reads the *International Tribune* for a small-town family drama.'

'Believe me, I wish that's all it was,' Jonny replies.

'Well I'm the doctor in this conversation and I can tell you that's all it is.'

But Jonny knows he can't afford to let this line of questioning drop. 'What would it take for you to establish the exact cause of this allergic reaction?'

Michelle frowns. 'Time. Money. And in case you haven't noticed, there isn't much of either going spare around here. Gill will already have told you that. It's all she talks about.'

Paloma taps his arm. 'Tell her about Jane,' she says. 'Gill already knows. It's only a matter of time before she tells Michelle too. They may not talk all the time but they're damn well going to talk about this.'

Michelle stands up, folding her arms. 'Tell me what? And who the blazes is Jane?'

Jonny pauses, exchanging a glance with Paloma and willing her to stay quiet. In the cold light of day his encounters with an assailant as unexpected as Jane still feel hard to believe. Short of dragging her off the island himself, the only verifiable proof that they occurred at all are his sweaty fingerprints on a fucking gun. He doesn't want to share those details any more widely than absolutely necessary. But this story isn't just about one dead child now. It's also about a former secret government agent breaking cover over a classified mission in the same location that may have harmed many more. He has to find out if the two events are connected.

'Gill also told us you are big into trees and plants,' he says instead.

'Microbiology. Yes. What's your point?'

Jonny hesitates again. He's a journalist. He doesn't deal in rumour and speculation. His theory about what may have happened on Blackwater Island in the past having something to do with this most recent death is still just that – a theory.

'I suppose I'm just wondering if you can be any more specific about Blackwater's ecosystem. I get that it's impossible to be definitive without more time and money. But could you narrow it down – for a layperson like me? What are the common naturally occurring toxins that might be found there?'

Michelle's eyes narrow. 'What's it to you?'

'I have no intention of dragging your private family business into it,' Jonny answers carefully. 'But there's a bigger picture coming into focus here. I'm just not going to speculate about what it is at this point.'

Michelle considers this, picking some non-existent lint off her white coat. 'So you want me to answer your questions without telling me why you're asking them.'

'Basically, yes.'

'And in return I can expect details of our family's private business to remain private.'

A statement, not a question. Jonny nods regardless. 'You've already been enormously helpful,' he adds for good measure. 'You don't have to tell us anything else if you don't want to. But you'd really be helping us out if we could lean on your expertise a little.'

The professional reference seems to defuse the tension. Michelle returns his nod before standing and walking out into the corridor, motioning that they follow. She pauses in front of a large picture framed on the wall.

'Fungi,' she pronounces with relish, waving a hand at the picture. It's one of several painstakingly detailed watercolour illustrations of different kinds of mushrooms with information lettered in neat boxes next to each. 'They make good eating. But there's no room for error in the wild. Never eat a mushroom you're not sure of. At best, you'll be vomiting for hours. At worst, you'll be dead before you get a chance to eat anything else.'

'What about things that are less obvious,' Jonny asks, still peering at the illustrations. Amanitas. Death Caps. Destroying Angels. Who knew there were this many varieties of deadly mushrooms? To think he usually enjoys eating mushrooms however they come.

Michelle turns and gestures at another frame on the opposite wall, this one filled with whimsical depictions of berries and flowers. 'Lilies. Foxgloves. And I'm sure you've heard of poison ivy,' she adds.

Jonny nods again. 'What about rare bacteria. Stuff you can't see.'

Michelle's eyes gleam. She folds her arms, straightening up authoritatively. 'Now you're talking. Some of the world's deadliest biological agents are found in nothing more than bog-standard soil. Which, on Blackwater, is most definitely not bog standard, so—'

'Like what?' Jonny interrupts, but Michelle is losing herself in blissful detail.

'—it's fair to say it could play host to all kinds of bacteria we wouldn't routinely see in this part of the world. It's important to remember, though, that the bacteria themselves aren't necessarily harmful. It's just that some can go on to produce highly poisonous toxins when deprived of oxygen.'

'Such as?' Jonny tries again.

'Clostridium botulinum. Bacillus anthracis. Both commonly found in soil, dust – or even river or sea sediments. Now, like I said, botulinum toxin is only produced when the bacteria itself is starved of oxygen—'

'Starved of oxygen?' Paloma echoes. 'How is that possible in the open air?'

Michelle gives her a sympathetic look. 'I know it sounds counter-intuitive, but we're talking at microscopic levels. Some dirt trapped inside a can, for example. Or a spore unwittingly ingested into the human body. And it doesn't have to be as complicated as that. Stagnant soil can do it. It's that straightforward.'

'You mean like mud?' Jonny asks in horror, pulse rocketing as he thinks about the glistening black mud from which the Blackwater river takes its name. His boots are still caked in the stuff.

Michelle nods. 'That'll do it too. But don't get me wrong. You don't wade around in botulinum toxin. It doesn't form in puddles. It isn't easy to find because you'd be dead before you could see it. A single gram of crystalline toxin, evenly dispersed and inhaled, can kill more than a million people. Bacillus anthracis, now that's a different story—'

She stops as Jonny gasps. 'One million people?'

'In theory, yes. Be grateful this is a theory that's never been tested in practice. Bacillus anthracis behaves differently, of course. It's more of an immediate threat to livestock than humans. The bacteria produce spores that can live in the ground for years. Easily ingested while grazing. Throw in some bodily fluids and the bacteria activate, multiply and spread. And there you have it.'

'There you have what?'

'Anthrax,' Michelle replies, staring at her pictures reverentially.

Chapter Thirty-One

Jonny turns cold. A black site on a tidal island. A former mercenary cast out over a classified mission that went wrong there. An innocent child dying due to a catastrophic reaction to an allergen or toxin in the same location years later. In an environment with perfect conditions for cultivating anthrax. 'Can you ... can you test for that?'

Michelle frowns. 'Test what?'

'Is there a test that can determine exposure to anthrax,' he clarifies hurriedly, mind suddenly racing a mile a minute trying to connect everything he knows.

'In broad terms yes, but it's complicated. There are different kinds of exposure. Inhalation anthrax is the most dangerous. Unless it's rapidly treated, ninety percent of patients will die—'

'But I thought you said the bacteria live in the soil,' Jonny interrupts as he spots the mud all over his boots again and tries not to panic. 'If that's the case, how can it be inhaled?'

'It would need to be synthesised and then aerosolised in some way,' Michelle answers. 'You can't inhale the stuff if it's still in the form of a spore in the ground. It would only be able to enter the body through a pre-existing wound on the skin from there.'

Synthesised. Aerosolised. The puzzle in Jonny's mind is starting to fit together in an increasingly disturbing way. Did the classified mission that failed on Blackwater years ago involve illegal experiments with biological weapons? Recalling the cutaneous lesion she had described on the small boy's body, a sickening rush of adrenaline makes him shiver. Did that child accidentally come into contact with a lethal dose of anthrax?

'Right, I see,' he says, unintentionally brusque, head spinning. 'Thank you again. You've been really helpful. I know this has been a difficult conversation. Again I can assure you we have no intention of reporting anything to do with your family's private business. The *International Tribune* is not that kind of newspaper.'

Michelle takes the hand he extends, still frowning. 'Alright, then. And if you see my sister, do let her know she needs to answer my calls.'

'I will,' Jonny answers, avoiding her eye.

They hurry away down the corridor and out into the street.

'Anthrax,' Paloma whispers as they scurry away. 'I can't believe it.'

'I can,' Jonny replies grimly. 'Jane said she was cast out over a mission that failed. She told me Blackwater was the place where it all went wrong for her. Its location is hardly strategic unless you're a Viking. It only makes sense as a site for black ops if the mission had something to do with its environment. And weaponised effectively, anthrax is deadlier than a fucking bomb.'

'But isn't the development of biological weapons illegal all over the world?'

'Yes, but that doesn't mean it isn't happening in secret. No sovereign nation worth its salt is going to take the risk of assuming all others are abiding by international law. It would also explain why hired guns like Jane were involved in the first place. The mission must have had to be completely deniable. It can't have implicated even the most clandestine arm of the military. So they used people like her.' He slows, scanning the street in vain for a telephone box. 'We have to call Lukas. And get back in touch with Gill as soon as we can.'

But something else is bothering Paloma. 'How has Jane managed to operate out there undetected for so long, though? The place has registered status.'

'Which we know isn't genuine,' Jonny replies. 'It's just convenient. The environment is unique enough that no one questions its designation as a wildlife reserve.'

'But how is Jane getting her equipment, for example,' Paloma persists. 'Or even just her basic supplies. She isn't living off marsh grass. She can't be working alone. So who's helping her? And why? That mad old woman in The Saxon? We already know it must have been her that warned Jane we were on our way the first time.'

Jonny stops dead at the mention of Judith, oblivious to the rain starting to fall softly around them. 'I wonder if Judith knows something about the original mission. Something that she feels guilty about but also implicates her in some way, so she can't talk about it directly. It would explain why she was so bitter but also seemed to want to talk to us.'

'It would also explain the ghost story,' Paloma agrees. 'And why she would tell Jane that we were coming.'

He starts to walk again, speeding towards the end of the alley. 'We've got to go back to Eastwood. We've got to try and talk to Judith. She might be able to explain what Jane is actually still doing on Blackwater.'

'Do you think that's why she disappeared last night?' Paloma asks, hurrying to keep up with him. 'So we couldn't ask her any more questions after we'd encountered Jane?'

'I hope not,' Jonny answers, turning on to the main street. 'We've got to find her. She's the only person we know down here who might be able to help us figure this out.'

'There!' Paloma points to a garage a few doors further down. Jonny breaks into a jog at the sight of some motorcycles parked up in the forecourt, waving down the mechanic emerging from inside in a pair of grubby overalls.

'Excuse me,' he pants. 'Are any of these bikes available for hire?'

The man regards them with suspicion, wiping his hands on a blackened rag.

'They're not available for anything, son. They're in for a service. This is a garage, not a dealership.'

Paloma points to something further inside the garage. Peering inside, Jonny spies a decidedly more ancient-looking motorbike in a corner. 'All of them?' she asks. 'Even that one in the back?'

The man frowns, twisting around to look over his shoulder. 'That old rust bucket?'

'Yes,' Jonny replies, pulling his wallet out of a pocket and proffering all the cash he has. 'We need to be somewhere fast. We're desperate.'

The sight of the money in Jonny's hand seems to completely change the man's countenance. He claps a grimy hand on Jonny's shoulder. 'If it's fast you want then you better take one of these babies after all,' he says, gesturing at the nearest motorbike. 'You got a licence? These engines are top whack.'

'I do,' Paloma answers before Jonny can. He busies himself pointedly counting out a hundred pounds from the bills in his hand. He'd rather be the one in the driving seat. But he knows full well he doesn't have a licence. He's not sure whether Paloma does either but he can hardly quiz her about it now.

'Could we take two helmets as well?' he says, pressing the cash into the man's oil-stained hand.

'Helmets are extra,' the man states. 'I've not got very many, see.'

'Really.' Jonny resignedly passes over his last twenty. 'Thanks. We appreciate it.'

The man disappears into the garage with an ill-disguised smirk, returning with two sleek black helmets and a shiny set of keys.

'Here you go. Have her back in four hours, mind. We're closing early for the festivities tonight.'

'We will,' Paloma replies, the rest of her thanks muffled into her helmet.

Thumbing a key into the bike's ignition, she kicks the starter motor to life and waits for Jonny to climb on to the back. The man folds his arms, by now openly smirking as he stands and watches them. Shoving his own helmet on to his head to hide his irritation, Jonny climbs on board, steadying himself on the hand rails either side. Paloma tips a hand to her helmet and nods at the man before executing a neat turn in the garage forecourt and accelerating away. The motion throws Jonny forward. He instinctively wraps his arms around her rather than hang on to the hand rails, and immediately feels more optimistic about absolutely everything.

Chapter Thirty-Two

Jonny is so revitalised by zooming down the road on the back of a motorbike with his arms around Paloma that he is almost disappointed by how quickly they get back to Eastwood. Screeching to a stop outside The Saxon, he is further encouraged by the amber light glowing through its small windows. Jumping off the bike, he leaves Paloma to park up, pulling off his helmet as he runs inside. The place is deserted save for Judith hurrying away into the dark recess behind her grimy bar.

'Hey,' he shouts, rushing across the sticky carpet, Paloma catching him up seconds later. 'Judith. Wait.'

She pauses in the doorway, back still turned. 'What do you want?'

'To talk,' Jonny pants, pulling up short at the bar. 'We need your help. And I think I can help you too.'

'With what?' Judith answers. Jonny can see her face reflected back at him in the mirror on the wall below her set of ancient optics. Even in the shadows her expression is unmistakable. Resignation, anger, fear.

'Inka,' Jonny replies, staring at the pencil drawing hanging beside the mirror. 'The ghost of Blackwater. Except she isn't a ghost at all, is she?'

When Judith finally turns to him, her once-flinty grey eyes are shining with unshed tears. 'I can look after myself. I don't need any help.'

'Well I do,' Jonny tries again. 'I know Blackwater Island isn't just a haunted swamp in the middle of the river. And I know Inka isn't a ghost, because I met her myself last night. And I think you've met her before too. That's why you drew her picture and turned her into a legend. You couldn't tell anyone the real reason why she's still out there. But you also couldn't stay completely quiet.'

Judith looks at the floor. Jonny watches a tear fall, a bead of light disappearing into the dark.

'I'm as intimidated by her as you are,' he continues. 'She told me her name was Jane Doe. I've only ever heard that name in the context of unidentified dead bodies – just like the child found dead on Blackwater last week. The truth is that I think she is part of something incredibly dangerous that could potentially still harm a lot more people. But we might be able to stop it if you tell me everything you know.'

Judith rests a gnarly hand on the doorframe. Jonny is suddenly painfully conscious of her fragility.

'No one else can die,' Paloma adds. 'A child has – just think about that. Nothing could be worse.'

Jonny watches Judith shrink into herself, her hand shaking against the wall now.

'I've never told anyone about this,' she finally whispers. 'But I can't keep it in no more. It's too much. It's all I can think about. It's like I'm suffocating. The guilt...' She trails off into silence.

Jonny sags against the bar, emotion suddenly threatening to overwhelm him. He knows all too well what happens when people feel suffocated by guilt. He can almost hear his mother screaming to him from some netherworld, begging that he forgive her for deserting him. Paloma puts a comforting hand on his arm but he can barely feel it.

'I know what you mean,' he manages to choke out. 'Honestly I wish I didn't, but I do. Which is why I also know that nothing good ever comes of keeping secrets that will harm people. I can't promise the truth won't have any consequences. But I am bound to protect my sources. I'll do everything I can to help you.'

Judith takes a shuddering breath. 'I deserve all the consequences. Truth is, I deserve everything that's coming to me.'

'Why?' Paloma asks. 'What happened?'

She turns and steps into the shadows at the rear of the pub. They follow without being asked. Sitting down heavily on the bottom step of the staircase, she takes another gulp before she can begin.

'The first time I saw her I thought I was imagining it. It was dark. The mist was up. I was born here and never once saw anything happen anywhere near Blackwater.'

'What exactly did you see?' *The mission that failed?* Jonny wonders.

'It was five years ago. Summer. A hot night. No wind. The kind of night where sound carries for miles. Especially sounds like ... like ...' She trails off again, hanging her head. 'I was out by the water with the dog. Old Monty always had a nose for trouble. He was the one who saw the boat. I'd never have known it was there if he hadn't barked at it. It was dark. The mist was up. And this boat was designed to be invisible.'

Instantly Jonny is remembering his warzone training course and pictures of the small, black rubber inflatables used by the Royal Navy's elite maritime counter-terrorism unit.

'I thought I was seeing things,' Judith continues. 'It was that dark and the boat was black. But the dark looked like it was moving. All black shapes, like they were a group of wet seals or something. But then Monty growled. He was an old dog, half blind, never usually made a sound. Gave me the collywobbles it did. We came back, opened the windows, turned out the lights, got into bed. And then I heard it.'

She pauses, sighs, stares into the middle distance. Jonny waits, resisting the urge to prompt her again. But then Paloma steps forward and sits on the bottom step next to Judith. 'Take your time,' she says, putting an arm around the old woman's shoulders.

'We know this isn't easy. We're very grateful to you for trusting us with your side of the story.'

A little of the anguish leaves Judith's expression. But only for the briefest of moments. 'He was only a boy,' she eventually says. 'Can't have been more than two, three years old.' She has to stop there, covering her eyes, shoulders starting to shake.

Paloma comforts her for another moment before looking up at Jonny with an infinitesimal nod.

He picks up the thread. 'I don't understand,' he says softly. 'What did you hear?'

Judith lets out a long, shaky sigh before she continues. 'A scream. It cut the night. Turned my blood cold. It was only the one. But I knew. Someone was in trouble. And Monty knew it too. He was up, ears flat to his head, nosing at the door. We ran out and back down to the water. That's when we saw them. I thought she were a man. She had on one of those rubber suits; it covered her whole body, came right up over her head. She was just standing there in the shallows, holding a boy in her arms. He was so pale he practically shone bright. But it didn't last long. Because he was dying. She just shoved him into my arms and said there'd been an accident. Then she disappeared back under the water. And the boy was blue and cold before I could do anything for him. He died in my arms. A child I never knew. I still don't know what killed him. But I think it killed Monty too. Because he wouldn't stop licking the boy. And then he just collapsed. Went all stiff and just kind of fell backward.'

She stops for another shuddering breath. Looking back into the bar, Jonny can see the old dog bowl, still waiting by the door, caked in dust. The sight is almost unbearably sad.

'I buried them together,' Judith starts up again. 'I couldn't think what else to do. I know I should've called the police. I go over it in my mind every minute of every day. But I panicked. It was pitch-dark. I had no idea who the boy was or what'd happened to him. I had no explanation for the person in the water, I weren't even sure whether I'd actually seen a boat or not. And I was half mad over Monty. He was my best friend, my only living family, and he was gone, just like that. I'd only just finished burying them when she came back—'

'She came back?' Jonny interrupts, he can't help himself despite Paloma's warning look. 'You mean Jane came back?'

Judith nods at them both. 'She came back for the bodies. Said they were evidence. Said a whole lot more lives were at stake than just theirs if I ever told anyone about it. And said I'd be implicated in the whole thing if I did.'

'Evidence of what, exactly?'

But Judith just shakes her head. 'I don't know. After that night, I didn't see her again for months. And I couldn't go to the police. I had no proof of anything – the bodies were gone, and Monty was an old dog. He could've died for any number of reasons. And the truth is that I didn't want to know. Because by then I was already an accomplice. I'd hid the bodies. And I didn't want to know any more. When she finally came back again, all she said was that she was as angry about it all as I was, and would get her revenge on behalf of all of us. And I believed her. Because the thing is, I think it was her that screamed in the first place. I don't think I heard the boy. I think it was her. I think she screamed in shock.'

Chapter Thirty-Three

Jonny's mind races. 'It all fits,' he says slowly, considering what he knows, examining it from every angle. The former mercenary cast into the cold. The mission that failed. The catastrophic reaction to a naturally occurring allergen or toxin that must have killed an innocent child five years ago – and then another as recently as Christmas Day.

'What fits?' Judith asks, a hunted look in her eyes as she gazes up at him. 'What do you know about this woman?'

'That she apparently spent almost thirty years working for the government in secret,' Jonny says. 'And that she's been left with nothing since a mission went catastrophically wrong a few years ago.'

Judith's eyes widen. She leans into Paloma. 'The boy who died?'

'From what you've told me, I think so, yes. Like I said: it all fits.'

Judith covers her face with a shaking hand again, hunching even smaller on her step. 'So why did he die? What really happened that night?'

'I think the Ministry of Defence used Blackwater to conduct illegal experiments with biological weapons. They had to use secret operatives to do them because there couldn't be any record of them actually taking place. And they used Blackwater because it's already loaded with naturally hazardous biological agents – they couldn't officially manufacture the weapons either, you see. Something obviously went wrong – as you witnessed – and Jane was cast out afterwards. I think she's been plotting some sort of revenge since, but only decided to make herself known when she found a second child's body in Blackwater's wilderness last week.'

Judith regards him with horror, still shrinking into Paloma's arm. 'You think that's why this other child died too? Because of an accident with some secret weapon?'

Jonny nods before something else suddenly occurs to him. Something even more disturbing than illegal experiments with biological weapons killing innocent children. 'The boy who died five years ago. Who was he? Where was he from? What happened to his family? Everyone knows each other around here. This is a tiny community. Someone must have seen something.'

He watches Judith swiping at her eyes with an angry hand. And suddenly he's picturing another desolate figure, unable to move on for grief, swiping at his own eyes with an equally angry hand as Jonny unknowingly looked at a photograph of his missing son that he'd found in the footwell of the man's car as he gave them a ride back to Eastwood.

'David Marshall,' he says slowly, remembering the faded snapshot of the small boy holding an ice cream. 'The man living on the private land directly opposite Blackwater's southern shore. The police told me his little boy wandered off on to the causeway five years ago and never came back. He was never found. No one around here saw a thing. Even the missing posters of him were torn down all over town.'

Judith positively shrivels at the mention of David Marshall's name. She reaches for Paloma, but she's already pulling away and getting to her feet, expression suddenly rigid. Jonny becomes dimly aware of the fact he is starting to shake, barely able to contain his fury.

'Except you saw something. You've known all along what happened to that poor kid and you've never said a word. Not even to spare his father the agony of wondering for the rest of his days. Did you take down all his posters yourself, too?'

Judith lets out a pitiful cry. But Jonny is unmoved, thinking of the piles of posters he found in the dark in Judith's room the previous night. The scale of David Marshall's pain at his young son Matthew wandering off on to the causeway, never to be seen or heard from again, is horrifying enough. But to find out that someone has deliberately chosen to stay quiet about what really happened? Something more occurs to him. He reaches for the phone mounted on the wall by the door to the saloon and is as sickened as he is unsurprised to find the line reconnected and the dial tone blaring into his ear.

'And of course your fucking phone works just fine now. Because you're the one who unplugged it last night. You were terrified we were about to find out your secret. So you disconnected your phone and bolted.'

'I kept all the posters,' Judith cries. 'They're all still in my room. I never threw them away…' She trails off into uncontrollable sobs.

But Jonny is still so consumed by the horror of what David Marshall has been through that it takes him a minute to register Paloma tugging on his arm and ushering him away.

'Leave her be. Come on,' she murmurs to him. 'She is punishing herself enough without us piling in too. She's told us everything we need to know. It's not our job to be judge and jury. It's our job to get the facts straight.'

Jonny follows her reluctantly back into the pub, still looking over his shoulder at Judith slumped and crying piteously in her squalid back hallway. 'This conversation is very far from over,' he hisses at her before making his way out of the deserted saloon.

Outside, the rain is intensifying. Paloma heads straight for the bike parked in wet grass beside the road. Jonny is still torn between staying to confront Judith or continuing to try and tackle Jane.

'Wait,' he calls to Paloma.

She turns to him with a quizzical expression, helmet halfway to her head. 'What for? We need to go and call Lukas. And we can't very well use the phone in there.' She gestures back at The Saxon.

Jonny starts to pace around in small circles. 'We can't just let Judith get away with it, though.'

'Get away with what? All that old woman is actually guilty of is silence. I can't help but feel a bit sorry for her. It sounds like she was a witness to something far more than she was an accomplice to anything.'

Jonny has to resist a sudden urge to scream into the wind. 'How can you sympathise with someone who chooses to stay quiet about such a thing for so long? That poor man is still wondering what the hell happened to his son.'

Paloma walks back over to him. 'And I won't rest until we're able to tell him exactly what did. But we need our information to be bulletproof first. We already know there must be powerful people working very hard to cover up exactly what happened here in the past. We need to talk to Lukas. We're going to need the *Trib*'s full support before we ring any more alarm bells. It's a lot harder for government officials to face down a massive international news operation than it is to intimidate a single reporter. Especially on a matter that they'll claim is in the interests of national security.'

But Jonny still can't bring himself to leave. 'We can't just ditch this and go straight back to London. We still don't know what Jane is planning to do about it all herself. Trust me, she is absolutely steaming with rage over how she's been treated. Having met her, I can assure you she is the definition of volatile. We also now know she swore to Judith she would get revenge on her behalf too. Her bunkers were stuffed full of equipment. Computer monitors, electrical cables, chip sets, circuit boards. And they weren't sitting around unplugged and covered in dust. They were in use – I could hear them whirring and humming. To be working underground in a very damp environment they must be state-of-the-art. Jane is doing something with them out there. And there is no way she's doing it alone.'

'Well the only person we know for a fact she's been in league with at some point is still sobbing her eyes out in there.' Paloma waves at the pub. 'And I don't see a frail and broken-hearted old woman like Judith being able to funnel the kind of hardware you're describing across a river unnoticed, do you?'

'Exactly. So where is Jane getting it from? And what is she using it all for?' He looks vainly down the road towards the river. The estuary mist is impenetrably thick.

'Well there's nothing much of anything around here except water,' Paloma says, following his gaze. 'Which is actually mud half the time. The estuary is a literal dead end. Remember what Gill told us about its nautical position? That it opens out into a very strategic area of the North Sea? We know container ships make a point of steaming straight past the river mouth.'

How Jane may have come by all the equipment in her bunkers hits Jonny now. 'That's it,' he mutters, running a hand through his damp hair, thinking about the kind of cargo some of those ships are carrying.

'What is?' Paloma demands.

Jonny pulls the map from the top pocket of his rucksack, pointing out the wide blue mouth of the River Thames just a little further south. 'Look. I'm willing to bet the containers on the ships passing in range of here are bursting with valuable cargo. This estuary is right between the gateway to London and all these massive ports further north.' His finger moves to point up the east coast at Felixstowe, Hull and Newcastle. 'Like you say, we've seen ships going both ways.'

'You think Jane is somehow intercepting goods as they make their way into port?'

'That, or they are being delivered to her in the oyster baskets we keep finding tied up and lined with plastic. I saw a load of them stacked up in her bunkers too.'

'You mean like a dead drop?'

'Yes. You can't cultivate oysters in waterproof baskets. So they're obviously not for oysters. We've been looking at a subterranean mailbox network.'

'But you can't fit a computer monitor in an oyster basket,' Paloma counters. 'And even if you're right, you're completely missing the point. We still need proof that anthrax was weaponised around here once upon a time. So we need to run down whether exposure to it is ultimately what killed the boy last week. For that, we'll need to get Michelle to run some tests, which, by her own admission, are going to take both time and money – and more importantly are going to raise a shit load of eyebrows. We have to protect both ourselves and our investigation before we do that.'

'You're the one who is completely missing the point,' Jonny shoots back. 'Jane could blow the whole thing up before we get a chance to do anything else if we don't deal with what she is plotting first.'

Paloma lifts and drops her hands in despair. 'Well we can hardly do that while we're standing around on some rainy street in the middle of nowhere.'

He walks back over to the bike. 'Actually, we're exactly where we need to be,' he says. 'Or close enough.' He slings his leg over the saddle.

Paloma hesitates. 'Where are you going?'

'To the nearest port. And Felixstowe is closer than London. You don't have to come with me if you don't want to. But I'm not finished here yet.'

Chapter Thirty-Four

The hurt on Paloma's face is obvious. Jonny is suddenly overcome with frustration. The last thing he wants to do is leave her behind. But he can't help feeling she is holding him back. He's the one who witnessed the scope of Jane's operation on Blackwater. It feels way too big to ignore.

'Look, you just told me you want to go back to London.'

'No, I told you we needed to call Lukas. Now you want me to leave? Aren't we in this together?'

'No. I'm the one Lukas sent down here to investigate this. He only told you to come meet me to make you feel better,' he adds before can think better of it.

'To make me feel better?' Paloma echoes disbelievingly. 'How can you say that after everything we've been through? Do you really think that's why I'm still here? I want to be here. I want to be here with you.'

Jonny stares back at her. 'You've been pretty explicit in the past about not wanting that at all.'

Paloma pales further. 'I told you that our friendship means too much to me to risk it for anything. I didn't say I never wanted to see you again.'

So then why did she kiss him? Jonny wants to ask so desperately that he almost feels nauseous from holding back the words. But he can't ask. There's no possible answer that he feels even remotely ready to deal with. Even if she says she loves him. Because then what? The person who was supposed to love him most in the world chose to take her own life rather than live with past mistakes.

'Well I don't want to risk it either,' he finally says. 'That's why you should go back now. Because you're right about needing to talk to Lukas. But I also know that I'm right about Jane.' He jerks his head at The Saxon. 'You were far nicer to Judith than I was. She'll let you call Bill and wait for him inside. I won't be far behind you, don't worry.'

He stuffs his helmet on his head and kicks the bike into gear before Paloma has a chance to say anything else. He can't bear to look at the hurt on her face for a second longer. His entire life has been a series of betrayals of the worst kind. His work is all he can truly count on. And his feelings for Paloma have already impaired his professional judgement once. That can never happen again. He zooms away from The Saxon and back up the road towards Maldon, picking up signs for Felixstowe almost immediately.

Gunning the engine, Jonny bends low over the motorbike's handlebars, trying to recapture some of the exhilaration he'd felt as they'd pelted down this same road in the opposite direction an hour earlier. But the driving rain is starting to feel like hail. The coast wind is whipping through his wet clothes like a lash. And Paloma's obvious distress at being left standing alone outside The Saxon is still all he can see in his mind's eye, despite trying to concentrate on the road ahead.

He accelerates, running red light after red light on the largely deserted streets. What does it matter? He already knows the single police officer based in the area does exactly the same in her car. And immeasurably more significant rules have been broken with impunity around here. Still, he feels increasingly beaten down with every passing mile. Why the fuck did he think that abandoning Paloma in the pissing rain in the arse end of nowhere was a reasonable thing to do? Does he really care more about a news story than her? Isn't that the exact opposite of how he feels? How the hell is he going to explain himself to her? A sign pointing the way back to Eastwood flashes past on the opposite side of the carriageway and for the briefest of moments he considers turning back, even though he already knows that he won't. Because he can't. Being let down by someone he cares about is not something that Jonny can survive again.

He grips the handlebars with renewed determination. The only way he will possibly be able to justify his behaviour to Paloma is if it results in an invaluable and hopefully explosive new piece of information. He has to make sense of the equipment in Jane's bunker. That should explain what she is actually still doing there. Where is she getting it from and what is she using it for? By the time he reaches the outskirts of the port, his conversations with Jane are playing through his mind like a repeating chorus. *I was a hired gun for thirty years and all it's left me with is blood on my hands ... It's finally time to make some people pay for that.* But how?

Following the signs to the port itself, Jonny pulls up in the car park just shy of the entrance. Out to sea, huge container ships are hulking on the horizon, puffing columns of smoke into the iron-grey clouds overhead. Inland, passenger ferries are steaming in and out of the terminal on the opposite side of the estuary – Harwich, Jonny remembers, recalling the map in his rucksack. And on the vast quay itself, rows of giant containers are candy-striped across the tarmac.

Hoping keeping his helmet on will make him look like a courier delivering something, Jonny strides purposefully towards the quay. He skirts around the barriers to the car park without incident and then up the vast access road towards a skyline punctuated by huge steel cranes. In the distance, a buggy scoots back and forth between the rows of giant containers. A low-rise building comes into view at the front end of the quay. And with it, the lone figure of a docker with a clipboard, pacing in a small circle with a decidedly dejected air.

Jonny walks towards the official with as much authority as he can muster. In the almost five years he's been a journalist he has learned it is usually far more productive to beg forgiveness than ask permission. When the official looks up, he starts to wave him away immediately.

'No foot traffic on the quay!' he yells, brandishing his clipboard. 'Stop right there!'

Jonny stops, taking off his helmet and holding his hands in the air.

Running over, the docker is instantly out of breath. 'What the hell do you think you're doing?'

'I'm so sorry,' Jonny begins, but the official is still talking.

'You got a permit? Actually, don't answer that. There's no permit for wandering around on the quay like some tourist—'

'Actually I'm a journalist,' Jonny interrupts, dropping his arms and spreading his hands wide. 'I'm sorry if I haven't followed the right protocol. I'm looking into a local black market in computer electronics and wanted to find out more about what kind of goods pass through this port.'

The official is shaking his head. 'Journalist, tourist, whatever. You can't take another step on this quay unless it's backward.' He points inland.

'I really am sorry,' Jonny tries again. 'I won't take up too much of your time. It sucks being at work over the Christmas holidays, doesn't it. I bet you're all as fed up as we are.'

The man scoffs. 'This port handles almost half the freight into the whole of the United Kingdom. No one cares about Christmas. And now everyone is working round the clock in case our computer systems melt down at midnight tonight.'

'Because of the millennium bug?'

The official sizes him up. 'Yes. The systems are already overloaded with counter-measures. Offshore congestion has never been so bad.'

Jonny looks around the quay, playing for time. 'It feels pretty quiet around here for an industry working round the clock. I guess not everyone is having to work all hours.'

The man scowls down at his clipboard. 'On your bike, now, go on. I could get in a lot of trouble just for talking to you.'

'I definitely don't want to cause you any trouble. But it doesn't look like there's anyone who can see us talking. And if they could, they'd just see you telling me to leave.'

The man sighs, proffering the clipboard. 'Take this, would you? At least make it look like you're signing for something.'

'Is that how it usually works?' Jonny asks, unclipping the pen attached to the top of the board. 'It's actually possible to come directly on to the quay and sign for something?'

'Sometimes. Only for small stuff, mind. Special deliveries. That kind of thing. It's unusual. But it happens. We don't know what's being signed for, just that it's OK to let it go.'

'Who tells you it's OK?'

'There's paperwork. We don't write it. We just get it. And we get fined if stuff doesn't make it on time.'

'Dockers get fined personally? That doesn't seem fair.'

'Too right it doesn't. We're the ones doing all the donkey work. And then the brass take it out of our wages. Now we've got this bug on our hands and everything is delayed no matter how hard we work. The big shippers prefer a delay to a diversion. Of course they do, because port workers are the ones who end up paying for some of it.'

'Do you mind if I write some notes down on here?' Jonny taps the pen on the clipboard. 'I don't want to get my notebook out in case anyone is watching.'

The official nods back. 'Go on then. But you didn't hear any of this from me.'

'Of course,' Jonny answers, folding the form on top of the clipboard in half so he can make notes on the blank side. 'That part's easy. I don't even know your name.'

The man looks nervously over his shoulder towards the low-rise building. 'Well I'm only talking to you because of the fines.'

'I can understand that. It feels very unfair if the delays are due to factors beyond your control. Is it fair to say that paperwork might sometimes fall through the cracks to make sure shipments are delivered on time? I'm not accusing you of anything. But if dockers are personally fined for delays, it follows that certain details might get overlooked on occasion to avoid that.'

The man shakes his head. 'We can't. There's another fine if the piece of paper goes missing.'

'So what happens if someone shows up here demanding a shipment that you can't release?'

The man shifts from foot to foot. 'I've said enough. I thought you were looking into a local black market in electronics and whatnot. I don't know anything about that.'

'No, but you've given me enough to explain how a black market like that might be run,' Jonny answers, thinking about all the ways in which dockers could be intimidated into handing over shipments without the requisite pieces of paper in place. 'You said everything is delayed at the moment. What happens then – is there a priority system for certain types of cargo? Do containers get diverted after all, and if they do, where do they go?'

'Cars go south. Industrial materials go north. That's about as sophisticated as it gets.'

'What about into London? That's the nearest option, surely?'

The man bristles. 'Listen, London may be the capital but its port facilities are the smallest of the lot. Poxy as you like. The only goods that ever go up the Thames are your electronics.'

Jonny seizes on this, picturing the nautical route south from Felixstowe, directly across the mouth of the Blackwater river. 'Any idea what kind of electronics?'

'Computers, mainly. Circuit boards, microchips. High-value stuff. London has the security arrangements for all that.'

Jonny's pen stills. 'Security arrangements? You mean like police escorts? Why?'

The man shakes his head, grabbing his clipboard back. 'More like secret service. You know the type. Folks with faces that wouldn't stick out in a line-up. You'd never know they were there, but they are. They have to be. Because if a circuit board gets stolen, you can bet it will turn up inside a homemade bomb.'

Chapter Thirty-Five

Jonny's blood runs cold. Instantly he is picturing the circuit boards cabled together inside Blackwater's bunkers. Was he looking at a homemade bomb? *The mission that failed.* All this time he's been concentrating on finding out what it actually involved when he should have been focusing on the consequences. He should have known a woman like Jane wouldn't bother deliberately blowing her own cover and tipping off the police about one dead child unless it was part of a far bigger plan. And Detective Inspector Gillian Peters might be speeding across the water to confront her right this minute with no idea of the scale of the danger she's heading into. He looks around the quay as if a telephone box will simply materialise from acres of grey concrete.

The official eyes him dubiously. 'You alright?'

'Yes, thanks. You've been really helpful. Can I use your phone before I go? It's just I need to call someone pretty urgently.'

'Don't push your luck, son. No way I can take you inside.' He gestures at the building behind them. 'It's bad enough that I'm talking to you outside. If you want a phone, your best bet is the box by the side of the road out of the car park...'

He fades as Jonny breaks into a run, hurtling along the vast access road. Finally reaching the car park, the bike is mercifully still where he left it. And beyond, a red speck in the distance, is the unmistakable outline of a telephone box.

Jonny jams his helmet back on with one hand, scrabbling for the keys to the bike in his pocket in the other. He has to call Gillian Peters. And if he can't get hold of her, he'll have to try and intercept her instead. Kicking the bike's engine into gear, he zooms out of the car park and back up the road towards the phone box. Slinging the bike and helmet on the verge, he is inside in seconds, digging around in his pocket for Gill's dog-eared calling card.

The line rings out until a harsh beep puts him through to an automated service – the one that Jane must have encountered on Christmas Day when she delivered her anonymous tip-off, he realises.

'Gill, it's Jonny. Are you there? Can you hear me? If you can hear me, please pick up. It's urgent. Gill?'

Nothing. He tries again.

'OK, Gill, I'm just going to assume you can hear me, or that someone else can, and will either pick up or get a message to you some other way. Do not go back to Blackwater Island under any circumstances. You've probably spoken to your sister by now, so I'm going to guess that you know who Jane Doe really is. And I'm sure it's all unbelievably difficult to take, and that all you want to do is find your brother and confront him, but please don't go to Blackwater Island again yet. I think Jane might be building a bomb there. Just … just stay where you are. I'm coming to find you now.'

He cuts the call, dialling emergency services as soon as he hears the tone. A bomb threat on the Blackwater river. An armed and dangerous woman on the loose. An immediate need for tactical reinforcements, and lots of them. The operator's disbelief is palpable. But there's no time for Jonny to remonstrate or beg to be taken seriously. He's back outside the phone box as soon as he's through the basics and grabbing hold of the bike again. All he can think about is finding Gill and making sure no one else perishes on Blackwater Island.

The miles scud past with dizzying speed, Jonny's mind whirling at a similar rate. He tries to remember the exact details of what he saw inside Blackwater's tunnels and bunkers. Multiple computer monitors. Yards and yards of cable. Dozens of circuit boards and chip sets. Could Jane be rigging the bunkers themselves to hide evidence of the mission that failed? Or is she building a bomb destined for somewhere else entirely?

Adrenaline suddenly surges through Jonny like an electrical current. What is Jane Doe angriest about of all? *I was a hired gun for thirty years and all it's left me with is blood on my hands.* And who is ultimately to blame for that? The machinery of government flashes through his mind as he pictures the historic institutions headquartered barely fifty miles away. The Ministry of Defence. The Security Service. Downing Street itself. All a stone's throw from where hundreds and thousands of people will gather to celebrate Millennium Eve in a matter of hours. Along with hundreds of news crews. Including Paloma – and all because he just told her to go back there. Is Jane planning an attack in the heart of London? He screeches back into Maldon on a wave of barely suppressed panic.

The police station is deserted. There's no sign of Gill. Vaulting over the counter, he grabs the phone on the desk, punching in the number for the news editor on duty.

'It's Jonny,' he says before the person at the end of the line can speak. 'I need to talk to Lukas immediately, is he there? It's urgent.'

He can hear shouting in the background as the phone is passed around before Lukas's clipped South African accent comes on to the line.

'Glad to hear from you, buddy. What's going on? I need you in position pronto—'

'Is Paloma back yet?' Jonny interrupts. 'Has she told you anything?'

'We haven't spoken other than to discuss heading down to Tower Bridge to get ready for the fireworks later.'

Jonny's stomach churns at the prospect of Paloma in potential danger – and the fact he might have put her there himself. 'You've got to turn her around. Get everyone out of the centre of town as quickly as you can.'

'What the hell are you talking about, Jonny? We don't have time for this—'

'Just listen to me for a second, OK? I know I should have called in earlier, but once I found out what's really going on down here I couldn't stop for long enough.'

'Down here? Down where?'

'On Blackwater Island. Remember? The place that neither of us had ever heard of before – where the body of a child was found on Christmas Day.'

'You mean you're still there?' The incredulity in Lukas's voice is plain. Jonny instantly regrets calling him. He doesn't have time to explain. He just needs to sound an alarm.

'Yes. Because Blackwater Island is supposedly an uninhabited wilderness reserve sitting innocently in the middle of the Blackwater river. Official permission to visit is tied up in paperwork a yard long. So when I finally worked out where it was and got myself ashore to investigate, imagine my surprise to find a former mercenary hiding out in an underground network of bunkers and tunnels full of weapons and computers.'

He stops there, suddenly out of breath. But Lukas is finally listening. 'Start again,' he says. 'Blackwater Island officially has protected status and yet you found some retired hired gun holed up there?'

'Exactly. Right where the child's body was found. She told me to call her Jane Doe. Said she was the one who tipped the police off to the fact there was a body to be found in the first place. Said she'd been working off the books for the government for years until she was cut off after a classified mission went wrong there. Said it used to be a black site and was fortified for marine training exercises during the Second World War. She's furious about how she's been treated and I am worried she's about to do something crazy in revenge.'

'That's why you're so exercised about our crews in town? But presumably you called the cops in short order after finding her?'

'No. Because there's only one police officer down here in charge of the entire area. With no official jurisdiction over Blackwater because of its protected status. Now I know what you're thinking: a child turns up dead on an uninhabited island and police somehow miss an armed fugitive hiding near the crime scene? It only makes sense if the authorities are deliberately looking the other way. Which in turn only makes sense if we're looking at a conspiracy on a large scale. That's why I'm still here. I've been trying to run down exactly what happened on Blackwater in the first place. But what I also should have been doing is worrying about how Jane intends to avenge it now. And that's why I'm worried about our crews in Central London. Because she's most angry with the top of the British establishment. And she's an expert in covert tactical operations.'

'But why would this woman tip off the police to a dead body in her exact location if she didn't want to give herself away in the process? Surely she knows you're going to make her presence known at some point and armed police will swarm the place.'

Something else suddenly occurs to Jonny. Dread takes hold as he pictures the circuit boards all cabled together inside Blackwater's bunkers again.

'What if that's exactly what she wants?'

'For armed police to swarm the place?' Lukas repeats disbelievingly. 'Why on earth would she want that?'

'So she can blow them all to hell,' he says, looking around the deserted room as if the harder he looks, the more likely it is that the security officers he just insisted that emergency services deploy as a matter of urgency will stop at the station rather than head straight to Blackwater Island. Beyond the open door, he becomes aware of the wail of sirens, calling to him like an alarm in the distance.

Lukas swears loudly before continuing. 'Do not go doing anything stupid, Jonny. Under no circumstances are you to go haring off to try and save the day. It is not your job to be the hero right now. It is your job to report the facts. I'll take care of our crews in Central London. But I need you to promise to take care of yourself...'

But Jonny is already slamming down the phone, rushing around the counter and back out to the bike.

Chapter Thirty-Six

Out in the open air, the sound of sirens approaching is unmistakable. Gunning the bike's engine, Jonny screeches out of the station courtyard just as three large police vans barrel past back down the road towards Eastwood. Falling in behind them, Jonny squints in vain at their darkened windows. Is it possible they are heading somewhere other than Blackwater Island? His breath catches as he spots The Saxon up ahead, amber-lit windows flickering like candles in the distance. But there's no time for him to pull over and see if Paloma is still there waiting for Bill. Because the vans are hurtling past at a clip, heading straight for the dirt track down to the river. And he knows there is only one place they can go on to from there.

Accelerating into wet grass alongside the track, Jonny manages to draw level with the van up front before he is forced to stop at the river's edge. The wind is up and the tide is high, dark water churning menacingly against the reeds lining the bank. Ditching the bike in the grass, he turns around just as black-clad officers pour out of the van, spreading out along the shoreline, save for two men who are either side of him and frogmarching him away before he can say a word.

'You need to come with us for your own safety,' one says, bursts of static belching from the radio at his belt. 'This is an active police operation.'

'I know,' he says, dragging his feet, trying to slow them down. 'I'm the person who called in to report the threat. There's an armed woman hiding out on Blackwater Island and I think she might have a bomb.'

'That's why we need you well away from the area, son. We'll have to arrest you if you don't comply, so don't struggle.'

Digging his heels into the mud, he searches the haze hanging over the estuary. Dusk is falling. The light is already low. The mist shrouding Blackwater Island is impenetrable.

'But I can help. I know where this woman is hiding. You won't find her without me. My name is Jonny Murphy, I'm a reporter with the *International Tribune*. I came here to investigate the death of a child on Christmas Day—'

He stops at the sounds of splashing by the shoreline. Officers are moving towards the sound like a wave. And then Detective Inspector Gillian Peters emerges, using two wooden oars to propel herself up through the reeds on the river bank.

'Gill,' he cries, seized with relief. 'Over here. It's Jonny.'

But Gill is immediately swallowed into the gaggle of officers at the water's edge.

'Wait,' he begs the men to his either side. 'That officer knows me.'

'I don't care,' one answers, giving him a shove.

Jonny is suddenly furious. 'Why – because you don't care about what happens down here either? This area has been deliberately ignored for years. I know because that officer told me herself. And now I happen to know why. And it's a whole lot to do with the woman waiting to ambush you as soon as you set foot on Blackwater Island.'

The man is reaching for his cuffs when Gill shouts: 'Let him through.'

It's all Jonny needs to hear to take his chance. Wrenching himself free as the men's grip slackens, he rushes back down the bank and straight over to a soaking-wet Detective Inspector Gillian Peters.

'Gill,' he pants. 'Are you OK? You're not hurt?'

She nods, adjusting the lip of her hat. 'I'm fine. I found them.

The pair of delusional druids that, courtesy of my sister, I believe you now know about, too. But we don't have time for that now—'

'I know,' Jonny interrupts. 'That's why I've been trying to reach you.' He gestures at the officers beside them. 'Did you find Jane as well?'

Gill shakes her head grimly. 'No. She's either still hiding or she's got away – and if she has, we need to find out exactly where she's heading. I found the bunker, trapdoor open, light blazing into the sky. And inside I found my brother and his chosen life partner on their knees, praying to the God of trees.'

Jonny peers past her but all he can see is mist. He hears the clank of more doors opening behind him, a senior commander barking instructions. A black rubber boat is being hauled out on to the grass along with some heavy equipment cases.

'Where are they now?' he asks.

'I had to leave them there.' A flicker of anguish crosses Gill's face. 'They're ... they're rigged up to a bomb. It's on a timer set to go off at midnight. This lot are here to disable the device and free them.' She gestures at the black-clad officers swarming around the equipment cases. 'But that's not the worst of it. I found maps of Central London. Detailed plans of Millennium Eve celebrations, even a blueprint of Tilbury Docks and a port-police shirt and badge. I think there might be a far bigger bomb on the move.'

Jonny reels, the blessed relief he can still trust his instincts jostling with the terrifying consequences of them being right. 'Describe exactly what you found. Then I can tell you what might be missing, or where else Jane could be hiding.'

'I found the entrance to this bunker a little way up the slope on the island's north side. I couldn't miss it with the light beaming through the undergrowth. She'd obviously left it like that deliberately.'

'So you've only been inside the one bunker?' he asks, thinking about the second, deeper tunnel network.

Gill nods. 'Yes. I could see a bunch of tunnels leading off it. Where do they go? Quickly, now.'

'I only went through a single passage. It came out via another few bunkers on the south side of the island. The entrance is inside an old building, which I'm sure has line of sight to the back of David Marshall's house on the opposite shore. But there is a second network of tunnels that comes out through the roots of a giant tree to the west. She called that network the Deep State. It's much harder to find.'

Gill stops him with an outstretched hand, turning to relay this to the commander readying a dive team. Another boat is being hauled out of a different van, along with some more cases. Jonny thinks through all the items he saw in the bunkers and tunnels when he first encountered Jane.

'Was there still a load of electrical equipment all over the place?' he asks Gill. 'Computer monitors, circuit boards, loads and loads of cables?'

Gill screws up her face trying to remember. 'I don't think so. But I didn't look that hard. Once I realised there was a live bomb in front of me that's all I could focus on. It looked like a relatively simple device. Which also worries me. The hardware you're describing sounds impossible to miss. So where's it all gone?'

Jonny tries to picture exactly what he saw. 'I don't know, but I think Jane's already left the island. She's got a far bigger target than Blackwater. I think the bomb she's left tied to your brother and his wife is to buy some time to get away.'

'And she obviously wants us to think she's headed into London,' replies Gill. 'It's like she deliberately left the maps out for me to find. But what if they're just a decoy? Tell me what you've found out about her so far. You said she was cut off after a mission failed?'

'Yes, and that she tipped you off because no more innocent people were going to get hurt on her watch. She said Blackwater was the place where it all fell apart for her. So it's obviously where the original mission went wrong. And it turns out that The Saxon's landlady, Judith, witnessed that failure and Jane has been paying her to stay silent about it since—'

Gill erupts into a volley of swearing.

'For what it's worth Judith claims she doesn't know exactly what happened,' Jonny adds hurriedly. 'But we don't have time to worry about her right now. Because I think the failed mission may have involved experiments with biological weapons, and I'm pretty sure your sister can confirm that for sure if she runs a few more specific tests on the allergen or toxin that she's already established killed your nephew. I don't think the maps are a decoy. I think Jane's target is the heart of the British establishment. My guess is she's going up the Thames to Whitehall. And it's Millennium Eve. The river is going to be packed.'

Gill barks urgently into her radio. Listening to the rapid back and forth just makes Jonny feel more unnerved. Jane's bomb could be laced with anthrax as well as a massive electrical charge. The potential fallout could be hundreds of square miles. And thousands of people are already gathering on the banks of the Thames to party. There's a dazzling array of fireworks being readied on the water. And there are reporters and photographers deployed across the city to document every single moment. He shudders at the thought of Paloma right at the heart of Jane's potential target.

Something else Jane vowed comes back to him then, snagging inside his mind amid the frenzy. *No more innocent people are going to get hurt on my watch.*

'Wait,' he says to Gill, but she's still yelling into her radio. A boat jostles him on its way into the water, black-clad officers moving like beetles in the rapidly advancing dark. When Gill turns back to him, there's no escaping the flash of fear in her eyes.

'Something's not right,' he says, barged again by a second boat being readied for launch. 'I don't think mass casualties are part of

Jane's plan. She kept saying that no more innocent people were going to die on her watch. I just don't think her revenge is going to take the form of killing hundreds of people. We've missed something, I just can't think what it is...' He trails off at the sight of Gill swapping her police hat for a black helmet.

'Doesn't matter. There's a bomb on the island that I saw with my own eyes. Two more potential casualties are trapped. We have to act on the information that we have.'

Another officer hands her some body armour. He tunes out the alarm inside his mind almost before it has a chance to ring. He will not sit this out for any reason on earth. 'I'm coming with you, right?'

'Yes,' the commander says, a second rubber boat sliding sleek into the water. 'You need to stay with us. Nothing can leak. Mass panic in town could cause a stampede.'

Gill passes a flak vest and helmet over to Jonny. 'And we need your input,' she adds, despite the commander's frown. 'You're the only one who's ever encountered this woman in person.'

The officers climb on board the boat. Gill turns back and beckons him with a black-gloved hand. But his feet are suddenly rooted in the wet grass. It may not be his job to be the hero. But it damn well is his job to get the facts straight. And he's going to do that, no matter what it costs him.

'So I have to come with you, is what you're actually saying? Because you can't risk a journalist going rogue and reporting anything until you're ready.'

'Right again,' says the commander. 'And she's right, too.' He nods at Gill. 'We do need your input. So get in unless you want me to arrest you for obstruction. We've got a long way to go.'

'We're not going to Blackwater?'

The commander's mouth sets in a hard line. 'No. We're going to London.'

Chapter Thirty-Seven

Jonny clambers on board. The boat whirrs gently to life. Gill turns down the volume on her radio as they cast off into the dark. The atmosphere is so tense it feels like they're operating in some alternate universe. The first boat takes the lead, cutting out gently through the water towards the middle of the river. The mist starts to thicken almost immediately, a layer of salty damp clinging to Jonny's face. Swooshing through the water, the boat ahead swings out in a gentle arc towards Blackwater.

'This feels like a trap,' he whispers to Gill, picturing the explosives rigged up inside Jane's bunker suddenly bursting into a fireball. 'Don't those officers need backup?' He gestures at the first boat, disappearing rapidly into the dark. 'What if something goes wrong when they try to disable the bomb on the island?'

'There will be nothing we can do for them if it does,' Gill whispers back. 'Try not to think about them. Just try and think like Jane. We've got to put ourselves in her shoes if we want to find her. We've found maps of Central London in her bunker. Hard evidence of bomb-making materials. And you say she claims to want to avenge herself against the most secretive arm of the British government. That's more than enough to suggest that this swamp may not be her only target. If we're wrong and she's still hiding underground then the first team will handle it. If she isn't, then she must be on the water. The tide is high. So her obvious first step is by boat.'

'But what if it's just a boat to a nearby access road?'

Gill shakes her head, hunching as she leans towards him. 'Think like Jane. You say she's an elite covert operator. Why would she risk a road move? She'd need to get off the water undetected and then commandeer a vehicle. Or use associates to bring her one – another risk. And she knows the few slow roads around here will already be policed – she'll have assumed that by now you'll have given away her location. My gut is that she'll stay on the water. It'll be much easier for her to avoid detection.'

'Think like Jane,' Jonny mutters to himself. The boat is still cutting its straight line across the river. 'OK. So she's on the water. Paloma and I abandoned the boat we first used to get to Blackwater. She could be in that and headed towards the Marshall land.'

'What kind of boat?'

Jonny racks his brain. 'Small. Wooden. And we took the oars to help propel us back through the mud. But I suppose substitutes can be fashioned out of driftwood easily enough.'

'Especially on an island covered in woodland.' Gill's eyes gleam at him through the dark. 'OK. So let's assume that's the boat she's in. So she can't be moving that fast.'

'And a knackered old wooden boat isn't the ideal environment to transport an explosive device,' Jonny adds, brightening. 'Everything will get soaked. So maybe she isn't moving with a bomb either.'

'But she could easily be moving with component parts,' Gill cautions. 'She knows exactly what she's doing. We can't discount anything yet.'

Jonny's heart sinks as the boat begins to turn towards the mouth of the Blackwater river. 'That reminds me. I think she's been getting her supplies off the ships being processed at Felixstowe. It handles over half the shipping into the entire country. I went there this morning. Managed to walk on to the quay itself completely unchallenged. Maybe that's where she's headed first. To pick up whatever else she needs.'

But Gill is already shaking her head. 'Think like Jane. Why would she turn fifty miles in the opposite direction to London? Especially in some substandard rowing boat with a pair of makeshift oars?'

'Someone could be meeting her on the water,' Jonny replies, thinking back to his conversation with the official at Felixstowe port. 'Container ships are idling offshore for hours at the moment. Everything is delayed because of worries about the millennium bug.'

Gill thinks about this. 'If so, then they'll meet at the mouth of the river itself. Or at least on the shore beside it. She'll want any exchange to be well clear of Felixstowe's operations.'

She squints into the dark as the boat completes its turn towards the sea. Jonny follows her gaze. The outline of Blackwater's southern shore is dimly visible up ahead on the left.

'And if she's meeting someone on the water, she could also easily be switching boats,' he adds. 'She'll need to if she's in the rowing boat we took to start with.'

'Think like Jane,' Gill repeats, shaking her head again. 'Why would she risk meeting anyone at all? We know she has access to both explosives and electrical equipment. We've seen evidence of both with our own eyes. So what's to say she hasn't built a small engine?'

The realisation dawns on Jonny with a whiff of their boat's own ignition fuel. 'You're right. If she can build a bomb then she can damn well find a way to kit out a boat too.'

'She's headed into London,' Gill states. 'I'm even more convinced of it now. The maps and schematics I found must mean something to that effect. But I think she's travelling light to evade detection and that she's either going to stop for whatever else she needs along the way, or her remaining component parts are already waiting at her final destination. We're not dealing with some backstreet petty criminal here.

We're dealing with a mastermind in black ops. What are we missing? Think like Jane.'

Think like Jane, think like Jane, think like Jane, Jonny repeats, racking his brain. Black mist swirls over Blackwater as it passes silently by on the left. Jonny turns, staring into the fog, wondering whether Gill's bomb squad has reached the bunker yet, picturing the device's digital timer ticking down with alarm. Then something else suddenly occurs to him.

'Tell me again about the bomb you found on Blackwater. It's rigged to go off at midnight, right?'

Gill nods. 'Yes. And it looked like a simple enough device to me. Limited charge that I could see. Frankly, I'm sure I could have disabled it under the right circumstances. But I couldn't take the risk in such a confined space. Not even with the druids praying to the God of trees,' she adds bitterly, looking away.

'But she knew we'd find it,' he persists. 'And she ambushed me. I didn't discover her hiding place. She wanted to be found. And she wanted you to find her too – she deliberately left her trapdoor open. So why give us a chance to disable the bomb? Why give us time to save the day?'

'Profound psychological torture. I don't know,' Gill grumbles.

'But what's the significance of midnight,' he wonders, thinking through all the events planned to celebrate Millennium Eve. The parties. The countdown clocks. The enormous fireworks displays set to dazzle around the world. And then it hits him.

The River of Fire.

Fireworks. Gunpowder. Explosives. Rigged up the whole way along the Thames.

Jonny gasps into a gust of freezing wind as they speed up towards the North Sea. When he turns to Gill, there's no mistaking the shock on her face. He must look completely possessed.

'It's Millennium Eve. The biggest New Year's Eve party the

world has ever seen. She's trying to delay us for long enough to get her hands on some fireworks. And with the amount I know they are planning to fire along the banks of the Thames, she'll have access to enough explosives to bring down the Tower of London.'

Chapter Thirty-Eight

Horror crosses Gill's face. Frantic instructions ricochet between her and the commander, the sudden burst of sound at odds with the cloak of night. He turns up the engine, leaning down hard on the motor. Instantly water starts to foam at the sides of the boat. The mouth of the Blackwater river is rapidly upon them.

Gill scrabbles with her radio, gloved hands slipping. Beside her, the second officer is also readying his. Bursts of static punctuate the roar of the motor. 'Tell me everything you know about the fireworks display,' she shouts. 'Every detail you can think of, however irrelevant it may seem.'

Jonny fights to steady himself as the boat banks steeply south around the headland. 'The organisers are calling it the River of Fire. Massive rockets are being rigged up along four miles of the Thames. The route starts at Tower Bridge and ends in Vauxhall.'

'Hang on.' Gill holds up a hand, braying into her radio. The commander is bent low over the motor, pushing the engine so hard it howls. Jonny wipes salt from his eyes, thinking back to the *Trib*'s endless meetings about millennium coverage. He'd been so desperately looking for fresh angles on the millennium bug that he'd zoned out the details of the parties.

'I think the fireworks themselves are being set off from barges on the water,' he shouts. 'I don't know that for sure. But I remember being told that the idea is to make it look like the whole river is on fire. There are going to be such massive crowds that setting up exclusion zones to detonate the things on land was impossible. They're estimating a million people are going to show up.'

His breath catches as he considers this. A million people, most of them drunk, laughing and joking, with no idea of the potentially fatal position they're in. Including Paloma. He racks his brain for more useful detail, anything that could help the security forces intercept Jane. What had Lukas said when they'd been running through the logistics of the event? Gill is still shouting into her radio.

'Four miles, you said?'

'Yes. Starts at Tower Bridge. Ends in Vauxhall. That bit of the Thames is covered in major landmarks. The Tower of London, the Royal Festival Hall, the entire South Bank, Big Ben, Whitehall, Westminster Palace. It's all about maximising the beauty and impact of the display.'

Gill and the second officer exchange looks before issuing more instructions into their radios. The engine starts to keen in Jonny's ears. To his right, the dim outline of the coast begins flashing past. He pictures the nautical route from Blackwater into London with a rising sense of dread. They've got miles to cover before they reach the mouth of the Thames. And a whole lot more miles than that to get all the way into the city. Jonny and Gill are the only people with a measure of Jane's next move and are stuck on the water with no means to communicate other than a couple of radios – which, judging by Gill's increasingly frantic expression, are becoming progressively useless.

'What else?' she shouts. 'Come on. Think like Jane. Who is lighting all the fuses?'

Jonny screws his eyes shut, trying to remember. 'A computer on the shore is going to send radio cues to the operators on each barge. So she'll have to get past the operators to get her hands on the explosives.'

'So if we take her out in the process then we risk taking them out too,' Gill bangs her radio unit between her hands, scanning the stretch of coastline speeding past. 'Sitting ducks, the lot of them. I can't believe I've been so stupid. We have to get off this fucking boat. This is exactly what she wants. For us to be marooned miles away in the fucking North Sea when we realise what she's doing, with nothing other than radios to communicate with.'

Radios. Jonny's eyes fly open into a jet of seawater. 'The technicians on the barges all have radios,' he yells triumphantly. 'That's how they're going to communicate too. We just need to get a message to the right people and we should be able to warn every single boat that is taking part in the firework display.'

'But these fucking things aren't going to work for ages now.' Gill waves her radio towards the murky outline of the shore. 'This whole marsh is also a massive nature reserve. Not just Blackwater. Good for nothing other than bloody birds. We've got miles to go with patchy transmission. And even further before we can dock anywhere useful.'

Jonny wipes his streaming eyes, searching the narrow shadow of nearby land as if the harder he squints the more likely it is that the end of an immaculately tarmacked road with a police van waiting at its end will simply materialise from thin air. 'Where the hell are we?'

'Don't ask,' the commander shouts back. 'It's either dock at Southend as soon as we turn inland again or keep going up the Thames.'

Jonny considers this. 'Think like Jane,' he murmurs to himself under the scudding engine. She can't bend time and space. If she's on the water, she's travelling at best at a similar speed to them. And she knows that the discovery of a live bomb on Blackwater will have prompted heightened alerts to go out across London immediately. Security arrangements at all the parties with a view of the fireworks were already through the roof. She must have a plan to evade them. Commandeering a barge loaded with explosives on the most crowded and overlooked section of the

Thames is going to be hard to pull off covertly, no matter how seasoned the assailant is. He closes his eyes for a moment, forcing himself to sift through what he remembers Lukas saying about the firework display during their last editorial meeting. If only he hadn't spent so much time investigating potential computer glitches.

There his mind sticks.

'The whole event is computerised,' he shouts. 'My news editor was told it's being run from an operations room at Tilbury Docks. Didn't you also say she had a port-police shirt in her bunker? The radio cues are being issued by a computer program written months ago. I was due to interview a pyrotechnician about it yesterday in the context of the millennium bug. It was another example of a system that could potentially go to shit. I don't think she's going to physically commandeer a barge. I think she's going to find a way to issue a radio cue that sends a barge to her. And no one will question it, because the orders are being issued by a computer to start with.'

Gill stares at him disbelievingly. 'You mean you think she's going to hack into the whole system? Rewrite the program for the event itself?'

Jonny nods vigorously, showering water everywhere like a wet dog. 'It's possible, isn't it? There were more computers in her bunker than anything else. In fact, she as good as told me—'

'Told you?' Gill interrupts. 'What do you mean, she as good as told you? She gave you specifics on this plot that you haven't thought to mention until now?'

'Of course not. But she did say something sarcastic about the dawn of a new digital age. And that there was a new kind of arms race under way these days that was putting people like her out of business. I think what she was really referring to is the start of digital warfare. Computer systems control almost everything now. Hacking into one is a lot more covert than holding a gun to someone's head.'

Gill turns her radio over and over in her hands. 'You could be right,' she says grimly. 'Is Tilbury Docks where the barges are being rigged up, too? The simplest and least suspicious thing for her to do is issue an error message at the latest possible moment to prompt a barge to return to port and then she can get her hands on the explosives.'

Jonny thinks hard. 'I don't think that's a detail that's been made public. There are dozens of barges involved. Tonnes of fireworks. The logistics are mental. Everything is massively complicated.'

'In which case it probably is Tilbury,' the commander says, exchanging a glance with Gill. 'It's the closest big port to the centre of London capable of handling an operation on that scale. It has a deep-sea cruise terminal. Over a hundred thousand international passengers pass through it every year. There's a police station on the quay. Its entrance is still guarded by Tilbury Fort – ancient artillery positions cover the river.'

'At least that's a whole lot of security she'll have to get past,' Jonny says, only slightly comforted. 'How far is it from here?'

'I'm not sure.' Gill scans the dark ahead. 'I've never taken a boat out past the estuary because of those damn cruise liners.'

She pauses, squinting at the land to the east. Jonny follows her gaze, momentarily encouraged to find the glow of lights shining in the distance further down the coast. Gill suddenly lets out a shout, putting one hand on the commander's arm while pointing with the other. Instantly the engine slows, sputters, then dies. Eerie quiet descends.

What is it? Jonny wants to ask, but doesn't dare puncture the silence. It suddenly feels as if even the waves settling around them are holding themselves back from making any sounds at all.

'There,' Gill whispers after a moment, pointing towards land. The commander murmurs in agreement.

Jonny squints at the shoreline. What can they see that he can't? He leans forward, training his gaze into the shadows, searching for any variation in depth and perspective. The boat rocks gently as Gill shuffles closer to him, pointing with increasing determination.

'That shape,' she mutters. 'There, do you see? This whole area should be flat as a pancake.'

A soft scuffle from the second officer, and then an object is thrust between them – a nightscope, Jonny realises, with another little jolt of adrenaline. She holds it up to one eye before passing it to him. Jonny sees what she means the instant he looks through the lens.

There's a boat abandoned in the shallows.

A kind of boat that Jonny is absolutely sure he has seen before.

Chapter Thirty-Nine

Jonny hands the nightscope back to Gill with a grim nod. She lifts it back up to one eye to have a second look.

'It's a boat,' she whispers. 'Wooden, by the look of it. And upside down. Like someone's tried and failed to submerge it.'

Chills run down Jonny's back. 'It must be her. Why else would we find a rowing boat abandoned somewhere as random and remote as here.'

'If it's her, then we've got her strategy completely wrong. There's nothing here except mud. We need to go and take a closer look.'

She gives the nightscope to him again before turning to the commander. Overhearing their discussion about readying their defensive weapons doesn't make him feel particularly confident. 'Jane isn't the sort of person to try and fail to do anything,' he tries to point out. 'If she wanted to submerge the boat, she'd have submerged it. There's a reason it's been left like that. We need to try and work out what it is before we go in all guns blazing.'

But the officers are too focused on their weapons to pay him any attention. He peers back through the lens at the alien-green outlines of the mudflats ahead. The boat's silhouette suddenly couldn't be more obvious, wooden exterior shining with the unmistakable gleam of water on varnish.

'What the hell are you doing here, Jane,' he mutters to himself, flinching as their boat's engine whirrs gently back to life. Putting the nightscope back in his lap, the shoreline nears in a matter of seconds – so flat and featureless bar the silhouette of the boat abandoned in the shallows that it's hard to distinguish where the water ends and land starts.

The commander cuts the engine again, reaching down into the floor of their boat for two sturdy plastic oars. Handing one to the second officer, they row the last few metres, propelling them as far forward as possible until the water finally gives way to mud and they come to a complete stop.

Silence descends again. Jonny holds his breath. The endless quiet and dark are like none he's ever experienced before. They're barely fifty miles outside London yet it feels like they've arrived on another planet. He forces himself to concentrate on the familiar outline of the boat capsized a few feet away. It looks unremarkable save for the fact it is there.

Gill leans towards the commander. 'We're going to have to get out. I can't see anything from here. Cover us, OK?' She looks back at Jonny. 'Come on.'

She gets out of the boat and lands awkwardly in the mud with a squelch. Jonny shivers as he follows suit, freezing water instantly soaking into his boots. They slip and slide the few feet over to the abandoned lump of wood. A gentle click and Gill trains the soft red beam of a tiny hunting torch up and over the boat's capsized silhouette. It looks undamaged, its back end still largely submerged in muddy water.

Leaning down, Jonny pokes a finger into the mud at the boat's base, running it as far along the edge in each direction as he can without unbalancing himself.

'What are you looking for?'

'A motor. If Jane's used this boat, then it has to have an engine of some kind. All I can remember about the boat I first saw on Blackwater is that it was a plain rower, which would never make it this far. Check for a rudder where you are?'

Gill moves the beam downward to no avail. Jonny sidesteps

along the boat's edge and tries again. Nothing but salty mud stinging the grazes on his hand.

'Hang on,' Gill says after a moment. 'Let's try and right it. We should be able to lift it up and out if the mud is soft enough to get your finger in underneath. Then we'll be able to tell for sure.'

'OK,' Jonny answers doubtfully, planting his feet as steadily as he can. Darkness descends again as Gill clicks off the torch, tucking it into a pocket. Leaning forward, Jonny shoves his other hand into the mud too, hooking his fingers under the boat and hefting with all his might. Gill does the same. An unearthly sucking sound rents the air as they heave the side of the boat and push it over. It lands with a soft smack, a crunch of plastic and a gleam of silver. Yanking off a muddy glove, Gill scrabbles for her torch. A second later its red glow illuminates the small engine mounted at the end furthest up the bank.

'Unbelievable,' Jonny whispers, shaking his head.

'On the contrary,' Gill replies, torch beam trembling slightly as she trains it on the motor. 'We know the woman we're dealing with is capable of building far more complex devices than this. She's an expert. And this is the work of an expert.'

'So what's she doing here,' Jonny wonders, looking reflexively over his shoulder. He can't see anything other than their immediate surroundings – mudflats and marsh grass.

'I don't know,' Gill replies, clicking off her torch. 'And I'm inclined to agree with what you said to start with. This isn't a woman who tries and fails to do anything. If she wanted to submerge this boat, she'd have submerged it. So she either doesn't care if anyone spots it, or she wants them to.'

She flicks her torch beam at the other officers. 'I think we need to look around, sir.'

The commander nods back, climbing out into the shallows with his colleague. Together they haul the police boat further out of the water until it is firmly deposited in the mud. The soft clicks of weapons being checked punctuates the silence.

'But if she's left her boat visible deliberately then we're just walking right into her trap,' he says.

'We don't have any choice. We have to find her. And we've just discovered our biggest clue yet.'

Gill clicks off her torch and they are plunged into darkness. Something reaches into Jonny's chest, grabs his neck and squeezes it.

Fear.

'Peters, you're with me.' The commander's whisper rasps through the silence. He brushes past Jonny to meet Gill up front. Jonny senses rather than sees the other officer take up a position next to him. Overhead, the clouds part to reveal a sky full of stars, bathing the marsh with ghostly shine.

They begin to inch forward in pairs, the two armed officers on opposite sides. Jonny concentrates on staying upright, the muscles in his legs burning with effort. The mud underfoot is unrelenting. The only one without night-vision goggles, he just has starlight to guide him, flickering with the movement of the clouds.

Up ahead, Gill pauses. Jonny tenses, bracing for some sort of impact. What has she seen? A click and a soft-red glow illuminates a hillock of marsh grass. They start to move again, torch beam arcing from side to side until it catches on a large rocky outcrop of some kind in the distance.

Gill and the commander stop dead. Gill moves the torch beam down to her feet. Jonny's heart begins to pound.

'There's something out there,' Gill whispers, dim-red light pooling in the mud underfoot. 'I saw a solid shape. Could be a squat tree. Could be a pile of rocks. But this is all supposed to be marshland.'

Jonny stumbles as he steps up alongside her. The commander and the other officer fan out to their either side, weapons out.

'So what do you actually think it is?' Jonny asks. 'Can you light it up again?'

'No. Because I think there's a chance it's a building. And there might be someone hiding out inside.'

Jonny stares into the dark, willing the clouds to part again. He thinks of Blackwater's fortifications, all largely hidden by rocky outcrops, tree root systems or ancient trapdoors. The unmistakable sensation that they're walking into a trap takes hold. Gill starts to move forward again, keeping her light low. The ground is beginning to harden as they move further from the shoreline.

'Watch carefully,' she whispers as they pick up the pace. A quick flick of her torch and Jonny instantly sees what she means. The solid outlines of an outhouse or shed of some kind are nearing with every step.

Wordlessly, the commander moves in front of Gill. The other officer takes up a position behind Jonny. The building's silhouette is becoming more obvious the closer they get – low and square, with a darker shadow in the wall facing towards them; a doorway, Jonny realises. He flinches into the sudden crack of a twig underfoot, stopping dead on the spot and holding up his hands as both Gill and the commander spin round to confront him. He shakes his head in apology, but they've already turned away, taking advantage of the pause to silently survey the building that's almost upon them.

The commander holds a finger to his lips, pointing at something on the ground. Gill reacts instantly, kneeling to examine it before standing again and moving over to the cover of a tufty mound of marsh grass. Jonny follows suit, the fourth officer moving round to the front to work with the commander. Crouching next to Gill, Jonny stares at the object she's rolling between her fingers – cylindrical and shiny with a rounded end. A bullet.

Beyond the clump of marsh grass, both officers have their weapons drawn. One step, then another towards the darkened doorway at the front of the building. A rustle, a sudden flurry of movement, then a beam of red light, flashing once, then twice. Some sort of deliberate signal. But of what? On cue, Gill grabs Jonny's sleeve and pulls him to his feet. They hurry over to the building and its darkened entryway, smoked-earth smell of the damp inside hitting Jonny immediately.

The commander whispers unintelligibly to Gill, sweeping a beam of red light inside the building. Jonny peers past. A small single room. Stone walls. A dirt floor. A dilapidated roof with open gaps to the night sky. Gill rolls the bullet between her fingers, showing it to the commander. Something snags in Jonny's mind amid the tension. Suddenly he's back inside a very similar shed, with the pungent smell of fertiliser thick in his nostrils instead. His warzone training course. He stares at the bullet again, mentally assessing its size and shape, trying to remember what he knows about ammunition. Long. Thin. Sharper than he'd first thought. More of a fit for a rifle than a shotgun? Some kind of understanding seems to pass between Gill and the commander. She puts the bullet into a pocket with a decisive nod.

The commander steps carefully inside the shed. Gill follows. But Jonny is rooted to the spot. He steadies himself against the building's stone wall, trying to surface the seed of a thought forming in his mind. Why would an unused hunting-rifle bullet be lying on the ground in a marsh? If he's certain of anything it's that Jane is not armed with an ancient hunting rifle. The beam of red light flashes again – once, then twice. Another signal. The other armed officer brushes past, heading inside. But Jonny still can't move. Overhead, the clouds warp and shift, sending starlight filtering through the gaps in the building's roof, illuminating Gill and both other officers hunched over a spot in the middle of the dirt floor.

And Jonny suddenly knows exactly what they've found, barrelling back to the bunkers on Blackwater and the ancient iron trapdoors hiding their entry and exits.

'Don't,' he tries to say, but the words just stick in his throat. There's a faint scraping sound as Gill and the others scrabble over something on the floor.

And then – the blinding white noise and flash of an explosion.

Chapter Forty

Jonny is running. His legs are moving as if operated by someone else. Muscle memory has kicked in from years of hypervigilance. *Fight for your life.*

A cry rings out in the distance. Then another. Or is it the explosion still keening in his ears? The urge to turn back and check on Gill threatens to derail him. But from the moment he saw Jane's abandoned boat, he sensed they were walking into a trap. It's the reason he was standing far enough away from the blast to stay on his feet. So he needs to use them, and fast. He has to get help. He has to get away.

A squelch underfoot and his conviction gains. Mud is now slowing him down. He must be nearing the shoreline. Their boat can't be far away. Thundering on through the marsh, a hard, cylindrical object suddenly trips him headlong into the shallows. Surfacing a second later – the nightscope, nudging gently against his wet leg. Scrabbling back on to his feet, he splashes on until a rubber shape rears in front of him like the nose of a walrus.

Jonny is inside the boat and using his hands to paddle out to sea even as he realises the key is still in the ignition. A simple turn and the engine whirrs to life. Steering away from the shore, his relief is short-lived. He's managed to get away, but he's alone, heading into the water in the pitch-dark with no idea of what to do next.

Keep calm. Focus on practical details. Jonny forces himself to concentrate on things he can control. He's in the North Sea, not the Blackwater estuary. So he needs to stay as close to the shore as possible to avoid unpredictable currents. If he keeps land to his right, he'll keep heading south towards London. He saw the glow of lights in the distance before they stopped. The Thames estuary can't be far. Safe places to dock will surely follow. Along with telephones to use. People to ask for help. And he knows this boat can complete the journey. It is a boat built for war. Something else that training course taught him. He grips the tiller with renewed determination. He has to keep going.

Foam laps at the sides of the boat as his mind turns back to Jane. All the signs pointed to her heading to Tilbury Docks to commandeer the firework display to devastating end. None pointed to an explosion in an old shed in the middle of another nature reserve. What is her ultimate goal? *No more innocent people are going to get hurt on my watch*. Everything Jonny knows is telling him that mass civilian casualties can't be part of Jane's plan. But what about police officers? *I didn't say anything about sparing fucking deluded fools*. Isn't that exactly how she feels about the state's security services? He accelerates, trying to drown out the cry still echoing in his ears. He may have saved himself, but he's on his own now. All he can do is try and make it count by getting help as fast as possible. He's just a journalist. All he's trained to do is find out the truth. He isn't trained to fight hand-to-hand combat.

Just a journalist. Jonny is suddenly raging. This fucking bogland has been hiding evidence of a botched and illegal black ops experiment into biological warfare. An experiment that has killed two children and left an already incredibly dangerous woman so angry that she's bent on revenge. And now Jonny is stuck on a boat in the middle of the North Sea with no means to tell anyone about it and far more pressing matters of national security on his hands. *Just a journalist*. Maybe that's why Jane keeps letting him get away – because he's just a fucking journalist. All he does is amplify information. He doesn't actually do anything about it.

There his mind sticks. If Jane wanted to silence him, she's had ample opportunity. But she's done the exact opposite. She ambushed him – then she let him get away. She's let him get away on multiple occasions. Why? So he can tell the world how dirty British black ops really is? She hasn't given him enough information to do that yet. Or was it just to draw in the victims she really wanted – state security officers? But taking down a few country cops in the middle of a random swamp doesn't fit the picture either. Jane is angry about something that happened years ago directed by the very top of the British establishment. Jonny leans down on the tiller, pushing the boat's engine so hard it howls. He has to get into London. Every theory he has about what Jane is really up to leads to the heart of government.

A minute passes, then ten, then fifteen. The sky clears. Moonshine lights up the water. Gradually the shadowlands of the shoreline become more jagged and defined – grassland taking hold over mud. The glow of a city starts to push higher into the sky. A disused railway line emerges, followed by a scatter of buildings. More light takes hold, and with it, the beginnings of civilisation as the North Sea meets the Thames.

Jonny banks right, cutting out towards the middle of the river to pick up as much speed as possible. Another minute passes, then ten, then fifteen. The Thames begins to undulate through its trademark twists and turns. Then it starts to narrow. The settlements thicken. More boats appear. And finally the blocky silhouette of Tilbury Fort emerges to his right, with its ancient, dormant artillery positions facing out on to the river exactly as the commander described. Jonny heads for the docks, remembering the police station the commander also mentioned, which stands on the quay itself.

Sirens blare through the air as soon as Jonny enters the waterway into the main terminal. Seconds later, he's entering some kind of internal harbour divided into docking lanes already thick with boats. Ploughing past a giant cruise liner, its towering shadow menacing in the dark, another siren sounds in three short, sharp bursts. And then the low oblong of a barge strung with fairy lights starts gliding out of the lane ahead. He banks a hard turn inland, narrowly avoiding a second barge docked on the opposite side of the lane, before coming to a juddering stop by the wet quayside.

He's barely taken his hand off the tiller before two security officers are upon him.

'I need help,' he shouts, holding up his hands. The siren sounds again, suddenly deafeningly close by.

'You most definitely need help,' one of the men barks back, reaching into the boat to haul him out. 'You've just violated at least fifty port regs.'

'I'm sorry,' Jonny replies, allowing himself to be manhandled up and out on to the wet dock. 'But this is an emergency. An explosion just went off in a marsh not far north of here—'

'Shut up,' the man snaps, pulling a pair of handcuffs from a pocket.

'But three police officers are injured. You need to send help immediately. There might still be an armed and dangerous fugitive on the run. All officers in the South-East need to be put on high alert...'

He stops as the two men round on him. 'We already are,' one says. 'Some loony is threatening to blow up the firework display. And here you are fitting the exact description.'

Jonny's heart plummets like a stone through water. 'What?'

One of the men mutters into his radio while the other cuffs Jonny's hands together. 'You heard. You'll have plenty of time to beg for mercy once you're inside a cell, where you belong.'

'But you don't understand. I think these officers might be seriously injured or worse. And this suspect poses a very serious threat to the public—'

'Young, white, male, delusional.' The officer's grip tightens.

'Travelling alone, possibly in a police boat. Pretty sure we're looking at him, right now. You're coming with us.'

Think like Jane. Jonny is suddenly reeling. He thought he'd evaded her trap. But now he realises he's walked straight into another one. Jane knew he wouldn't blindly open a trapdoor after what happened to him on Blackwater that first time. Once her explosion had taken out Gill, Jane must have used her police radio to update the alert issued to all security operations in the entire city. Look out for a young, white male gabbling about some lone-wolf plot to blow up the fireworks display. Likely to show up on the water. Jonny might even laugh if the position he's in wasn't so serious. It's as brilliant as it is deranged.

'I swear you've got the wrong guy,' he begins, struggling to free himself. 'I'm just a journalist. I'm no threat to the public.'

'Like I said. Delusional.'

Jonny stops fighting, allows himself to be frogmarched along the dock.

'But I'm not armed. I'm definitely not dangerous. I'm not even resisting arrest. Please listen to me.'

'Yeah, yeah, yeah. You've never seen a gun before. Let alone handled one. We've heard it all before. You're whiter than the driven snow. Come on, move it.'

Handled one. Jonny's heart kicks at his chest. That fucking gun that Jane handed over in the bunker. Something else she thought of long before he did. Somewhere out there is an unlicensed state-of-the-art firearm covered in Jonny's fucking fingerprints.

'I know my rights,' he says, with as much conviction as possible. 'You need to let me make a phone call. I can clear all of this up in minutes.'

'You'll get your phone call just as soon as we've made ours.' The officers exchange self-congratulatory looks. 'The clock's ticking and we need to get this show back on the road.'

Fairy lights on the passing barge flicker in Jonny's peripheral vision. 'You mean the firework display? You can't let these barges leave. You mustn't. Please listen to me. There is a very dangerous woman playing all of us. Thousands of lives are potentially at stake. There's a chance that some of those barges are rigged with bombs, not rockets.'

He tries and fails to gesture at the barge in the nearside lane, arms still pinned against his sides. The officers smirk back and forth.

'It's like you're reading from a script, son. That's exactly what we were warned you might say. A senior commander from out of town just showed up here to give us the exact details.' The man looks across Jonny to his partner. 'We best flip a coin for who gets to call this in. Lots of glory waiting. Maybe even a bonus.'

'Fuck off, Jerome,' the other man grumbles. 'You got the crown last time.'

'You don't know what you're dealing with,' Jonny begs, by now so desperate to convince them he doesn't care how he sounds. 'This is a public emergency. You've got to keep looking for her—'

'Delusional is right,' Jerome interrupts with a flash of yellow teeth. 'Pack it in, now, would you? Some of us have got a party to go to. You have the right to remain silent – I should have said so at the start. I suggest you take it. Otherwise anything you say can and will be used against you in court.'

'But—'

'Leave him with me.' Another voice cuts in. A voice Jonny is absolutely sure he has heard before. He tenses, squinting at the officer walking swiftly towards them. Can it be…?

'Sorry, ma'am.' Jerome immediately dips his head, slackening his grip.

Jonny freezes on the spot.

For there, right in front of him, wearing a pristine port-police uniform and snapping a pair of shiny silver handcuffs around his wrist, is Jane Doe.

Chapter Forty-One

Jerome and his partner fall away. Jane grabs Jonny's arm. The siren sounds again in three more short, sharp bursts.

'Turn that fucking thing off,' she barks at the two policemen. 'We've got our man. He's exactly as I described to you. Now go fill in the paperwork. Use your usual commanding officer's details. I won't be sticking around.'

The officers scuttle in one direction while Jane guides Jonny in the other. He's struck completely dumb. Even after spotting that boat abandoned in the marsh he couldn't shake the feeling that she might still show up at Tilbury. But the possible reasons why are rendering him mute with horror. Fireworks. Gunpowder. Explosives. A devastating attack on thousands of innocent people.

Jane is leading him towards a small building at the far end of the lane. He regains the power of speech when he realises it's actually a huge shipping container. But by then Jane is already silencing him with a gloved hand over his mouth. The inside of the giant container is fitted out like an office, computer hardware on every desk, cables trailing all over the floor. A light flicks on. A door slams. He is suddenly able to gasp for breath. A click – and then blood rushes back to his hands as she releases the cuffs around his wrists.

Jonny props himself against a corrugated wall, trying to make sense of it. The container is deserted. Only one computer is actually on. It can't be an operations room for an active op. Not least a firework display involving more explosives than the country has ever seen before. He stares at Jane tucking the cuffs back inside a pocket. Tangled silver hair. Flinty steel eyes. The same woman, without doubt, that he encountered twice on Blackwater Island. Except how has she managed to get herself from there into a uniform at Tilbury police station via another dungeon in a different marsh without so much as a smear of mud on her jacket? She stares back at him with an expression akin to satisfaction, even pride.

'I've said it before and I'll say it again. You're good.'

Finally Jonny locates his voice, uses it. 'Good? What do you mean, good? How the hell did you get here? And what did you do to Gill?' A black thought suddenly occurs to him. 'Is that how you got hold of another police uniform – by taking hers?'

Jane scoffs. 'Of course not. And Gill is unharmed. Her companions too. There's nothing for you to worry about. You can trust me on that.'

'But there was an explosion. I was there. It was only because I wasn't standing as close as Gill that it didn't take me out.'

'No, there was a bang and a flash. It was just a stun grenade. I rigged it to go off if that trapdoor opened. It won't have hurt anyone. Just slowed them right down.'

'Do you honestly expect me to believe that explosion was just some harmless delaying tactic? You left a bomb behind on Blackwater too, for fuck's sake.'

'That wasn't a bomb, either. It just looked like one. And by the time your precious Gill found it, a bomb was exactly what you were all expecting. Sometimes all it takes is a terrifying idea. Then imagination does the rest of the work. Looking at wires and a timer attached to those two goons she already hated was all she needed to believe it was real.'

The distant cry Jonny is sure he heard as he fled from the marsh sounds in his mind. 'So where's Gill now? What have you done to her? I heard her ... I heard her scream...'

'I did nothing to her. I wasn't even there.'

Jonny shakes his head. 'But we saw your boat.'

'No, you saw *a* boat. And you decided it belonged to me. Just as you found a trapdoor and assumed I was hiding behind it. When in actual fact, you saw a boat I had left there and a bunker I had rigged up—'

'With some innocent little flashbang?' Jonny interrupts, still unwilling to believe the explosion in the marsh was ultimately harmless. She lets out a brittle laugh.

'There you go again. Imagination is a powerful thing. I've already told you it was just a stun grenade. I rigged up a few more in various other locations. Had to plan for different scenarios. No way of being sure where folks were going to end up once you'd raised the alarm and knew some would inevitably head up the Thames as well as swarm all over Blackwater. You probably just heard her calling after you.'

Jonny watches in a trance as she reaches for the radio clipped to her belt and twiddles with a knob before calmly speaking into it.

'Operations, this is Tilbury. Suspect in custody. Drunk and disorderly. Confident there's no threat to the public. Are Blackwater officers all secure? Repeat, are Blackwater officers all secure?'

A beat, then: 'Tilbury, this is Operations. Copy suspect in custody. Blackwater officers all secure. Device was a dummy, over.'

She snaps off the radio and stares back at him.

Jonny shakes his head again. 'Then how did you get from Blackwater to Tilbury undetected? Where did you get that police uniform? Do those other officers – Jerome and his pal – have any idea who you really are? And how could you possibly have known that I would show up here too?'

Jane shrugs. 'I didn't. But I knew you wouldn't head blindly into a bunker after what originally happened to you on Blackwater. I updated the alert so you'd be apprehended wherever you showed up. And how I got here or got my hands on this police uniform is of no concern to you. All that matters now is why.'

She pauses, appraising him with that curiously satisfied expression again before turning to the lone computer humming on the desk behind her.

'What are you doing?' Jonny asks, as she lifts the lid of the scanner next to the monitor to remove a creased and faded piece of paper before turning back to the keyboard and pressing a few buttons. 'What is that document?'

'Proof. They've been lying to you for so long that there needs to be verifiable proof,' she mutters, putting the page on top of a few more loose pieces of paper beside the scanner before bunching them together and folding them into her pocket. 'Do you believe in fate?'

'Absolutely not,' Jonny replies, heartened to be finally sure of something. 'I'm a journalist. I deal in facts. I don't deal in random coincidences.'

Jane nods approvingly. 'Smart. Like I said, you're good. The fact you ended up at Tilbury testifies to that. Commandeering a police boat alone and sailing through the North Sea in the dark takes some balls. I'm glad. Means I'm finally going to get to tell my story to the right person. To think that when all this started, I wasn't planning to tell it at all.'

Jonny stills. 'Your story?'

'Yes. You *are* still a journalist, right? Surely you're still bursting with questions? Well, I'm here to answer them. We've got all the time in the world now the proof is finally safe.'

The mention of time unnerves Jonny all over again, part of him still convinced that something terrible is going to happen on the stroke of midnight.

'Proof of what?' He balks as he checks his watch. 'What the hell have you done?'

Jane shrugs again. 'Nothing. I told you right at the start. No more innocent people are going to get hurt on my watch. But guilty people are going to pay for the ones that did. In fact, they already have. All it took was a few computers and a couple of dodgy codes and *bam* – everyone thinks Doomsday is about to dawn.'

Jonny pictures flaming boats crashing into the crowds banked by the Thames in a blaze of fire and fury with a rising sense of dread. 'You mean I'm too late?'

Jane's expression softens. 'Look at you. Still sure the world is about to explode around you when in fact it's all just in your head. These days it's imagination that's the new weapon of mass destruction. We're entering an age where information can travel almost as fast as the speed of light. There's a totally different arms race under way now. The battle to control information is everything. People like me have to reinvent ourselves. And the best part about this new era? Plant a bug in a computer and no one dies. But millions lose their minds.'

Computers. Misinformation. The dawn of a new digital age.

Jonny gasps as he finally realises what Jane has been planning and executing with all her computers on Blackwater. Months of investigative reporting flash through his mind to finally pause on three simple words.

'The millennium bug.'

Jane nods back, smirking. 'I've been working on it for years. And the computer system isn't even going to come crashing down. Everyone just thinks it might.' She checks her watch with another smirk. 'Still thinks it might, in fact, even though the other side of the world is well into the new millennium already and nothing has imploded. But corporations have wasted billions. Software engineers have aged decades. All computer programs have had to be reassessed. All because imagination has run away with everyone. And not a single shot has been fired. I didn't even try that hard. That reporter who wrote about the Doomsday bug a few years ago did most of the work for me. Imagine what might happen in the future, when computer hackers get really good.'

Jonny's mind spins through his encyclopaedic knowledge of how the panic started.

'That old woman in Minnesota,' he says. 'The one who was invited to join her local kindergarten when she was one hundred and four, all because her birthdate confused a computer program. You did that?'

Jane shakes her head. 'No. But I found out about it. And it got me thinking about what might happen if something like that occurred on a grander scale. Just like it got others thinking. So then I got a more high-profile reporter to investigate it.'

Jonny pales. The idea that a job dedicated to pursuit of the facts might also be somehow to blame for a hoax of such epic proportions is almost too much to bear. 'You mean you tipped off the journalist who wrote about the Doomsday bug?'

'Indeed. That wasn't all it took, obviously. He was a good reporter. I knew he wouldn't just write about something so abstract without more facts. So I started to build an actual bug. Deliberately tripped up a few more systems. Destabilised some more software in key industries that always grab headlines – travel, defence, finance. Tipped off some more well-placed folks to potential consequences. And then imagination took over, as I always knew it would.'

But Jonny still can't quite believe it. Hired guns like Jane have been contracted to fight some of the bloodiest battles around the world for decades. Can her revenge for something so brutal really be as simple as a computer virus? And if so, what the hell is she still doing in some empty office on Tilbury Docks?

'Let me make sure I get this right. You're the architect of the millennium bug. And it's just a giant hoax?'

'Depends on how you look at it,' Jane says, flinty steel eyes starting to shine. 'Can an idea ever be a hoax? That's all the millennium bug has ever been. The prospect of something happening that no one really understands. But the feeling of being completely helpless and panicking in the face of something you cannot control is inescapably real. And the struggle to stay on top of it is often the most damaging of all. Well, I'm the one who's finally in control of things now.'

Years of struggling to suppress his own emotions are immediately flashing through Jonny's mind. Growing up alone with his mother. Losing her when he was nine. Discovering he was never meant to be alone, that he wasn't even in the fucking womb alone – that there's a twin sister living somewhere else in the world who he still has no way of finding. A series of betrayals that have left him only able to live on the margins, too scared of finding meaning with anyone or anything that could let him down. He suddenly feels like he understands at least a fraction of what it must have taken for Jane to abdicate her entire existence to the state's most shadowy arm. And more than just a fraction of how she must have felt to be cast out and left with nothing just because of a simple mistake.

'So you proliferated the prospect of total systems meltdown in revenge for ... what, exactly?' he asks. 'And what are you doing here if your job is already done?'

She taps the pages folded into her top pocket. 'Everyone in authority in this country is about to go online to check whether their systems are still working. Now the document I've just uploaded is what they'll see first. I wanted to do it just before midnight for maximum eyeballs. And I had to do it from a system with an electronic file-sharing network already in place, like an international passenger terminal. Thought I'd have to find a way into an airport, but then I thought of Tilbury. To think I spent months watching those damn cruise liners steam past before I realised. Like I said, there has to be proof.'

Jonny stares at the computer humming behind her, still trying to process this. 'Proof of what?' he asks again. 'Can you show me the document?'

She straightens the hat over her silver curls. 'I'll tell you everything, but not here. We've got to get moving before I'm expected to have you banged up for the rest of the night. Come on.'

She opens the trailer door into the night. Jonny hesitates. Despite all he's suddenly come to understand about Jane, his own trust issues are still embedded deep in his bones.

'Where are we going?'

When she turns to him, there is the merest hint of a smile on her lined and determined face. 'We've got fireworks to watch.'

Chapter Forty-Two

They slip out into the night. The quay is deserted. Jonny checks his watch – less than thirty minutes till midnight. Jane turns to him with a pair of handcuffs in her gloved hands.

'It's just for show,' she murmurs, snapping them around his wrists. 'Remember, I'm supposed to have apprehended you. And there are two keys – look.' Something flashes silver against her leather palm. She gives one to Jonny, tucks the other into a pocket. 'Take this in case we get separated. I'll unlock them as soon as we're in the boat.'

Jonny hesitates. The idea that the imminent firework display might be rigged with bombs hasn't fully dissipated yet.

'Trust me,' Jane says, as if she can read his mind. 'The best way to disappear on a night like this is to hide in plain sight. The waterways are already packed.'

She moves quickly into the shadows. Jonny follows, hanging his head, trying to look defeated while adrenaline is coursing through his veins like a live circuit. A small, rubber patrol boat is moored alone at the far end of the quay, hidden by the hulking cruise liner in the adjacent lane. Jane climbs in, Jonny follows. She removes the cuffs almost as soon as he does. The boat's engine whirrs to life.

Head down, Jane cuts through the centre of the lane before banking right towards the waterway leading out into the Thames. Jonny lifts his face to the wind, exults in the salt spray on his face. They are quickly back out in the open river and accelerating fast towards the centre of London.

Jonny stares into the black water foaming at the sides of the boat, completely oblivious to the barges loaded with fireworks scything past to their either side. Miles pass in silence as he tries to find the words to begin questioning her. He almost can't bring himself to start. And it's as if Jane has lost her voice too. The secret government mission that went wrong. The innocent children that died. He's suddenly not sure whether he's ready to hear the truth about what really happened.

'It made sense in the beginning,' Jane finally says. 'We were told the tests themselves would be harmless. And we weren't the kind of people expected to worry too much about potential casualty counts anyway. We were trained not to give any thought to collateral damage.'

Jonny leans forward, finding his voice too. 'What made sense? The mission that failed?'

Jane nods. 'Yes. The foundations were laid decades earlier. It all started during the Second World War. Fear that the Nazis were developing biological weapons was overwhelming. Britain had to respond in kind. I can still kind of understand it on those terms.'

Jonny takes a sharp breath. He was right about the clandestine development of biological weapons. Blackwater's rare and fragile wilderness has been at the heart of this mystery all along.

'I forget the exact date,' Jane continues. 'But there was a suggestion at some point during the war that the Nazis were experimenting with using mosquitoes to proliferate malaria in enemy territory. Apparently they never seriously considered it. And it was thought to be largely impossible anyway. But the suggestion alone was enough to kick start a biological arms race, even though on paper, germ warfare was officially outlawed. Just the thought of a potential swarm of deadly insects was enough to sow panic. Developing and experimenting with various pathogens took years, and it all happened in test tubes in labs. But then the time came to see how they would work in practice. And that's when hired guns got involved. Because the whole thing had to happen completely off the books.'

She leans down hard on the tiller, engine's roar muffling her sigh.

'By then the military had already conducted a series of tests involving dummy bacteria. The exact details of those were classified, of course. But they were all run by the Ministry of Defence. And officials used the entire country as a testing site. They started with confined spaces – releasing simulated agents on the London Underground during rush hour. Similar tests went on in tunnels running under government buildings in Whitehall. Then they got bolder. Took on huge chunks of the English countryside. Coastal areas got especially whacked because scientists were able to operate from military ships anchored off shore. It was all to pinpoint the contaminant radius of an aerosolised biological agent and how much damage could be done by a single ship or aircraft. At that time they were most concerned about the Russians unleashing clouds of deadly germs over populated areas. The Cold War was anything but fucking cold. Early results indicated that one aircraft flying along the coast while spraying its agent could contaminate a target over a hundred miles away and cover an area of ten thousand square miles. Local residents had no idea they were being treated like guinea pigs. Military personnel were briefed to tell anyone asking that the trials were part of research projects into weather patterns and air pollution. And the top brass were always ready to argue that the tests would ultimately save lives should Britain come under chemical or biological attack.'

She pauses to wave an official-looking badge as she overtakes a barge. Jonny is transfixed with horror at the thought of the populations of whole cities having no idea that the air they were breathing had been deliberately contaminated to find out how vulnerable the country was to germ warfare.

'But we had to test the real thing,' Jane continues. 'And to do that we had to find a new testing site that was remote, uninhabited and isolated but also accessible from the mainland. I know what you're thinking. Blackwater is barely fifty miles away from London. There must have been dozens of far more remote spots to conduct top-secret weapons tests. But Blackwater had a secret weapon all of its own...'

'...because it was already host to some of the world's deadliest biological agents,' Jonny finishes for her.

'Correct,' Jane says grimly. 'Bacillus anthracis. Otherwise known as anthrax. Naturally occurs in soil loaded with minerals and organic matter. Blackwater's soil is so rich in both that it may as well have been a petri dish. The key thing, though, was harnessing it into a weapon of mass destruction. The real damage is done when a high concentration of the stuff is inhaled directly. Coming into contact with a couple of microscopic spores isn't exactly advisable, but it's easily treated. That's all scientists ever found to be naturally present on Blackwater. But by then the few people involved were so excited by the advantages of the environment itself that they overlooked some of the risks of experimenting so close to populated areas. Blackwater's ecosystem was genuine. Nothing needed to be manufactured to justify designating it a wilderness reserve and closing it to visitors. The paper trail was straightforward. And the place was covered in old fortifications that had previously been used for marine training exercises. It was perfect. Until it wasn't.'

Up ahead, Jonny can see the lights of Central London, the unmistakable silhouette of Tower Bridge frosted and shining against the dark night sky.

'So what went wrong?'

Jane hunches over the tiller, wiping salt spray from her face. 'We built a very small explosive device. Surrounded it with cattle cakes.'

'Cattle cakes?' Jonny asks in astonishment.

'Little patties of cattle feed,' Jane explains. 'One of the first biological weapons to result from research done right after the Second World War. The idea was that Royal Air Force bombers would drop anthrax-laced cakes on to enemy fields. Grazing cattle would infect themselves and then either die, or spread disease amongst the human population. The goal was to both wipe out food supply and cause the enemy to eat infected meat. Not the most sophisticated of weapons systems. Would have resulted in millions of civilian deaths.'

Jonny is appalled. 'Then why did you use them?'

Jane hunches even lower. 'Because this was a completely black operation and these were items that already existed. The development and production of either biological or chemical weapons has been officially outlawed for yonks, remember? And this country had signed yet another piece of paper attesting to its sovereign compliance as recently as two years earlier. The goal was to establish the size of the contaminant radius of a very small cloud of anthrax. We knew the exact concentration of those cakes. We knew the exact size of the charge we were using to explode them. All we needed was a trigger. The apparatus was built with almost zero external input. We were even able to control for weather conditions. Blackwater's atmosphere is so damp that it slows wind right down. Another unique advantage of the place.'

Jonny barrels back to Judith's description of what she saw and heard twenty years ago: *A hot night. No wind.*

'We trapped a few wild rabbits. Spaced their cages along a vector to establish the exact perimeter of a deadly cloud. The device was detonated remotely. We were all vaccinated in case of exposure. No one was supposed to be in range,' she adds, the merest note of a tremor quavering in her voice.

'Except someone was,' Jonny replies roughly. The thought of David Marshall's young son Matthew lost on the causeway and wandering into a deadly biological weapons test is almost too much to bear. But he can't let himself be consumed by emotion. 'A little boy was in the wrong place at the wrong time, right? And a dog,' he adds, thinking of Monty's water bowl still waiting by the door at The Saxon. 'But they should never have been in danger in the first place. I bet you don't even know their names.'

'Of course I do,' she finally says. 'I've never forgotten them. Because no one was supposed to be there. It was an accident.'

'That you've stayed deliberately silent about ever since,' Jonny fires back, still absorbed by David Marshall's unspeakable loss. 'And you've been paying the witness to this so-called accident to keep quiet about it, right? The landlady at The Saxon. She doesn't know the whole truth but was so scared of the fact she was an accomplice to something she doesn't understand that she agreed to never say a word – until now. Even though her dog died on the spot and you both know that little boy's father has been a hermit since his son disappeared. You could have spared him years of agony. You might have saved a different child's life if either of you had come clean sooner,' he adds, thinking of the small boy found dead on Christmas Day after a catastrophic reaction to a naturally occurring toxin.

Jane replies with a desolate nod. 'I buried the bodies afterwards. I wasn't supposed to; they should have been incinerated during the decontamination operation, but I couldn't let that happen. I knew I'd be finished professionally, but I didn't care.' Jonny remembers Judith's account of Jane returning for the bodies and describing them as evidence. 'So I hid in the reeds and watched the rest of them search until they gave up and completed the rest of the decontamination. Then I went back to make sure the bodies weren't disturbed. By then there was zero risk of inhalation exposure. Even though anthrax spores can survive decades in the right kind of soil, they aren't deadly in that form unless the symptoms go untreated. And the place was uninhabited. Officially closed to visitors and tied up in miles of paperwork. But I should have known better than to assume there was still no risk to the public.'

'You all should have known better,' Jonny retorts. Something else occurs to him. 'What happened to the other people involved in the mission?'

'Still making a living off the books, as far as I know. I was the only one that couldn't live with what happened. I was coming to terms with the consequences of a lot of other missions at the time, as well as what went wrong on Blackwater.'

Her hand stills on the tiller. The engine slows to a low putter. They are idling in waters so choppy from the dozens of pleasure boats and barges banked all around them that it feels like they might capsize.

And then – a deafening bang. Fireworks begin exploding in the night sky with battlefield ferocity. Showers of luminous sparks rain down over the city centre, embers dying as they hit the black water. A menacing rustle behind them and a wall of flame rushes past along the river bank as rockets fire from their barges in perfect sequence. The River of Fire, he thinks, picturing an operations room back on Tilbury Docks full of jubilant software engineers high-fiving to have escaped the prospect of catastrophic computer meltdown. Jane begins to steer again as soon as the flames have ripped past, banking hard left towards the river's southern shoreline. Jonny hunches reflexively as they cut across a pleasure cruiser. Fireworks are still dancing overhead. No one gives them a second look as they slip past some houseboats and into a narrow waterway inland.

Jane steers them expertly to a small dock, exchanging nods with the police officers arrayed on the shore. All of them transfixed by the fireworks still popping further down the river. Cutting the engine in the shallows, she turns, exhorting Jonny with a hand.

'Follow me,' she says, pulling her handcuffs out of a pocket with a meaningful look at the officers behind her. 'Make a fuss and it's bracelets again.'

Scrambling to his feet, Jonny wobbles out of the boat, desperate to get back on to solid ground. Jane takes his arm and marches him purposefully away from the shore and into a side street crowded with revellers.

'Here,' she mutters, taking the document out of her top pocket and shoving into his hand as they walk. 'This is the only paperwork that's ever officially existed about the mission. You'll need it to prove what I've uploaded isn't a fake. People will already be racing to find a way to take it down and pretend it never existed. I suppose it's lucky this all happened when secret documents still had to be written down on paper. Soon enough there will be no physical record of anything – it'll all live online in some alternate universe. The numbers written at the top are a grid reference.'

Jonny is momentarily thrown off balance by the jostling, and whoops and cheers, of the drunken crowds partying all around them. When he rights himself, Jane has let him go.

'A grid reference for what?' he asks.

'Where I buried the bodies,' she answers, turning to face him. 'You'll need them to prove it all too. And you'll be able to give David Marshall a semblance of a gravesite, at least.'

Jonny puts the wad of fragile paper into his pocket. Jane busies herself straightening her hat and smoothing down her uniform, looking every inch a police officer on duty during the most loaded New Year's Eve in living memory. Telling her he is professionally obligated to report a source if he suspects them guilty of a crime now feels as ridiculous as it sounds.

'So what are you going to do? Just disappear as if you never existed?'

'I haven't officially existed for years,' Jane replies. 'That document will prove it to you and anyone else who reads it.

Which, since you work for the *International Tribune*, will hopefully be millions of people. To think I wasn't planning on giving it to anyone when this all started. I was just focused on creating a digital battlefield and thought I could do it all by myself. I've lived my whole life feeling better off alone.'

Jonny's hand closes around the document in his pocket. 'So then why are you giving it to me?'

'You cared,' Jane replies simply. 'You showed up to try and find out what really happened on Blackwater. And you didn't stop at any cost, not even in the dark on a boat by yourself in the North Sea. The minute you arrived at Tilbury Docks was when I decided it was worth telling you everything. The rest is up to you. My guess is you're the kind of person who will go into battle if it's over the truth.'

And with that, she turns and disappears, swallowed up by revellers dancing and singing as they celebrate the dawn of a brand-new age.

Chapter Forty-Three

Jonny stares numbly into the crowd. Party hats whirl. Streamers fly. Whoops and whistles rent the air. Two revellers grab his arms and try to twirl him between them before clattering off, cackling. All around him, people are celebrating together. But somehow Jonny has never felt more alone. He instinctively grips the pages in his pocket as if their presence might bring him some relief. He's finally in possession of a news story fit to beat the new millennium. Surely he should feel something other than hollow inside?

He starts to walk, trying to find a way through the throng. A plastic beaker crunches underfoot, its contents sloshing over his boot. He needs to find a telephone. He needs to find a way back to the newsroom. He needs to make a copy of these precious pages in his pocket before anything happens to them. He needs to tell someone about everything that's just happened to him! No, not someone, he realises, pulling up short as he reaches the water's edge. He needs to tell Paloma. This story means nothing without her.

Jonny looks desperately up and down the river bank, pleasure boats twinkling as they float on the water like lucky charms just out of reach. Jane's parting shot rings around his mind. *I've lived my whole life feeling better off alone.* Is that the real reason why she finally decided to share her story with him? Because she recognised someone who has always felt exactly the same and has pushed everyone away for fear that they'll let him down in the end? He peers into the night sky, suddenly seized by the urge to scream at the heavens. From the moment he learned his mother took her own life he resolved that caring too deeply about another person would never be worth the risk of them deciding they don't feel the same way. But all it has left him with is a brand of loneliness so crushing and profound he must wear it on his face. Now here he is, all alone, with no one left that cares about him other than a former mercenary trying to make peace with herself.

He turns towards the hordes of people streaming in either direction across the frosted silhouette of Tower Bridge. Hundreds of people that look like they know exactly where they are going. And Jonny suddenly has absolutely no idea of how to get himself to where he needs to be. Why did he tell Paloma to go back to London without him? Why did he push her away just because he's not sure she feels exactly the same way about him as he does about her? What she actually said during their agonising conversation the night before he left to go on that stupid course was their friendship was too precious for her to risk. Isn't that also true of how he feels? The job may give him purpose. But his life is meaningless without her in it. She only came down to Eastwood because she didn't want to be alone either. Not because she cared about a news story more than she cared about him. He has to find her. And she's here somewhere, he realises with the pop of a flash bulb on the boat opposite. She said she only had a security pass for the press pen at Tower Bridge.

Jonny is suddenly moving at speed. He pushes his way through the crowds on the river bank and makes for the access staircase to the bridge itself. Revellers are streaming up and down the wharf, streamers popping and drinks flying with almost every step. His heart thumps as he spots a photographer laden with equipment hurrying up the stairs with a protective hand wrapped around his camera's long lens. Another skipped beat at the sight of an army of television crews ranged in an enclosure on the opposite side of the steps. He breaks into a jog, ducking round the gigantic concrete foot of the bridge and skidding to a stop beside a security guard at the entrance.

'Excuse me,' he pants. 'My name is Jonny Murphy, I'm with the *International Tribune*...' He trails off, fumbling for the press card still mercifully stuffed below the precious pieces of paper in his pocket.

But the security guard is already putting out a gloved hand. 'This is television crews only, son. Snappers are across the water.' He points over the river, and Jonny is on the move immediately, shouting his thanks over his shoulder.

Up the concrete stairwell and out on to the walkway on the mighty bridge itself. Scything through the crowds pausing to take in the breathtaking sight of London's most celebrated landmarks lit up against the night sky and back down the steps on the other side of the river. Straight into a security guard waiting in an almost identical position to the first.

'Jonny ... Murphy...' he pants again, waving his press card. '*International ... Tribune.*'

The guard frowns down at the identity badge in his hand. 'You got a security pass?'

Jonny's heart plummets. He pictures his neat pile of security accreditations for the different press pens along the river bank still waiting for him to collect from Lisa on the news desk in London.

'Not on me, but there are *Trib* staffers already here. If I could just come in for a second I'll find someone who can vouch for me, you can even keep my press card until I come back.'

The guard returns his card with a rueful smile. 'Sorry, son. I can't help you. I can't let anyone in without prior security clearance...'

But Jonny is no longer listening, as he's spotted Paloma in the scrum of photographers just inside the gate. Screaming her name, his heart lurches as she runs over immediately.

'Jonny! Are you OK? We've been worried sick.'

Jonny recalls his fevered exchange with Lukas warning of a potential security threat to the celebrations in Central London.

'Lukas is out looking for you, I think he's probably still in Westminster—'

'You know him?' the security guard interrupts with a frown.

'Yes,' they both answer in the same moment.

'He's one of our reporters,' Paloma adds breathlessly. 'Can you let him in?'

The guard shakes his head. 'No. But I can let you out. That OK?'

Paloma is already nodding, looping her camera around her neck. Jonny is seized by a feeling so unfamiliar it almost makes him dizzy. A kind of happiness and relief so profound that he can feel his chest swell. They walk quickly away from the entrance, pausing a few feet from the gate.

'I'm sorry,' he starts before she can ask him any more questions. 'I shouldn't have told you to leave me alone back in Maldon. Or said that Lukas only told you to come and meet me to make you feel better. I wasn't thinking clearly. I've been completely self-absorbed. You deserve far less selfish people in your life than me.'

'Well, you're the only one I really want,' she replies, squeezing his arm. 'But don't worry about that now. What else did you find out after I left? Did you get the whole story? The fireworks weren't even that spectacular.' She gestures dismissively between the river and the press pen. 'And the view from here was shit.'

Jonny's laugh practically bursts out of his chest. 'Yes. But I'd have got there a lot faster if I hadn't tried to do it all by myself. Come on. Let's go and find Lukas. We've still got a lot more work to do.'

Epilogue
Maldon, 7th January 2000

Bill's black minivan idles at the kerb outside Maldon police station. Rain is pelting down relentlessly from the iron-grey sky overhead. Pulling up the hood on his jacket, Jonny peers past the thudding windscreen wipers at the Blackwater river in the distance. The tide is high and the only thing he can see through the estuary mist are thick laces of black-and-yellow hazard tape roping off all the visible areas of coastline.

'The entire channel must still be closed,' he remarks, picturing the scenes he and Paloma had witnessed during the first week of the new millennium. Medical confirmation that microscopic spores of anthrax were to blame for the death of a child barely fifty miles away from London triggered an emergency response of epic proportions. Paloma's pictures of decontamination teams in their white hazmat suits on the Blackwater river were licensed to news organisations around the world. Signs warning of deadly hazards are up around the shoreline. Maldon remains deserted. Eastwood is still under an evacuation order.

'I should hope so,' Bill replies with a shudder. 'I doubt anyone is going to voluntarily take a boat out on this river again in a hurry.' He nods dubiously at the thick sheaf of newspapers Jonny is readying to tuck underneath his arm. 'Those won't last a second in this rain. Shove them under your jacket or something.'

'I can roll a couple into my camera bag,' Paloma pipes up from the backseat, reaching for the copies in Jonny's lap. He stares at the headline bannered along the top, feeling curiously deflated.

'The Secrets of Anthrax Island'. There is still so much more to report about Britain's secret biological weapons programme. But the row over potential risks to national security is threatening to win out. Ministry of Defence officials have had Lukas locked in meetings about it for days.

'Thanks,' he says. 'I don't know why I'm bothering, to be honest. Gill's got bigger things to worry about than reading about herself in the fucking newspaper. And she won't want to be reminded yet again about the nephew she didn't know she had until he was dead.'

Paloma squeezes his hand. 'You don't have to give it to her if you don't want to. And if you do, she'll be grateful you've thought to save her a copy.'

Jonny gazes out of the window at the rain-soaked and deserted pavement. 'I don't know about that. This area was neglected long before residents found out about the deadly biological agents lurking nearby. It'll still take years to recover even with the government ploughing a load of financial compensation and other sweeteners into the place.'

'You can't fix everything, son,' Bill says. 'Kids died around here as a result of careless government experiments. It's a matter indisputably in the public interest. You had to report as much as you could.'

Jonny watches raindrops explode on the tarmac. 'I know. And I'm happy we have. I just wish the outcome could be different, that's all. No one around here will believe the authorities have made the area safe. Development of biological and chemical weapons will continue in secret. No other countries are going to pause their efforts no matter how outraged they say they are about the evidence we're reporting. The fact that a child died as recently as last week is already just a footnote. His name should be up in lights or at least printed on a tombstone somewhere and we still don't even know what it was.'

Paloma slides the passenger door open. 'We don't need to know. It's none of our business. But it definitely is Gill's. He was her nephew. And was one of two children who paid the highest price of all. She won't rest until he's memorialised properly. And David Marshall will do exactly the same for his son Matthew just as soon as we've given him that grid reference.'

Jonny taps the piece of paper folded neatly into his shirt pocket, feeling instantly revived. He'd memorised the numbers scribbled at the top of Jane's classified document as soon as he read them. The semblance of a gravesite for little Matthew Marshall.

'You're right. And for once we're getting to deliver news that someone wants to hear.'

'Exactly,' she says, climbing out into the rain. He follows her with renewed determination.

'I'll wait here,' Bill shouts after them. 'Take as long as you need to.'

They hurry up the gravel forecourt towards the station entrance, stopping just inside the lobby. Gill is already walking out behind the reception desk to greet them. Jonny is momentarily distracted by the hubbub in her previously deserted station. Uniformed police officers are moving industriously between her overstuffed filing cabinets, murmuring back and forth as they pore over pieces of paper.

'Morning,' she says, shaking both their hands, winter-blue eyes snapping with conviction. 'Things are moving pretty fast around here.' She gestures at the officers behind her. 'Making up for lost time and all that. Do you have your vaccine certificates? I know you had them done before the decontamination operation. But I still can't let anyone inside the cordon without proof of a vaccine.'

'Yes,' Jonny replies, pulling out a small booklet. 'We got jabbed first thing on New Year's Day in fact. The nurses said it made a nice change from dealing with yet another case of alcohol poisoning.'

Gill snorts, examining both his and Paloma's certificates. 'I bet they did. We heard exactly the same thing when we showed up for ours, too. Anthrax vaccines aren't exactly ten a penny.' She snaps the booklets shut. 'OK. That's all I needed. We're good to go. I'll just get my coat.' She hurries back behind the desk.

Jonny eyes the police officers moving around inside the station, hoping this is just the start of a hugely overdue amount of investment in Maldon and its surrounds. The area has been consumed by the secrets of Blackwater Island for far too long. Gill returns with a raincoat and a bunch of shiny new silver keys. 'Got a patrol car of my own now. Drives like a dream. Come on, let's get going. It's not far.'

They follow her back out on to the forecourt. A chirp of a car alarm and the doors of a new gleaming panda car pop open with a jaunty clunk.

'You two are the first civilians to ride in it, too,' Gill continues, climbing into the front seat. 'Unless you count that old landlady from The Saxon. Which I don't, because she's still got to account for far too many lies to be considered an innocent civilian.'

Jonny flinches at the mention of Judith, picturing her hunched on the stairs at the back of her pub as she admitted to witnessing the fallout of the secret weapons tests and to burying Matthew Marshall's tiny body, only to lie about it for years afterwards.

'What's the latest on Judith? Still being questioned by Ministry of Defence officials in London?'

Gill nods, throwing the car into gear and reversing out into the road. 'She most certainly is. Though, from what I hear, they'll go easy on her in the end. She had no idea what she'd blundered into. All she's really guilty of is keeping schtum about it. Unlike my clueless brother and his delusional wife, who are both still refusing their anthrax jabs,' she adds bitterly. 'It wasn't just deadly bacteria that killed their son. It was criminal levels of neglect. You won't find me crying if either of them end up dead from a treatable toxin.'

'Where are they now?' Paloma asks from the backseat.

'Under guard in a hospital isolation ward. Can't even mix with prisoners until they're officially certified free from anthrax, which they won't be until they've had their bloody jabs. Turns out praying to Mother Nature brings you zero redemption in real life. They'll miss their own son's funeral at this rate.'

The thump of her indicator reverberates around the car as she turns away from Maldon towards the privately owned land opposite Blackwater's southern shore, which has been in David Marshall's family for decades. Jonny is lost for a moment in the tragedy of two small boys dying eminently preventable deaths.

'I suppose it's comforting for the rest of your family to be able to lay him to rest, at least,' he finally says. 'What was he called? You don't have to tell me if you don't want to. I just can't bear thinking of him in this faceless and nameless way. He deserves to be remembered properly. Everyone should know who he really was. I won't report it, of course,' he adds hurriedly.

Gill takes a moment to reply, staring fixedly at the road ahead.

'I'll always think of him as Antony. Josh told me they called him Antaine. But I know what he really meant. They named him after Dad. If the big fella still knew his own name, he'd be pleased as punch. Shame about the massive stroke and catastrophic brain damage. But thems the breaks.'

Jonny's eyes meet Paloma's in the wing mirror. He doesn't need to see her face to know she is smiling.

'Antony,' she repeats. 'Then that's how we'll both remember him too.'

'It apparently means "priceless one",' Gill adds gruffly. 'Which, if I was a poet – or a fucking idiot – I suppose I'd find meaningful in some way.' She gives her head a little shake, dislodging the cap on her head.

'Well you're definitely not a poet,' Jonny replies.

'Or a fucking idiot,' Paloma adds.

Gill raises a small smile, straightening her cap. 'I most certainly am not. Anyway, enough about that. You two just focus on David Marshall. I'm not going to come in with you – it's not fair on the poor guy. Even though I arrived after he lost Matthew, he still associates me with failing to find him before it was too late.'

'It wasn't your fault,' Paloma says. 'You were deliberately put in a position that meant you'd never be able to find out what really happened to his son.'

Gill shrugs. 'Doesn't matter. He still needs someone to blame to be able to move on. And some secret mercenary operation on behalf of the Deep State isn't going to cut it. He needs a name and a face, too. He wants a judge and jury, a trial and a conviction. But he isn't going to get any of that. He's going to have to deal with this alone for the rest of his life. So let him stay angry with me.'

'But that's not fair,' Jonny says. 'And it also isn't true. You didn't fail him. The truth is you've done everything you can around here with the information and resources you've had at the time.'

Gill waves a dismissive hand. 'That's the problem with you lot. Journalists always think the truth is enough. But David Marshall wants justice. And he won't get it. You know that. His son died in a tragic accident as a result of tests that are supposed to save lives in the event of some unimaginable war. National security interests will prevail. No one will be openly prosecuted. The only charge that could stick is one of treason for breaching the Official Secrets Act by making the details public. And that's on Jane.'

'Then let him blame her,' Paloma says. 'She was part of the team that caused this tragic accident.'

Gill replies with a wry laugh. 'The ghost of Blackwater, you mean? Jane is long gone. No one's ever going to find her. Reminding him she's still at large is just going to make him feel worse. So I wouldn't bring her up unless you have to.'

She slows, pulling over to the side of the road.

'Right, here we are. You can walk the rest of the way; I'm not risking my new suspension driving over marsh grass. Go on, out you get. David will be pleased to see you. And I'll be here when you get back.'

Paloma opens the passenger door and gets out. Jonny follows, staring over the reeds into the thick mist swirling over the river. Blackwater Island is invisible. Paloma turns back to him with an outstretched hand.

'What is it?'

'Nothing,' he says, walking resolutely towards her, trying to forget about the legend of Inka and her wild silver hair.

Afterword

This book is a work of fiction. Blackwater Island does not exist. But details of Britain's secret biological weapons programme were declassified in 2002, revealing that potentially dangerous chemicals were released over vast areas of the country without ever informing the public. More than a hundred covert experiments were carried out over a period of some fifty years.

The remote Scottish island of Gruinard was used as an anthrax testing site during the Second World War. Prime Minister Winston Churchill tasked British scientists with finding a way to harness anthrax as a weapon. Sheep, horses and cows nearby all began dying mysterious deaths. Later a Ministry of Defence film showed dozens of sheep in exposure crates surrounding a remotely detonated anthrax cloud. Gruinard was finally certified as free from anthrax in 1990, almost fifty years after the original experiments.

A decade later in what became known as the Fluorescent Particle Trials, planes flew from North-East England all the way to Cornwall dropping huge amounts of zinc cadmium sulphide. The chemical's fluorescence enabled its spread to be monitored and determine the contaminant radius of an aerosolised biological agent. The government insisted cadmium was safe. But it was considered a chemical weapon by the Allies during the Second World War.

More than a million people along the south coast of England went on to be exposed to bacteria including E. coli in the Large Area Coverage Trials. Operations were run from a military ship anchored off the Dorset coast over a period of seven years. Similar bacteria were released during the Sabotage Trials a decade later to determine the vulnerability of large government buildings and public transport. Simulated chemical agents were released on the London Underground Northern Line and in tunnels running under government buildings in Whitehall.

The Ministry of Defence latterly commissioned scientists to review the safety of these tests. All reported that there was no risk to public health. But some families in affected areas remained convinced the experiments led to their children suffering birth defects, physical handicaps and learning difficulties, demanding a public inquiry.

When the details were declassified, a spokesperson for the government's scientific research facility at Porton Down said: 'Independent reports by eminent scientists have shown there was no danger to public health from experiments which were carried out to protect the public. The results from these trials will save lives, should the country or our forces face an attack by chemical and biological weapons.'

Asked whether such tests are still being carried out, they said: 'It is not our policy to discuss ongoing research.'

Acknowledgements

Four years ago, I spent a weekend with my family camping on the tidal island of Osea in Essex. A friend had booked for a group of us, and it sounded idyllic – only five pitches on the edge of a field, on an island only accessible by road at certain times of day or night. I raised an eyebrow at this. Our kids were constantly getting into scrapes on holiday, and we were wearily familiar with minor-injuries units at overseas hospitals. But at barely fifty miles from London, the place was hardly off the beaten track. What could possibly go wrong?

Osea was, as promised, magical. Bikes, beaches, forests, panoramic skies. Minimal infrastructure. Zero mobile-phone reception. It was like stepping back in time. Such was the excitement on the first night we all went to bed long after midnight. At 5.00 am I was woken by my daughter writhing and sobbing. Her entire body was covered in the most enormous hives I had ever seen – hundreds of raised red splotches. She was clearly suffering a violent allergic reaction – but to what? She had no known food intolerances. She'd fallen asleep in the same clothes she'd arrived in. And this was hardly an alien environment – we lived an hour's drive away.

We decamped to the nearest A&E as soon as we were able. A triple dose of antihistamines later and she was fine. We were told the most likely explanation for her reaction was an unfamiliar insect bite and that we'd never know for sure without a battery of extra tests – the nature of Osea's ecosystem was extremely rare due to its tidal position. By then there was no point. She was most concerned about how we were going return to Osea now the tide had come in again. She didn't want to miss another minute of fun. One water taxi later and we were back on the beach. I went to bed that night with my head spinning. The result is contained in these pages.

To that end I must thank our dear friends Tina and Edu, Debs and Ethan, Sheena and Ross and all the kids. Without our weird and wonderful trip to Osea this book wouldn't exist. Special thanks to Tina for her expert reassurance on allergies and EpiPens.

I am also, as usual, indebted to my long-suffering agent, Jon Wood, and editors, West Camel and Karen Sullivan, for helping shape my story into a coherent novel; and to the generosity of my fellow authors, and of the reviewers and bloggers who have given me such kind feedback over the years.

Lastly to my family: my parents, my brother, my husband, my children. I love you all more than words can say.